VINTAGE

David Baker

TOUCHSTONE

NEW YORK LONDON TORONTO SYDNEY NEW DELHI

Touchstone
An Imprint of Simon & Schuster, Inc.
1230 Avenue of the Americas
New York, NY 10020

First Touchstone hardcover edition September 2015

TOUCHSTONE and colophon are registered trademarks of Simon & Schuster, Inc. For information about special discounts for bulk purchases, please contact Simon & Schuster Special Sales at 1-866-506-1949 or business@simonandschuster.com.

The Simon & Schuster Speakers Bureau can bring authors to your live event. For more information or to book an event, contact the Simon & Schuster Speakers Bureau at 1-866-248-3049 or visit our website at www.simonspeakers.com.

Interior design by Akasha Archer

Manufactured in the United States of America

10   9   8   7   6   5   4   3   2   1

Library of Congress Cataloging-in-Publication Data

Baker, David, 1971-
    Vintage : a novel / David Baker.—First Touchstone hardcover edition.
        pages cm
    Summary: "A humorous and evocative debut novel about a food journalist's desperate attempt to save his career—and possibly, his marriage—by tracking an extremely valuable bottle of wine stolen by the Nazis over half a century ago"—Provided by publisher.
    1. Food journalists—Fiction. 2. Receiving stolen goods—Fiction. 3. Losers—Fiction. 4. Domestic fiction. I. Title.
    PR6102.A3375V56 2015
    823'.92—dc23
                                                                                                2015008747

ISBN 978-1-5011-1251-5
ISBN 978-1-5011-1255-3 (ebook)

For Liesbeth and Nelda, who cooked for us

VINTAGE

ONE

Bouillabaisse

This classic peasant stew was originally designed to stretch bonier and cheaper fish into a meal, but the addition of crushed garlic, herbs and fresh vegetables in balanced proportion have rendered it the poor fisherman's gift to humanity. Bouillabaisse has sent many a Marseilles sailor to sea with a strong back and a full belly, but it can also work wonders on a broken heart. It is a comeback meal, and with a dash of cayenne and saffron, even the most battered hearts can be restored with enough vigor to again brave the turbulent and storm-ridden waters of love.
—BRUNO TANNENBAUM, *TWENTY RECIPES FOR LOVE*

Not bad, not bad at all, Bruno thought as he wiggled his fingers above the keys. He cracked his knuckles. He was glad. It was starting to feel like a book. "Now, that's a hell of a beginning!" He actually said this out loud, drawing attention from the other diners at the bistro. He didn't care, though. He resumed typing:

Wine is life. It is essence. It is the inky-dark heartsblood pulsing out the rhythm of our species' slow crawl from the muck. Wine is the mystery behind every religion. It is the warmth of every sunrise. It is the chime of every bell that ever rang for a wedding or tolled for a funeral . . .

Bruno stopped his typing, rousing himself long enough to reach for his glass and sip the peppery velvet of his wine. He swished, coating his gums, and swallowed. Then returned to the keys:

Wine is civilization. It is what raised us up from feasting around carcasses and seated us at tables lit with conversation and laughter. Wine is desire. It is poetry. Philosophy. Science, nature, art. It is . . . humanity.

Bruno surfaced satisfied from his writerly fog. He reached for his wine once more to celebrate the words that now poured directly from his heart. But the glass was empty. *Damn!* He tipped the bottle. A single drop rolled off the rim. He looked around in a mild state of panic, realizing that he'd likely overstayed his welcome. But he wasn't about to leave the restaurant. Not now that he was finally making progress.

He blinked, staring across the room at a youngish blonde in a low-cut black cocktail dress. She glanced at him with what may have been intrigue or annoyance. Maybe it wasn't him at all that caught her attention, but the oiled Smith Corona typewriter propped on the table before him, next to the half-eaten plate of mixed brochettes and the empty bottle of the house red, an affordable Vacqueyras from the southern Rhône. He didn't care what she thought. He was about to submerge into the writing again. It had been too long. He'd worked too hard. He typed. The table shook. The bell on the carriage chimed in celebration of a new line. The typebars, gleaming with olive oil, clacked and hammered home. It was the music of composition. His blood ran with the fire of creation . . . and the Vacqueyras.

An El train whooshed past outside, blotting the evening sun. There was a dull murmur of conversation around him. Waiters slalomed between the small tables. In his periphery, Bruno could see the crowd in the vestibule, waiting for tables in the tight little restaurant.

La Marseillaise was more popular now than ever. The *Green Guide* gave it a perfect score and couples made dinner reservations six months in advance. This dismayed Bruno even though he'd had a hand in the establishment's success. He'd written the restaurant's very first review in the *Sun-Times* a decade ago. He'd described the meal as a "subtle spectacle," and declared Chef Joel Berteau, a humble cook from the French Merchant Marine with no prior experience in the restaurant racket, without even a green card, a "culinary magician of the highest order."

The upshot was that Bruno's adjectives had transformed La Marseillaise from a hidden gem into the crown jewel of Chicago's River North neighborhood. He couldn't afford to eat here anymore, especially not in his current predicament. But Joel Berteau had become a friend. Now that Bruno was back living with his mother, the chef offered him a sort of office . . . a corner table during the hours between the lunch and dinner rushes. Most days, a complimentary bowl of Joel's triumphant bouillabaisse would appear next to his notebook as inspiration to coax Bruno's chin out of his hands, to nudge his dormant fingers toward the pen or the typewriter keys. Occasionally Bruno would ask for a bottle of wine. Occasionally he'd get one.

Today, he'd already had two. He was celebrating the end of his writer's block.

The keys sang their clattering, literary song. Discovering his father's old typewriter in the closet beneath the spare pillows had been a stroke of good fortune buried within the larger humiliation of moving back in with his mom. The mechanical clatter gave a new sense of urgency and permanence to his words. Never mind that it annoyed the restaurant staff and other guests, who were now arriving for the evening rush: smart couples in relaxed cotton, first dates trying to impress, a salesman wooing an out-of-town client. All of them wore the self-assured air of folks who know where they belong. Bruno felt, and ignored, the occasional toe-to-head glance. The raised eyebrow. He was gruff. Stout. His unruly beard flecked with gray. His royal blue Chicago Cubs cap covering a thinning crown of bristly hair. His rumpled tweed jacket was neither new nor old enough to be fashionable.

And add to all of this the fact that he was typing. Noisily.

CLING! The carriage chimed another small victory. Finally, his new book was under way. After all this time . . .

"Bruno? Mr. Tannenbaum?"

The voice was at his ear. Whispered. Urgent. Bruno turned his head and scowled, but his eyes never left the bond paper.

"Mr. Tannenbaum!" The whisper morphed into a low, urgent order.

Bruno glanced up. A waiter with a beak nose supporting Versace glasses was bending down at his elbow. *How the hell can a waiter afford Versace?*

"Mr. Tannenbaum, you have to stop writing."

"What?"

"The table . . . we need the table now."

Bruno looked around. People crowded the entry. They spilled onto the street. They eyed him and his corner table. Prized real estate. When he'd arrived, the last diners were abandoning their lunches. He blinked. He looked at his page . . . a full page, finally a single full page. How many hours had it taken?

"Give me some more time. I'm working here."

Wine didn't usually make Bruno surly. But he didn't like this waiter, who was wearing glasses worth more than a check from Condé Nast for a freelance article on squid salads. Whoever this guy was, Bruno was a peg higher. After all, he was pals with Berteau. After a number of favorable reviews, Berteau had invited him into the kitchen. They'd spent many a late night at the table in back, uncorking Rhônes, experimenting on the stove and discussing the merits and failings of Twain, Proust, Fitzgerald and Flaubert: Berteau had done a fair amount of reading in the Merchant Marine, and one such evening had led him to make the offer: a clean, well-lighted place to work. It was an offer that Bruno now abused. But an offer nonetheless. And Bruno wasn't about to let this waiter challenge precedent.

The door to the kitchen flopped open. A waitress shouldered a tray. Bruno smelled the Mediterranean Sea. Inspiration struck and he resumed typing.

"Mr. Tannenbaum . . ." Versace said, as if speaking to a child.

"Can't you see I'm working?" Bruno must have shouted, because heads turned. The blonde in the low-cut glanced his way again.

"Mr. Tannenbaum, the chef would love to offer you his table in the kitchen. It would be an honor . . ."

Bruno wasn't listening. He knew he was imposing. But he also knew he'd been working for hours, days, years to carve out the first few words of a new book. He was writing again.

Writing something real. It was the first step in climbing out of the hole he'd been living in. He was making his comeback. And Versace wasn't going to derail him.

"Bring me more Vin de la Maison," Bruno ordered, swiping at the empty bottle and knocking it over.

Another waiter arrived. A pair of hands reached for his typewriter. They lifted it from the table. His hard-won sentences were being snatched away. He spun. He swung. He felt flesh and bone mash beneath his palm. The Versace glasses smacked the cobbled floor. There was a collective gasp.

Rough hands were on his shoulders. He was on his feet. Standing up so quickly carried the wine from his stomach to his head. He felt someone grabbing his jacket, muscling him toward the door. Then he lost handle on his consciousness.

*   *   *

Bruno came to with his cheek pressed to the concrete. A taxi roared past. A train rattled overhead. He sucked in a mouthful of oily exhaust, blinked and saw his father's typewriter lying upside down before him, the handle on the return broken. Tears burned hot behind his nose, but he sniffed them back.

He heard the door swing open. Big hands were on him again, but gentler this time, coaxing him to his feet. Joel was there. Bruno smelled the garlic, sweat and olive oil. The chef's apron was smeared, his toque askew.

"Bruno, Bruno, look at you." Joel shook his head. The large sailor steadied Bruno on his feet, then took a step back and scratched his sandpapery jaw. Bruno was a big man, but Joel was bigger. "I don't want you back. Not till you straighten yourself out."

"I am straight. I'm back at the top of my game."

Joel reached down and pulled the single page out of the typewriter. He began reading. Bruno watched, eager, expectant, as
Joel studied it.

When Joel finally looked up, Bruno's heart sank. The chef
folded the page and tucked it into Bruno's inside jacket pocket.
"I don't get it. Where's it going?" he asked. Bruno didn't answer.
He couldn't. There was a pause. Joel shook his head. "Try again,
Bruno. Come back when you're in a better place."

Bruno felt like a child as Joel squeezed his shoulder. He could
feel his friend's disappointment, like a cold, heavy weight, in the
chef's grasp.

Joel hailed a cab. It eased to the side of the street and he
helped Bruno in, setting the typewriter gently in his lap. Then he
turned and disappeared back into the maelstrom of the restaurant.

TWO

A Capon

Call the capon the king of the cockerels: this table bird has been gelded and fattened, and the result is the richest, most mouthwatering fowl that can cross your palate. To refer to him as a chicken is an insult. The capon is the perfect gourmet solution for finicky dinner guests, but careful preparation and pairing with an excellent wine also wins him a special place in the practices of seductive cookery.

—BRUNO TANNENBAUM, *TWENTY RECIPES FOR LOVE*

"Some Frog fishmonger thinks he knows good writing . . ." Bruno was saying.

"S'cuse me?" The cabdriver glanced in the rearview.

"Nothing."

Bruno huddled over the typewriter, cursing Joel Berteau. But in his heart, he knew his friend was right. He didn't even unfold the page that Berteau had stuffed into his pocket. How could anything be good after two bottles of wine? He had no doubt he was a decent writer. He'd written a very good novel twenty years before. It hadn't sold exceptionally well, but it earned strong reviews and was translated into French, Spanish and German. One draft, words pouring from his heart, adjectives tumbling from his palate. One draft, and his editor had requested only minor revisions. He'd written the book in France in his twenties, fresh out of college, after he'd spent his savings on a backpacking trip across Europe and then taken a job as a vineyard laborer in the Burgundian village of Pommard to raise funds for his return home. The novel was filled with so many rich vignettes of food and wine that it earned him a guest column at his hometown newspaper, the *Chicago Sun-Times*. This turned into a regular gig reviewing restaurants, then a spot on the local news and finally another book deal.

Bruno's second book sold much better. It was a collection of essays called *Twenty Recipes for Love*. It wasn't very good, in his opinion, but it caught the collective fancy of foodies. And it wasn't just the epicures who bought it: he was surprised that some of the folks in the working-class neighborhood where he'd grown up had read it. That's because it was clever. It had a gimmick: it would help you mend relationships or seduce your neighbor through food. They'd hired a cartoonist from *Playboy* to create vignettes introducing the chapters. "Hooky" was how his agent, Harley, had described it. It had given Bruno a shtick, and he'd been working it ever since. Bruno knew he was a good writer. No doubts there. But what he didn't know was how long it lasted: this state of good writerliness. He feared that being a good writer wasn't a constant. It wasn't a state or plane of existence. Maybe it was a pinnacle you reached only momentarily. What he feared more than anything in the world was that each writer had a limit. A tab. And when your credit ran out, you were done, the well was dry.

This wasn't a new fear brought on by his age. He'd felt it

early on, as soon as he'd started his second book. It was as if he knew whatever came next would be a sham.

Now here he was, an aging, sodden hack taking a cab to his mother's flat. He was broke. His only valuable possessions were a busted typewriter and the single page in his pocket. An opening to another unfinished book. A bridge to nowhere.

Bruno noticed the cabbie's bloodshot eye studying him in the rearview mirror. The man turned and offered a half smile. He was youngish, but weathered, with a scruff of a beard, bags under his eyes and wispy brown hair spraying out from under a newsboy cap.

"Hey," the driver said, "you're that guy, aren't you?"

"What guy?"

"The one who used to be on TV?" He smiled again, showing yellow teeth.

"It's been a while."

"Sure, I remember you. On the news. You did those pieces about the restaurants. Man, you used to tear some of those places to shreds. Close places down. I remember that. I loved it, man. You were ruthless."

"I also gave favorable reviews."

"Sure. But everybody does that."

They rode in silence for a while, the cabbie smiling to himself and glancing on and off in the rearview enough for Bruno to grow nervous about the man's distraction. It was as if the fellow were searching his memory for the vestiges of Bruno's fading career.

"So what are you doing now?" the driver finally asked.

Bruno grasped the typewriter uncomfortably. *I'm separated from my wife,* he thought. *I'm sleeping on my mother's couch.* "I still write a column for the *Sun-Times*."

"Yeah? But nobody reads papers anymore. At least I don't.

You should get a blog or an app or something. That way I could read it on my phone while I'm queued up at O'Hare."

"Of course. Brilliant." Bruno couldn't suppress his sarcasm. He loathed technology. He despised everything that sped up meals, everything that interrupted the slow pleasures of living. He hated televisions in dining rooms and in airport lobbies. He despised mobile phones answered between *il primo* and *il secondo*. And most of all he detested the insipid Internet and its so-called democratization, the fact that every asshole with an opinion could become a critic, that every restaurant could be exalted or decried by any untrained palate, the reviewer's only qualification being his ability to type with his thumbs.

But the cabbie hadn't picked up on Bruno's derision. "Hey, I remember now, you also did that book, right?"

Hope glimmered in Bruno's heart. Had the man read his first novel, *A Season Among the Vines*?

"Yeah, my lady's got that one. It was huge when we were in high school. If you wanted to act classy and get laid, you had to have that book."

The glimmer flickered and died. The book the man spoke of wasn't *Season*, but Bruno's second effort. The *hooky* one.

"What was that called?"

"*Twenty Recipes for Love.*"

"Yeah, right. That was great."

Cheeky and gimmicky though it may have been, *Twenty Recipes* had still carried a core of truth. He'd still been a writer then. At least it had made him famous.

"Hey . . ." the driver said after a pause. He was staring at Bruno full-on in the rearview at the same time that he swerved between cars on the Kennedy Expressway. Bruno gripped his typewriter tighter. "You can help me out."

"How so?"

"My girlfriend. She just got a promotion. She now runs the perfume counter at Marshall Field's."

Bruno smiled. The man was humble, maybe a little crass, but he still respected tradition. He refused to use the landmark Chicago department store's new name: Macy's. The fellow had a sense of history. Bruno appreciated this.

"And?"

"Well, I want to fix her a little something to . . . touch off a little spark, maybe heat things up in the sack . . . if you know what I'm saying."

"I do."

"So, can you help me out?"

Bruno searched the recesses of his brain, struggling to remember his prescriptions from *Twenty Recipes*. He'd divided the meals into function: first dates, rekindling the dying flame, celebrating the lasting commitment. It was silly pop psychology, but it had given Bruno a reputation as a sort of physician for relationships. *Oh, the irony.*

"How old is she?" Bruno asked.

"Thirty-five."

"Her favorite book?"

"She ain't really the book type. She reads magazines. You know. *People*. That kind of stuff."

"That's unfortunate. Movies?"

"She likes chick flicks. But the old ones. Ever see *Roman Holiday*?"

"Ah . . ." Bruno said, brightening and leaning forward, his mind whirring as the alcohol receded and instinct took over. "Have you been to Natasha's on Diversey?"

"Nah, but I know where it is."

"Good. Go there on a Thursday; that's when they get deliveries. First thing in the morning. You're looking for a fresh capon. Go large, eight pounds. You'll want to pick up some truffles and fresh sage. Get some good olive oil from Nick's down in Greektown. Taste it first. It should smell green and leave a tang in the back of your throat. You're going to want to make a paste of the oil and sage and rub down the whole bird. Roast it with new potatoes. Pick up a decent white, but nothing too showy. You don't want to upstage the fowl. Maybe a Vouvray, or a Grüner Veltliner. Better yet, get one of each. You getting this?"

"Getting it," the cabbie said. He was looking down into the passenger seat and scribbling, somehow managing to thread through the speeding highway traffic without looking at the road. Bruno didn't notice. His pulse surged. He closed his eyes and imagined the meal coming together.

"Now, you're going to want to go classy. Clear out a room and move the table to the middle. Use a white tablecloth. Don't skimp on the flowers."

"Gotcha, gotcha. White tablecloth. This is good stuff. Really good. Thanks."

Bruno leaned back, satisfied, at last, to be of some use. The cabbie nodded as he drove. Undoubtedly he was thinking of his girlfriend, the expression on her face when she returned home from her perfume counter to see the carefully arranged table, her breath on his cheek as he takes her into his arms, and then later . . . their bodies lying beside one another, glazed with a sheen of sweat . . .

Bruno leaned back and smiled, trying to remember what it was like to wake up next to a woman.

THREE

Tenderloin

While tenderloin is sensual by name and nature, the emotional application of this cut can vary greatly. Pork expresses comfort and confidence. Beef, unabashed extravagance. Prepare bison for your lover and you are taking a bold risk that could overwhelm and frighten. The tenderloin of a domesticated American elk, however, is perhaps the most versatile choice. The hint of wild game can remind the diner of forgotten desire, the buttery softness in the heart of a filet can connote the affection that lies just beneath a surface seared by years and difficult times.

—Bruno Tannenbaum, *Twenty Recipes for Love*

Bruno choked on a snore, jolting awake. He cracked his eyes, the light angling through the slats in the window shades arousing his headache. A family of porcelain ducks watched him from the lace doily on an end table. He was stretched on the couch, still wearing his rumpled sport coat, though his mother had tucked a warm fleece blanket under his chin.

He turned his head and spied his father's battered typewriter facing him from the coffee table; its keys formed a mocking grin. He could vaguely remember playing on the floor as a child while his father sat straight-backed on a creaking chair, carefully using the contraption to peck out a bank loan application. His dad had worked long hours for a kosher butcher on the far north of the city, and he'd held out hopes of one day buying the shop from its aging owner. He had been cautious and pragmatic like other North Side immigrants, and his sole daily luxury was a glass of reasonable Chablis that stood beside the typewriter, filled to a line on the side demarking four ounces, and not a drop more. Bruno had hoped that the ancient machine could somehow rekindle his literary fire, but it hadn't been the typewriter working its magic last night at La Marsellaise. It had been the Vacqueyras.

He smelled coffee and fresh bread in the kitchen. His mother had already left for work, but she'd left him well provisioned. A small carafe of coffee stood next to poppy-seed-studded *mohn-berches* on a plate beside a pat of Beurre d'Isigny.

He was late for work but refused to rush. The health risk of fretting over your day job was a lesson learned from his father's demise—the old man died of massive heart failure at work when Bruno was only seven. Bruno learned from that experience that life should be lived in the moment, filling the glass well past the four-ounce line, right up to the rim, because you never know when you'll wind up lifeless on the shop floor clutching a broom.

It was a warmish spring day and he took the El downtown, strolling through Millennium Park, his well-trained sniffer detecting a trace of pear tree blossoms above the exhaust and sewage, and then a hint of sweet lake air behind it. He was still feeling the joy of spring as he danced out of the elevator onto the ninth floor of the *Sun-Times* building.

Iris Hernandez at the reception desk smiled up at him through a mane of glossy black hair.

"Good morning," Bruno chimed, removing his sunglasses and winking. He'd always loved this compact fireplug of a woman who guarded the lobby.

"Good morning?"

"Heavens, I haven't missed lunch, have I?"

"Almost, but not quite."

"Speaking of lunch, any plans?"

Iris patted a neatly tied plastic sack on her desk. She smiled. She liked him. Or so he thought. She was an adorable twentysomething who lived with her mother and her six-year-old daughter in Garfield Park. She was single. Never been married. How some lout could impregnate her and then flee was beyond him. But then, could Bruno really judge?

This little lunch routine was something of a game. It wasn't quite flirting. Iris was nearly half Bruno's age, and Bruno was usually broke.

"My mother would kill me if I brought this home. She says wasting food is a sin."

"Sounds like something my mother would say. Wise women."

He offered a wink as he moved on, but Iris poked her head around the corner.

"Oh, hey, Grovnick is looking for you."

"Thanks for the warning."

Ernie Grovnick was Bruno's boss. He was the editor of the lifestyle page, a newspaper lifer. He was budget-conscious and excelled at appeasing upper management. He could write a mean headline. But he was also unimaginative and one of the larger pains in Bruno's ass.

Bruno wove through cubicles to his cubby in the corner.

The sterility of the newsroom was relieved by the floor-to-ceiling glass that afforded a generous view of the Chicago River, the springish breeze adding a lively ripple to the surface of the gray water. Unlike the others on the floor, Bruno's desk contained no computer. He worked with yellow legal pads and little black notebooks. It was the only civilized way to write now that Bruno's brief romance with his father's manual typewriter was fading. Bruno also felt that he was doing a service to the interns who input his words into their computers. Sort of like fine art students who make precise copies of a Rembrandt or Modigliani.

The rest of Bruno's cube was taken up by culinary magazines, his telephone, notes and files and a collection of essential resources, including *Le Guide Culinaire, The Professional Chef, Consider the Oyster* and *Beard on Food,* as well as the classic text on Russian cookery, *A Gift to Young Housewives,* which Bruno kept on hand largely for the effect of the title.

He licked the tip of his pencil and began to scribble on a notepad. He was formulating a concept for an article: all great restaurants began to fade as they approached the decade mark. La Marsellaise, turning ten this year, would be his first case study. *Ah, the might of the pen!*

He leaned back and drummed his fingers on his stack of books, staring down at the river, his dark and watery muse. His reverie was interrupted by the squeak of Grovnick's loafers.

He ignored the man until Grovnick cleared his throat.

"Um, Bruno, we need to talk."

"I'm working on a story, Grovnick." Bruno slowly turned the crank on his pencil sharpener, breathing in the metallic smell of ground lead, shredding spirals of paint and wood into its clear plastic tray.

Grovnick tilted the legal pad in front of Bruno. It was blank save for the words *ten years, decade, decline*. "Doesn't look like much of a story to me."

"Goddammit, Ernie, a writer does his real work here, not here." Bruno spun in his chair, tapping his head and then the legal pad.

"Excuse me for offending your artistic sensibilities, but I've got a dozen writers to pay. And I, unfortunately, do my real work here." He tapped his watch and spun. There were chuckles from the other journalists in the room. A few rolled eyes.

Bruno followed the circle of flesh at the back of Grovnick's head that shone through his greasy black hair. He noticed smirks and winks as he passed the cubicles.

Grovnick's office likewise had floor-to-ceiling windows, but its view of a neighboring building made it feel confined. The desk was stacked with papers and manila folders. There was a framed photo of Ernie in wraparound sunglasses hoisting a fishing pole in one hand and a toothy northern pike from a Minnesota lake in the other. There were photos of his college-age children. A crowded bookshelf indicated that the man had at least read a few worthwhile books. There was a copy of Mike Royko's *Boss*, one of Ebert's movie compendiums and Asbury's delightfully lurid ramble, *Gem of the Prairie*.

Bruno slouched in the chair across the desk from his editor like a rebellious teen in the principal's office. But now that they'd settled in, Grovnick's gruff demeanor changed. He fumbled with proofs on his desk.

"So, how's the book coming, Bruno?"

"It's fine."

"You're overdue, you know. You're a good writer."

"Thanks, Ernie." A compliment. Grovnick usually didn't

do flattery; it always seemed to pain or embarrass him. Bruno smiled.

"When I read *Season*, Bruno . . . holy shit . . . what was it, twenty years ago now? When I read that novel, I thought, *There's a guy who knows his grape juice. There's a guy who knows how to eat. How to enjoy life. And then tell other people about it.* Then when Harley called me up and said he had a guy in town who could do a food column, I thought, *Yeah, yeah, whatever. I got a million guys who can do food.* But then he said your name, and I didn't have to think twice about taking the idea up to the boss. Everybody knew you. You were a writer's writer. You had fans all across the business. I knew it was a good idea."

Bruno squinted at Grovnick with suspicion. This was beginning to sound like a eulogy. "What's this really about, Ernie?"

Grovnick released a long sigh. He looked right at Bruno, and then his eyes flitted away. "We're going to have to let you go."

Bruno laughed and started to get up. "Come on, don't waste my time. We've been through this before."

"No, it's real this time."

"That's what you said last time."

"The maître d' from La Marsellaise called. He said you made a scene."

Bruno froze, his hand on the door handle. "What's that got to do with anything? I was on my own time. I had to go somewhere to write. Ma had some girls over for pinochle . . ."

"Joel Berteau is a customer. He takes out full-page ads. You broke some waiter's glasses?"

"The whole reason Joel's little dive still exists is because of me. I discovered that fucking place! Were people lining up and down the street to get in before I started writing about that Frog?"

"They sent us a bill for the wine. And the glasses."

"Those sonofabitches broke my dad's typewriter!"

"The twelfth floor wasn't happy."

"My job isn't to make the twelfth floor happy. It's making the readers happy that counts."

"That's the other thing, Bruno. Your blog traffic hasn't been the greatest, either."

"Blog traffic? I don't even know what the hell that means! I'm a columnist, for chrissake."

"You were a columnist."

"Were?"

"Corporate wants you gone. It's a tough business. The Internet's slowly killing us. Death by a thousand cuts. Arts and Culture just cut four columns."

Bruno was beginning to realize that this was an actual firing. It felt different from the virtual firings he'd experienced in the past, when he'd storm out of the room and Grovnick would appear at his cube later in the day, his voice conspiratorial, like a defense lawyer. *I got you an extension, Bruno. I convinced them that they don't want to be seen dumping a top writer. Sends a bad signal.*

But there was a hint of sadness in the way Grovnick regarded him now. The middle manager sat slumped and helpless, merely an instrument of the forces that drive the world.

Bruno felt a tingle at the back of his neck. *Jesus, this is it.* How much lower could he get? He was already on Ma's couch. He was supposed to be helping Anna with the mortgage and the girls' college funds. He dreaded hearing the inevitable disappointment and condescension in his estranged wife's voice when he told her the next time he visited his daughters.

He had weighed the pros and cons of being fired before. It could be a good thing. Unemployment benefits, if he scrimped, would give him a few months to write. It would be a small price to pay for a full draft of his next book.

But he now recognized that impulse as a fantasy. Life without a net wasn't exactly exhilarating. It was terrifying. He didn't even have the opening of his new book. Being cast off by the paper would be a confirmation of his greatest fear: the end of his relevancy. An irrelevant writer was someone in need of a career change. And there was very little else for which he was qualified. Obsolescence, he realized, was humiliating. He felt tears pressing. He forced them back. He released the door handle and leaned against it, facing Grovnick. "Give me six months, Ernie. I just need to get a jump on the book."

"Sorry, Bruno."

"I'll do a contract. Half-time, no benefits. Just kick me a little something. Six months and I'll be on my feet again."

"We can't."

"I'm not going to beg, Ernie. Please . . ."

"You're already begging."

"No, I'm not."

"Yes, you are."

"Okay, I'm begging. Please, you wormy little sonofabitch. *Please*."

"No." Ernie handed Bruno an envelope.

"What's this?"

"Your final check. It's prorated through yesterday. There's a bit extra for vacation time."

Bruno took it and stared at it for a long moment, his heart pounding, experiencing a parade of emotions. He'd passed from denial to indignation, and then, strangely, he felt a ray of hope. After all, this was an early payday.

His stomach rumbled, distracting him from the hard ques-

tion of what he would do next with his life. His short-term
goal became lunch. There was an upside to everything, and he
now had actual money in hand, whereas a few minutes before
that had not been the case. Wasn't staving off despair a worthy
investment? He felt a little shiver of happiness that made the
world of unemployment a touch less bleak.

The gears began to whirr in the back of his brain. *Lunch!*
Nick's Fishmarket in the Loop flew coho salmon in daily. Perhaps that would be irresponsible. Maybe he should just go down
to Maxwell Street and get the greasiest Polish sausage he could
find. Then he could hit Natasha's and pick up groceries, the best
ingredients. Hunt down a bottle of Côte du Rhône or two. What
could he fix for Anna and the girls? He'd surprise them for dinner. He was now unencumbered, liberated from the long and
dreadful funerary wake that was the demise of the newspaper
industry. He was now free to write! A celebration was in order.

Ernie stood with his hands in his pockets, staring at his shoes.
He wiped his nose with the back of a sleeve. Bruno suddenly felt
a little sorry for the man. It wasn't his fault.

"Hey, Ernie . . . I don't want you to think that I never appreciated what you've done for me over the years. You're one of the
top editors around. I mean that."

"Thanks, Bruno."

Bruno engulfed him in a hug. He felt the small man's shoulders heave with a sob. *The sorry little bastard's going to miss me.*

"Bruno, you're one of the last old-school true believers. Used
to be our room was filled with guys like you. And holy smokes,
did we break some great stuff. This is a sad day for me."

"Of course it is," Bruno said, kissing Grovnick on his balding
forehead and spinning toward the door. "But don't worry about
me. I'll be back in top form before you know it."

But Grovnick caught Bruno's sleeve before he could slip out the door. He cleared his throat sheepishly. "Bruno, I wanted to ask you something."

"Fire away."

"Now's probably not the time."

"It's your last chance . . ."

"Well, it's kind of personal."

"Okay, then," Bruno said, grabbing the door handle and making to leave.

"Wait. It's Lois. I wanted to fix her a little something for our anniversary."

Bruno could read him right away. There was a hint of despair on the edge of Ernie's nervous smile. His eyes had the wild look of someone who was afraid to give up on life, the jaundiced haze of a man beginning to doubt the resilience of his marriage.

"How long's it been?"

"Thirty years . . ."

"That's not what I'm asking, Ernie."

"What do you mean?"

"How long has it been since you did the horizontal mambo?"

"Huh?"

"Since you and Lois were lathered up and rounding the last bend? Since you were screwing like teenagers in the back of Dad's Buick?"

"Umm . . ."

"Out with it . . ."

"Ah . . ."

"Come on, then . . ."

"Two years. Maybe three."

"And before that?"

"Used to be we'd get a room up in Door County every year on

our anniversary. But last couple of years . . . nothing. Neither of us have the energy, I guess. Or maybe . . ."

"Maybe what?"

"Maybe Lois has been stepping out on me. Maybe I don't do it for her anymore and she's been looking elsewhere for . . . you know."

Ernie slumped back in his chair, a beaten man. Bruno tried to suppress a smile as he eyed the photo of Lois on the file cabinet behind him. She was grinning beneath the butt-crack center part of her hairdo, the shoulder pads in her blouse hiding her neck and extra chins. The photographer's lights glinting off the lenses of huge round glasses supported by a knobby beak. Bruno couldn't actually picture her "stepping out" on Ernie. *Remember that love is in the eye of the beholder.*

"This is a hell of a time to be asking me for advice, Ernie."

"I'm sorry. It's just probably my last opportunity."

"Fine. It's been two years, you say?"

"Maybe three."

"Let me think." Bruno paced the room. Grovnick watched expectantly. Bruno stopped suddenly, stabbing his finger at the air. "Got it! Elk tenderloin."

"Really?"

"Absolutely. Fischer's Meat House down by the river. And don't let him sell you *aged*. That's just a euphemism for *rotten*."

"How do I fix it?"

"Stud with garlic spears. Brush with olive oil. Good stuff. Extra, extra. Roll in fresh-cracked black pepper, not too sharp, a bit crunchy. You want it seared on the outside but real pink in the middle. You're going for contrast here. Grill it. Soon as the juice is clear, you're done. Got that?"

Ernie scribbled furiously on a reporter's notebook. "What do I serve it with?"

"Grilled asparagus, of course. Don't be so dense, Ernie. And wild rice. You can get the real stuff, gathered by the Ojibway on lakes up in Minnesota. Natasha's has it."

"Wine?"

"Pommard Premier Cru. Maybe Volnay. Or an Oregon Pinot. Temperance Hill, or Yamhill County. Don't go cheap, Ernie—I know you." Bruno shot him a stern glance and Grovnick nodded earnestly. He snapped his notebook closed and glanced back at Lois's photo. He seemed relieved, as if a weight had been lifted.

"Thanks, Bruno, I . . ."

But Bruno was already halfway out the door. "Don't tell me you owe me, Ernie."

At his cube, Bruno swept his stack of legal pads into the trash. He didn't truly believe in notes and records. He stored everything important in his head. It was the best way to protect his sources . . . especially those he invented. He grabbed his stack of cooking books and headed for the door, whistling and planning lunch.

He stopped short as he passed Iris. Her eyes glistened as she stared into her monitor screen.

"Did you know, Iris?"

She opened her lips to speak, but no words came. Instead, she nodded her head. She brushed her hair out of her face. She glanced up at him. A tear welled and shivered in the corner of her eye, threatening to drop. "I'm sorry, Bruno," she whispered. "Oh, here. This is yours." She cleared her throat and handed him a stack of his mail: some overdue bills and a letter from *Gourmet* magazine. Anna had had his mail forwarded to the office after kicking him out.

He stuffed it into the inside pocket of his blazer and hovered. He realized he'd never embrace Iris. Inside his head he heard the sad strains of the prelude to the waltz in Tchaikovsky's *Eugene Onegin,* always one of his favorite operas. Iris rose from her desk and floated to Bruno like Tatyana in the opening of the second act. He slipped his arm around her, his hand at the small of her back, her forehead pressed to his chin, the fingers of their extended hands interlaced. He breathed in the smell of her hair. Lemons, the chemical tang of shampoo, car exhaust and all the must and splendor of a spring morning in Chicago. They swirled to the three-part meter and the office dissolved around them.

Her tear slipped, running down a long eyelash and dropping on her cheek, and his fantasy evaporated. He was simply standing across her desk from her. For a sad, awkward moment he wanted to bend down and kiss her. But instead he asked: "You sure you don't want to grab lunch? How about Trotter's? My treat. It'll knock your socks off."

Iris glanced back toward Grovnick's office. She smiled. She thought. Then she looked at her bundled lunch on the desk. "I can't, Bruno. Mom doesn't like it when I waste food."

"Of course. She's absolutely right."

Bruno bowed again with mock formality. He blew her a kiss. Iris laughed. He skipped to the elevator. He'd put up a brave front for the gang, but as soon as the doors closed and he began to sink back to earth, the weight of the moment bore down on him. His shoulders heaved and he buried his face in his hands and wept.

FOUR

Poor Cousin of the Artichoke

The magic of the humble cardoon lies in its contrasts. It's an ugly, thistle-like plant with unappetizing leaves. Even its brief flower is unspectacular. Much of the world considers it a weed. But beneath its scrubby exterior there is much to love. The delicate petals, steamed and buttered, pack more subtlety than the leaves of its artichoke cousin. The ancient Etruscans prized its braised stalks as much as today's Tuscan chefs. While often consumed for its medicinal properties, I recommend it as a reminder that beneath the thorny skin of an angry world lies the nourishment and comfort of those we find most dear.

—Bruno Tannenbaum, *Twenty Recipes for Love*

There is a certain magic in holding a double-bagged brown paper sack full of good groceries. It reminded Bruno of a hug from his grandmother. Standing on the steps of the brownstone where he had once lived, Bruno found comfort in the sack even while his knees threatened to buckle. He clutched the groceries and buried his face in the bag, breathing in the mix of flavors: earthy vegetables, the coppery tenor of fresh porterhouse cuts of Chianina beef, all wrapped in the clean, dull aroma of a new paper bag. Perhaps he lingered because that mixture of scents was glorious. Or more likely because he was afraid to go inside and tell Anna that he'd been fired. But admitting his unemployment was the right thing to do and he was proud of himself for being responsible, though this may have been canceled out by his purchase of a few hundred dollars' worth of groceries and wine for the evening's meal with money from his severance check. He figured he was facing a drought, so this was his last chance to cook and eat well for some time.

He swallowed hard and knocked.

But before his knuckle could rap the door again, it was yanked inward and a freckled, round-faced girl of eight stood looking up at him, blinking through a wild mop of mousy brown hair. Green eyes sparkled and she released a squeal, leaping into his free arm.

"Daddy!"

"Lamb Chop!"

She squeezed his neck until it cracked and Bruno was reminded that the desperate affection of your child is perhaps the finest sensation one can experience. This recognition conjured a deep sadness in his chest now that he could only be around her and in this house as a visitor.

"What's in the bag, Pops?" the girl, Carmen, said, peering inside. He held it away from her, chuckling.

"You'll have to wait. You gonna help me cook?"

"You bet!"

The house was tidy, almost pristine. Every time Bruno came it felt more foreign. At first his stacks of books disappeared.

Then the knickknacks he and Anna had collected as a couple started to vanish. Bruno used to keep empty bottles of some of the better wines they'd uncorked as decorations, but such trophies had long since been recycled.

Anna had also replaced many of the family photos. He noticed one now on a table in the foyer. It showed her and the girls at Disney World. Bruno would have been no more likely to take the girls to witness that gauche spectacle than he would have brought them to a McDonald's. Perhaps that was selfish and pretentious of him. But in the photo, they looked happy. A giant-headed Minnie Mouse hovered, out of focus, in the background behind the trio. They all wore broad, genuine grins. The photo seemed a demonstration of the fact that they were doing just fine without him.

Bruno's older daughter, Claire, drifted quietly down the stairs. She was more restrained and aloof than her sister. She stood on her toes and pecked Bruno on his cheek. At sixteen, she seemed almost a grown woman rather than a child. She was striking, her long blond hair fashionably haphazard, bookish glasses traded for contact lenses, and teeth perfectly emerged from braces to grace her with a smile she was not yet quite comfortable using.

"Claire! How are you, sweetheart?"

She shrugged and offered a half smile. Carmen frowned, not wanting to share her father's attention with her big sister.

"Why don't you get some pans out? We've got cooking to do."

"I've got to finish my homework, Dad," Claire said. It felt like a rebuke. *How could schoolwork be more important than dinner?* More evidence of Anna's disproportionate influence.

"I'll help you, Daddy," Carmen piped in. He smooched her on the cheek.

"Of course you will, kiddo!"

He headed into the kitchen and found Anna unloading the dishwasher. She wore a shortish business skirt. He set Carmen down and indulged himself in a long gaze at his estranged wife's posterior, longing to walk up behind her and place one hand on her hip, burying his beard in the back of her neck.

She must have felt his presence, because she started speaking before she turned around. "You're late."

"I needed to pick up a few things."

"The girls have school tomorrow."

"I'll help Daddy cook! We'll have it ready lickety-split," Carmen said. Anna turned and leaned against the counter. She released a long sigh. She wore her long curls tightly bound, but a strand had slipped free and hung in her eyes. She was pale and drawn. It seemed there were more lines of worry around her mouth than he'd remembered. He'd had a hand in creating a few of those back when their marriage had begun its decline. The extra week in Paris for "research" that could more accurately be described as binge-drinking, eating and a tad bit of copulation, and so he'd confessed in an article for *Playboy*. Why try to hide it? During another junket he was photographed with a model in Milan for some Italian rag. It had only been lunch, according to the caption, but Anna could read through the newsprint.

And then there was the money, which seemed to last no longer than his fidelity. There was always an expensive bottle of wine to invest in. A lavish dinner. The lifestyle didn't change as the funds dried up. His TV spot on the news only lasted a few years before folks grew tired of him. The newspaper didn't pay much for a washed-up columnist. The new book never came. The magazine articles appeared fewer and farther between.

Bruno's drinking increased. He slept until noon. He disappeared for more research trips, though he never seemed to return with a story. He finally came home to find a set of cardboard boxes melting from the rain on the front porch, a signal even Bruno couldn't fail to understand.

They'd had an amicable separation. There had been no demands. No rancor. No split time with the girls. Anna had instead insisted that he simply leave until he grew up. At first he was happy with the arrangement; it would allow him plenty of time to restart his new book and put his career back together, which would eventually lead to winning his family back.

That was two years ago.

In the meantime, Anna struggled to meet the bills. She'd taken on freelance bookkeeping work on the weekends. There was an after-school program for Carmen and college test prep classes for Claire. She socked away what she could for university tuition.

Bruno sent money at random, though due to the steady collapse of his career it amounted to even less than when he'd lived here. Still, he'd made attempts at being good. He came by a few nights a week for dinner. He took Carmen to gymnastics and jazz dance. He took Claire to Cubs games. He hadn't slept or even dined with any other women since the separation, though admittedly not for lack of trying.

Anna sighed. "Remember, Claire's got a test tomorrow."

"Then she needs a good meal in her belly!" He unpacked groceries. He unwrapped a bloody paper bundle, breathing in deeply the deep red steak. "Carmen, pepper!"

"Yes, Chef!" Carmen leapt into action.

She produced a pepper mill.

"We'll have everyone fed in no time." He winked at Anna as

he cracked pepper onto the steaks. "Carmen, we'll need risotto—two cups. Pronto!"

Anna left the kitchen wearing a straight-lipped smile that was either indicating amusement or masking annoyance. After all these years she was still a mystery. He dreaded telling her that he'd lost his job. But he thought that it might finally put him on a baseline footing. It provided clarity. If he could convince her it was a wake-up call, that he'd hit rock-bottom and now knew he had to change his ways, maybe he could start to play a bigger role in his family again. But first there was dinner.

He immersed himself in the preparation.

Bruno could remember the first time he cooked with Claire. It was a simple pizza margherita. She was three. It was a complete mess, but he recalled her amazement as she watched the miraculous transformation through the oven glass. As the girls grew, they spent more hours in the kitchen together, working their way up to cabbage rolls, cassoulet and brown sauce reductions. Dabbling in pastries and coating the counters in flour dust.

With Carmen's help, Anna's clean kitchen was again transformed into the staging area for an elaborate production. Carmen inexplicably used three pans to create one risotto dish. Olive oil coated the counters and peppercorns speckled the stove. Bruno reveled in the grand mess of it all.

Carmen turned on the kitchen radio and began dancing to some saccharine pop music as they worked, the beat heightened by the clatter of pots and pans. Ever nimble on his feet despite his size, Bruno hooked arms with Carmen and they do-si-doed. Claire passed by and rolled her eyes.

In truth, Bruno detested most of this contemporary music. He'd been an opera fan after he learned that James Beard, one of his personal heroes, had pursued an opera career before he began cooking. It started as an affectation, a way for a kid from a working-class Chicago neighborhood to pose as cultured, but it had grown on him. Bruno had once insisted that only great works should be played during the preparation of food, and this in his view included mainly opera, though Ella Fitzgerald, Billie Holiday and Lightnin' Hopkins were acceptable alternatives. One Direction certainly didn't make the cut, but then the girls were moving on without him, and the new default station on the kitchen radio served as evidence.

But when Carmen later paused mid-stir to switch the dial to a public station playing *Don Giovanni,* Bruno felt a warmth in his belly that, either by nurture or by nature, he'd somehow managed to remain present in his daughters' lives. Carmen dirtied two different cutting boards for the morels. She splashed milky, foaming broth and rice onto the stovetop while she attempted to sing along with Ottavio's aria, clutching the pan with one hand and her chest with the other.

Bruno sang, too. He prepared the meat carefully, trimming and molding it into shape with his fingers. He snipped parsley.

Claire drifted by the kitchen door again and peered in. Bruno caught her eye as he flopped a steak on the lightly floured board. He winked at her. She nodded and left.

Moments later, she showed up again, this time ostensibly for a glass of water. Bruno smiled to himself. She hovered over Carmen's shoulder. Despite his younger child's best efforts, she was making a hash of the risotto. Claire couldn't restrain herself.

"You need more oil."

"It's already in there!"

"It's not enough."

Claire sighed dutifully and took over from the sulking Carmen. A minute later the teenager was immersed in cutting fresh cardoons and humming along with *Don Giovanni*. Bruno grinned and uncorked one of the two pricey bottles of Barolo he'd brought, splashing himself a generous pour.

They fussed over the presentation. Anna was coaxed out of her office. She had changed and let down her hair, brown curls resting on her shoulders. Bruno thought he detected a trace of orange peel when she drifted past, perhaps the Annick Goutal perfume he'd bought to make amends after the Italian incident. It hadn't worked, but it smelled delicious.

The girls set the table and lit candles. With one hand on the dimmer and the other cupped under the bowl of a wineglass, Bruno dipped the lights as Anna scooted in her chair. The girls lingered in the dark kitchen, exchanging harsh whispers like the nervous scramble before a school play. Anna pressed her lips together, but a smile swelled in her cheeks.

The girls made their grand entrance, carrying serving dishes. Carmen set a clean white casserole dish before her mother and removed the top with a clink, revealing a mound of fluffed risotto garnished with a pair of cilantro sprigs, waxy morels glistening in the candlelight. "*Risotto al carciofi,* madam."

She curtsied and Claire took her place, laying out a platter of sautéed cardoons, the stalks piled in the middle, and the blades of the flowers arranged around the edges.

"*Cardi trippati.* They have medicinal value in some cultures. Some people think it's a weed, but Dad says, 'If it's—'"

"'If it's good enough for the ancient Etruscans,'" Anna finished, glancing at Bruno, "'it's good enough for us.'" He smiled. It was immensely pleasing to be feeling like a family again. It made Bruno think that splurging on this meal had been a masterstroke. He hoped it would help lessen the blow later when he told Anna about his job.

Claire disappeared into the kitchen and returned, straining under the weight of a platter of huge porterhouse cuts. "*La bistecca!*" she declared. Everyone watched her set it down. Clear juice welled under the steaks, the seared surface adorned with cracked pepper and rosemary sprigs, the traces of fat clinging to the side translucent gold and buttery. Bruno closed his eyes and inhaled the raw mineral bite of the cardoons intertwining with the rich animal texture of the steaks. He knew he'd be able to cut the Chianina with the edge of his fork.

Anna offered a genuine smile as they all sat. Food, after all, was a way into her heart as well. Bruno uncorked the second bottle of Barolo and poured himself a healthy splash. He reached over to pour for Anna, but she stopped him after a couple ounces, which didn't bode well. Claire proffered a wineglass half filled with mineral water, and he gave her a splash as well, a ritual they'd started when she was thirteen in hopes that a little exposure would keep alcohol from being some mysterious novelty as she grew older.

Carmen held up her own glass of sparkling water. "Can I try some, Daddy?" Bruno poured a dram into her glass before Anna could stop him, just enough to turn her seltzer pink. Carmen giggled.

Then there was an awkward pause as they all eyed the food and hesitated. It was as if they realized at that moment the reality of the situation. They weren't a nuclear family. This was a sham, an exception to their daily routine, evidenced by the fact that they'd taken out the good china.

But then someone's stomach grumbled and Carmen hefted a huge spoonful of risotto onto her plate. The dining commenced, and Bruno noted that Anna helped herself to one of the larger cuts of steak. A healthy appetite was a sign of happiness. Somewhere beneath her tough shell she was smiling.

The meal was by all accounts a success, and after they had finished clearing the table, Bruno met Anna in the kitchen doorway. She carried a stack of plates and he was swirling the last of the wine in his glass, rocking slowly on his feet. Her face was flushed, her cheeks rosy and youthful, a strand of hair slipping across her forehead. She smiled.

"That was amazing. As usual. Thank you, Bruno."

He figured that now was as good a time as any for his confession. He followed her to the kitchen, where she set the plates down next to the sink. She spun, surprised to find him close behind her. It was all he could do to refrain from leaning in to kiss her on the lips.

She looped her arms around his neck and pulled him down. She kissed him on the forehead, and then they pressed their brows together.

"Thank you," she said. "That must have cost a fortune."

"Life is short—"

"So eat like it means something," she said, finishing the phrase he had used to sign off from his television news segment. She rested her chin on his shoulder and pulled him closer. His heart beat so hard that he could feel it reverberate against her body. "It means so much to the girls to have you here."

"It means a lot to me, too."

"And I have to admit it gets lonely."

Bruno slipped one hand to the small of Anna's back, a familiar indentation, molded to fit perfectly. He squeezed her tighter. He felt a small opening here that he hadn't sensed in years. He began to second-guess his planned confession. Seducing his estranged wife would be so much more fun.

"So what did you think of the *bistecca*?"

"And cardoons? Chapter nineteen, right?"

He was surprised that she knew the book so well . . . better than even he did. But then, she'd been his first editor on every draft.

"So, did it work?"

"Hard to say."

"I think maybe we should test it out." He pulled away and pirouetted her, ending in a dip and a kiss. "What do you say?"

"It's a weeknight. I've got work to do."

"So true." Bruno sighed. "And Ma's got the couch all made up. You know how disappointed she'd be if I didn't show."

Anna laughed. Ella Fitzgerald was crooning silky strands on the kitchen radio, and they slow-danced, his bristly cheek pressed to her temple.

"You know," he said, "you're still the best thing that ever happened to me."

"Even after everything?"

"Even after everything. I'd do it all again," he said, pulling her closer.

"Bruno . . ." Anna offered halfheartedly.

"No strings attached," he said, pulling her closer. "You could kick me out in the morning."

"Why?"

"Because we're technically still married. And I'm charming as hell. And there's a half bottle of very good wine remaining. And I've been largely good . . ."

Anna stopped short and pulled away. "What do you mean, 'largely' good?" She was half teasing, but something must have crossed Bruno's face. She could always read him like a clean draft. "Bruno?"

It was certainly an opportune moment to confess. Bruno thought about it, and it was clear that Anna could see the wheels turning. The bad news could wait. It had been a long time since

they hadn't ended an evening with an argument or strained diffi-
dence, and he didn't want to spoil the moment.

"Oh, you know," Bruno said, pulling her close again. "I've
practically been a saint . . . aside from the occasional splurge."

"Like tonight's wine?"

"Precisely."

"It was very good."

"Perhaps you'd like to have some more."

"I've got work to do."

"Yeah. So do I."

"You do?"

"The book."

"Oh, of course."

They danced awhile longer, but the opportunity was gone.

The song ended and Anna switched back to the pop station,
which drew Carmen to the kitchen to help clean. Anna reminded
Bruno of an upcoming parent-teacher conference at Carmen's
school as she brushed off her apron. Carmen took a place at her
side and began to scrub a crusted baking dish while Anna smiled,
patting her daughter on her shoulder as Bruno stood there
suddenly feeling purposeless.

*   *   *

Later, Bruno lay on the roof of the house next to Claire, the clink
and tinkle of Anna and Carmen cleaning dishes coming through
the window of the floor below a soothing, merry sound. They
watched a satellite trace across the sky, fighting through the pink
haze of Chicago's ambient light.

Lying with their backs on the black tar shingles that were still
oozing the day's warmth had become something of a ritual for
Claire and Bruno. It was their refuge from a troubled household

when the marriage was going to hell. It also provided Claire respite from an overly energetic younger sister.

Bruno balanced his glass on his belly and swirled the last drop of his wine. He felt his daughter's presence next to him, radiating like the roof tiles, but this sensation was a blend of teenage immortality and worry.

"There's another one," Claire said, pointing out a second satellite. Bruno squinted through his wine buzz.

"I see two of them."

"I think you're tipsy."

"Probably." He smiled sadly and attempted to change the subject. "You should see the stars in Chianti. They're like nowhere else. The dark hillsides are dotted with lights so that it's hard to tell where the world stops and the heavens begin."

"I wish I could come with you sometime. On one of your assignments."

"Of course. Next time, let's do it."

"Really?"

He turned his head and looked at her, nodding and smiling. She was a little girl again. "Absolutely. As long as it doesn't interfere with school."

"I'm dying to go to Europe."

He didn't have the heart to admit that the prospects of some magazine expensing a trip to Italy were as remote as the satellites circling overhead.

They lay in silence.

"What are you thinking about?" she asked. Why were women always asking him this question? It's not something you can answer honestly. Could he tell her that he'd just lost his job? That he was no longer writing? That he was struggling to imagine a useful purpose for his life? That, despite lying here, belly full of a good meal and a favorite wine, next to one of his top three most favorite people in the world, on a warm spring night under the stars, he wasn't happy?

"How's school?" he asked, changing the subject.

"It's fine."

"Grades good?"

"Second in my class."

"Not bad."

"I don't want to be valedictorian. I don't want to be the kid who knows it all. Some kind of sideshow attraction. Salutatorian is a much better option for me."

"I suppose that's reasonable."

"Really?"

"Yeah, why not?"

"Mom says I shouldn't sell myself short. She also doesn't want me to go to culinary school. She says it would be a waste. Especially if I could get a scholarship to a university."

"Ah, I see. If you were valedictorian and had a free ride to a top school, it would make it difficult to justify the expense of cooking school to your mother."

"Yeah, right. What do you think?"

"Cooking at that level is tough. The hours are terrible. It's stressful. It's hard to maintain a family. And culinary school is expensive, and when you get out you're not guaranteed to make much money. Your mother is a pragmatic person. She wants what's best for you."

"But I've been saving. I added another two grand to my college fund since last year just from babysitting."

"I think you should listen to your mother," Bruno said, and he thumped his chest with his thumb, "but also listen to what's in here. Sometimes we are our own best advisors."

"I thought you'd want me to cook."

"I want you to be happy. So does your mom."

"Then why doesn't she let you come back home and stay with us?"

"That's complicated, honey." They lay there for a long time, watching the stars twinkling through the veil of city light.

FIVE

Kulebyaka

For generations industrious Russians have been fending off their brutal winters and obscene number of Orthodox fasting days with the help of the noble salmon. Kulebyaka, or Russian fish pie, is the ultimate meal for spiritual rebirth. Stuffed with leeks, rice and wild mushrooms, and wrapped in a flaking pastry, this hearty peasant dish will allow you a glimpse of spring from within a February blizzard. When prepared with earnest contrition, it promises a ray of hope in even the most hopeless of situations, mending marital spats or bringing estranged siblings together to break bread and begin at last the overdue thaw of hard and frozen hearts.

—BRUNO TANNENBAUM, TWENTY RECIPES FOR LOVE

Bruno awoke profoundly disappointed that he wasn't lying next to Anna. The evening before had been lovely, and he'd felt closer to her than in any time since she'd given him the boot. There was also the burden of the looming confession about losing his job. Anna was an accountant. There was no skirting the issue of his evaporating financial support. His head thrummed from the wine and his guilty conscience. The lace doilies and porcelain doodads of his mother's living room were an affront to his senses. He squeezed his eyes shut and tried to recapture sleep, but he felt his mother hovering over him.

"Bruno, are you sick?"

"No, Ma. What time is it?"

"Time for me to open the store. And you should be at work, too, no? You need a good meal. I fixed you a little something." She headed into the kitchen, a round, compact woman bundled into her powder-blue deli uniform, leaving a vapor trail of moderately priced, if old-fashioned, perfume.

What awaited Bruno in the kitchen was the full exhibition of a German breakfast, with a dash of Yiddish, the latter the influence of his father's side of the family. The small round table was laden with the fresh *brötchen* that his mother had always been able to produce as if by magic, and then the poppy-seeded *mohnberches*, her mother-in-law's recipe.

Aside from the breads there was a spread of quality preserves from the shelves of Ma's eponymous deli, Greta's European Imports, where Bruno had learned appreciation for imported fineries as a child. After her husband's death, Greta had employed his life insurance in a series of shrewd decisions, purchasing the kosher butcher shop where he used to work and transforming it into a high-end deli aimed at the neighborhood's changing demographics. She'd grown up in a German-speaking corner of France, half Catholic and half Jewish, which she felt gave her an ethnic flexibility, allowing her to pick and choose as the neighborhood Jews moved north, the Germans disappeared, the Poles encircled and the young urbanites and then hipsters encroached. It wasn't a smashing success, but it was a steady living. As a boy Bruno used to sit on a stool behind the counter after school, with a spiral notebook and a rubber-banded bundle of Black Warrior pencil stubs left over from Greta's bookkeeping duties. He would engross himself with sketches and scribbling for a large part of the afternoon until restlessness drove him into the aisles, where he'd begin to study the colored jars and tubes of mustards, jams and jellies, until he knew their names by heart.

Three wax paper squares before him on the kitchen table held scoops of *leberwurst*, thin-sliced lox and schmaltz, the latter being a clear, white, gloriously gelatinous globe of rendered goose fat that immediately set Bruno's mouth to watering.

He sat down to a small pitcher of coffee, his mother sitting across the table, her hands patiently folded, her lips pursed. He chose a roll and carefully ripped it apart, laying the open faces across the top of the toaster and depressing the plunger.

Greta pushed a pile of mail before him while he inhaled the buttery tendrils of the warming bread. He thumbed through the usual list of bills, chuckling over a new payment booklet for a car that had long since been repossessed. This reminded him of the mail that Iris had given him when he left the office, and he fetched the envelope from *Gourmet*. It was a check for an article he'd sent months earlier, a story on summer picnic fare that contained the (secret) recipe for his mother's favorite kosher potato salad, including exact measurements for the juiced dill, grated lemon peel and precision-cracked celery seeds, all ingredients whose inclusion Greta guarded jealously. Had she known of the betrayal, she would have turned on Bruno with a wooden spoon.

"What's that, Bruno?" Greta said, hovering over his shoulder and setting a soft-boiled egg in a porcelain stand before him.

"They're publishing my article," Bruno said guiltily as he spun the egg and cracked off the top with the edge of his spoon.

"A thousand dollars! You're such a fine writer." She kissed his blushing cheek.

The toaster popped. Bruno spread schmaltz on his roll. He sipped strong coffee and fingered his newfound fortune. He knew he should carry it directly to Anna as a sign of goodwill. But then he could also invest it in a bottle or three of excellent wine.

"Straight to the bank with that," Greta said, patting her son on the back. "You can stop on your way to work."

For once Bruno didn't have to cringe at the mention of work. He was beginning to concoct a new plan, one that required investors. The check from *Gourmet* and even his severance check from the *Sun-Times* were a good start. But there was more to do.

*   *   *

The Black Samovar was one of Bruno's favorite restaurants, not for the clichéd and barely passable Stroganoff, but for the burgundy leather barstools and cushioned booths in the lounge at the back of the cavernous room. It reminded him of the dark, faded elegance of the dining caves of his childhood before kitsch and irony became the norm in restaurant décor. The Samovar also boasted an impressive wine list, its owner being an aficionado of some of the more elusive Georgian wines, along with interesting Italians from the Friuli and Alto Adige. The polished bar was dim and mysterious, manned by a humorless hulk named Yuri, whose shaved head and handlebar mustache made him simultaneously cartoonish and frightening.

The corner booth was reserved for the Samovar's owner, Aleksei Gurgin, a former KGB officer who fled to Chicago after a colleague and onetime rival ascended to the presidency of Russia. He took a job at the bottom rung of the construction business and worked like a serf for several seasons until he realized that his KGB experience coupled with years of free market racketeering in the Yeltsin era had equipped him quite well for the streets and City Hall offices of Chicago. He started his own construction firm, one that specialized in the removal of asbestos . . . whether the client had invited him to remove it or not. His crew showed up in their chemical suits and set to work on old tenements, threatening the slumlords with visits from city inspectors whose services Aleksei had purchased in advance. It was a perfect scheme, turning Aleksei from a political refugee into something of an underworld success story and making him feel like a Russian Robin Hood.

He'd done well enough to open the Samovar on the North Side, as well as a posh tearoom downtown, a present for his Kazakhstani wife who liked to dabble as a pastry chef, among other things. He was earnestly interested in the restaurant side of his operation, and enlisted Bruno early on as a consultant to help him plan his personal wine cellar. He'd also paid Bruno for a favorable review or two over the years, a practice that Bruno considered less checkbook journalism and more like a form of patronage from a wealthy individual who was also a fan of his work.

Bruno squinted in the dim light at the entrance of the Samovar and Aleksei beckoned from his corner booth.

The Russian wore his customary pressed white shirt and cheap blazer that fit him like a uniform, sharp brown eyes sparkling beneath heavy lids that made him look perpetually tired to those who didn't know him well. What little hair he had was gray and militarily cropped. Calling for hot tea from Yuri and clearing the table of spreadsheets and ledgers that kept restaurant balances (mostly negative) as well as those from his more lucrative construction and informal loan businesses, he welcomed Bruno with a warm smile and gestured to the seat across the table. Bruno slumped into the chair.

"Welcome, my friend," Aleksei said as he fussed about pouring tea from a small samovar that Yuri produced and set on the table with a serving tray. "How are the girls?"

"They're good. Really growing."

"And Anna?"

"She seems to be doing fine without me."

"One hell of a woman. You really fucked that one up."

"Didn't I, though?"

"Perhaps we can help each other out," Aleksei said, sugaring his tea and leaning over. "Tatyana is opening a restaurant in Wicker Park. Russian peasant food. Siberian-themed. She's still a lousy cook, but once she gets something in her head . . . you know her. She's sent for her aunt, who supposedly makes the best *kulebyaka*. And in truth her *kotlety* isn't half bad."

Aleksei sipped from his cup and reached into his pocket for a roll of hundred-dollar bills. He peeled off a half dozen, licked his finger, double-counted, and then slid the pile across the table to Bruno, who gulped, eyes bulging.

"So . . . why don't you write up a nice review for me in the paper?"

"Actually . . ."

"Ah, I see the price of objective journalism has gone up!" He peeled off six more bills and added to the pile. Bruno eyed the cash hungrily.

"I'm not with the *Times* anymore."

Aleksei paused, shook his head, and then retrieved the bills with a shrug. "Sorry to hear that."

"Wait, wait . . . I'm hoping it'll be a good thing. And I have a great idea I wanted to share with you."

Aleksei tucked the money into his inside pocket, laced his fingers together and leaned forward on his elbows like a man who has suffered his share of great ideas.

"The papers are dying, right?" Bruno said, lowering his voice and looking around conspiratorially. "Everyone knows that. They're losing their relevance. That's why they couldn't stand me . . . guys like me, we're the ones people trust. And I plan to use that trust to start a consulting practice."

"You're going to become a businessman?" Aleksei was clearly trying to suppress a smile.

"Bingo! I'll set up an office. Gold nameplate on the door. I can advise restaurants. I can write menu copy, whatever. I'd start one of those . . . blogs . . . and I could charge people for reviews just like we've been doing, but go legit."

Aleksei leaned back and laughed.

"Do you even know what a blog is?"

Bruno's ears burned. In truth he rarely used the infernal Internet and didn't really understand it, but he'd heard plenty of talk about it. "It's like an electronic newsletter. Kinda like my column. I'd write on food and wine . . . the stuff I know best. But with no middleman . . . no Ernie Grovnick around to clip my wings or saddle me with shitty copyediting assignments. And I'll use the interest from the blog . . . the clicks or whatever . . . to fuel my consulting practice."

"Do you know how many food bloggers are out there? My wife's one of them. RussianFoodieGirl-dot-com. *Girl!* She's three years older than I am! Can you imagine? She's got fifteen thousand subscribers and nets a hundred thousand page views per month. She's using a photo from twenty years ago for the hero image—she was quite striking, you know—and spends half the day fending off Web trolls and deleting spam. She even set up a pay-per-click ad account, and you know what she makes every month? Thirty bucks." Aleksei dismissed the figure with a wave of disgust. "Blogs are old news, Bruno. Even if there was money in it, that ship left the harbor ten years ago."

Now, Bruno understood next to nothing of this . . . other than the mention of "spam," which reminded him of a favorite food cart in Portland, Oregon, that served Hawaiian street fare, which in turn reminded him that dinnertime was approaching . . . but he wasn't worried. The economic viability of the scheme wasn't his primary concern. He didn't need for this venture to actually be profitable. What he really needed was for Anna to see him make a legitimate, organized attempt . . . at something. If he showed up, cash in hand and a plan in the works, maybe she'd see him differently. If she saw him striking out in a bold direction, with good timing and some luck maybe she'd let him move back in. Then he'd work on some articles, pay Aleksei back and in the meantime he'd clean and cook and drink less and pick up the girls from school and prove himself indispensable . . . all while working on his next book, which he'd eventually finish and prove his worth to Anna. It was a harebrained scheme, to be sure, but it was the only one he had. Besides, weren't all schemes a little harebrained? Like spending everything he had upon graduating college on a plane ticket to Amsterdam with no idea what he wanted to do with his life other than the fact that he didn't want to wind up an overstressed shopkeeper dead before he could accomplish his lifelong goals of taking over the butcher shop or seeing the Cubs make the World Series.

But Bruno couldn't explain this all to Aleksei. Instead he offered, lamely, "Still, I think it could work."

"Sorry, Bruno . . ."

"I've already got some seed money, see," Bruno said, unfolding the check and holding it out to him. "I just need a couple grand more. You could be a partner."

"Another way to get on the IRS radar . . . no, thanks."

"Well, then how about a loan? I know that you offer . . . lending services."

Aleksei thought for an uncomfortably long moment. "I'd rather we remain friends," he said with a weary sigh. Then he regarded Bruno with a long, sad, heavy-lidded gaze that sent a shiver down Bruno's spine. Behind that sleepy expression, deep down, there was a hint of warning, or even malice. Bruno suddenly sensed then that owing money to Aleksei might be quite dangerous. He gulped.

"Um, I mean, how does that work?"

"Typically there is something of value that can be put up . . . as collateral. Something of substantial value. Perhaps a family heirloom. Or a business. Or one's . . . health. Whatever the case, I'm not sure that I'd be willing to take you on as a business partner or a client. In the former case it's always unwise to invest in friends. In the latter it can be . . . quite uncomfortable for all involved."

"I'm sorry," Bruno said, "I probably shouldn't have asked."

"It's okay," Aleksei said, waving his hand.

They sipped tea in silence, Bruno feeling a little foolish for having come here. Then Aleksei offered him a sympathetic smile.

"You know," he said, "I never properly thanked you for helping Tatyana with the wine list. It's been quite successful."

"Glad to hear it."

"And perhaps I can help your little venture in another way.

Let's call it your first official consulting project," Aleksei said, sitting up higher. "I've recently come into the possession of a wine locker, and I could use some assistance in cataloging and assessing the value of the contents. I'd like recommendations on what to keep and what to sell. In exchange, I'd offer you a commission. And you're welcome to take a few bottles for yourself."

Aleksei snapped his fingers and Yuri materialized at his elbow holding a manila envelope. He unfastened the clasp and dumped the contents on the table, sifting through the collection of papers and odds and ends.

"A former client of mine, an accountant originally from Minsk, amassed quite a collection. It seems his former employer was a connoisseur on a grand scale, though he ran into some trouble in Russian politics. This accountant made off with a few treasures and some schemes of his own. He borrowed money from me but encountered some repayment issues and had to forfeit the contents of this locker . . . among other things." Aleksei plucked a key attached to a leather wine-bottle key chain from the pile and tossed it to Bruno, whose heart began humming. The key chain bore the logo of Chicago River Wine Storage, where the better-off Chicagoans kept their oenological prizes. This locker might hold any number of treasures.

"I don't know what to say."

Aleksei waved off his gratitude. "Just some honest work for a fair wage."

Aleksei sifted through the contents on the table. There were a few coins, a wallet and a cell phone. Bruno tried not to think of what happened to the unfortunate accountant. Aleksei retrieved a waiter's corkscrew from the pile and handed that to Bruno, who took it in his hands. It was elegant, brushed silver, with a double eagle and some Cyrillic letters etched into the side.

"I'm sure you'll find that useful." Aleksei smiled.

"Of course," Bruno said, admiring the craftsmanship.

Aleksei retrieved a Rolex from the pile. He shook it and held it to his ear, frowning. "You wear watches?"

Bruno shook his head. Somehow the watch felt too personal.

"So, you're staying for dinner, right? There's fresh *kulebyaka* in the oven."

"I'd hate to impose," Bruno lied. His belly rumbled and his mouth began to water at the thought of the buttery crust that sealed the miraculous mixture of fish, leeks, rice, mushrooms. He sniffed and thought he could detect a trace of the aroma coming from the kitchen.

"Impose? Nonsense!" Aleksei clapped his hands and Yuri appeared again, this time bearing a bottle of vodka and two short glasses on his tray. "Enough talk about wine. Let's have a toast to our new little partnership!"

The toast carried them well into the night, and it wouldn't be until much later that Bruno would recall Aleksei drunkenly putting his arm around his shoulder and speaking carefully: "You know, this wine locker . . . there are those who have been showing great interest in its contents. Whatever you do, be careful."

SIX

Noble Rot

Compatibility is not only overrated but something of a scourge. With computerized dating or those overly earnest matchmaker friends (you both like movies and hiking!) it is easy to wind up with someone a lot like yourself, but where's the fun in that? Celebrate contrast. Fall in love with your opposite. Explore, disagree, fight, make up, make love. Open a Sauternes (cheap will do, but d'Yquem if you can get it) and pair its silky sweetness against good anchovies packed in brine with capers spread on toasted flatbreads. The contrast of flavors, from salt to acid and sugar all commingling, will create lusty tensions you wouldn't have encountered had you chosen to play it safe.

—Bruno Tannenbaum, *Twenty Recipes for Love*

Bruno's head throbbed. Actually, it shrieked. Had he been able to peel back his scalp and dump crushed ice directly onto the aching gray matter of his brain, he would have gladly done so.

Slats of light cut through the blinds, burning his eyes when he cracked them behind crusted lashes. He swung his legs over the edge of his mother's couch and pushed himself to a standing position. His brain screamed and the room spun counterclockwise as he lurched to the kitchen.

Ma had left for work but she'd left a pair of *brötchen* in the kitchen that were still soft in the center and some clear, gelatinous slices of *sülze* she'd made herself from the head of a calf. He ate the simple sandwiches, drank some cold coffee and started to recall shards of the prior evening.

He remembered tossing back an alarming amount of vodka with dinner at the Black Samovar, and then there were memories of strobe lights, neon and Polish techno music at a North Side club, followed by a march to an all-night taco stand with Aleksei, arms around each other as they sang Russian drinking songs. Bruno didn't remember how he got home, though he expected Yuri had a hand in the process.

Now, with the rolls and coffee stabilizing his hangover, he began to recall the task at hand. Something about a business plan began to emerge out of the fog. Yes, that was it . . . he was to provide evidence of his stability to Anna, which he would do simultaneously with announcing his . . . disengagement . . . from the newspaper. True, his request for funding had been denied by Aleksei, but his friend had provided him with some impressive-sounding terms like *page views* and *pay-per-clicks*. While this didn't make Bruno an expert, he'd never let that stop him from writing with authority before.

Tonight's parent-teacher conference should allow him some time alone with Anna. He'd task the girls with making dinner to distract them. He went to the living room and rolled a clean page onto the platen of the patched-together Smith-Corona and waited for inspiration. After a few moments he typed: *A Plan for the Growth of Tannenbaum Consulting.*

He skipped a few lines. He waited again.

He typed: *Executive Summary.*

A line skipped, a long pause.

Nothing.

Writing a business plan, it seemed, was no easier than writing a novel. Frustrated, he watched the rays of window light creep across the carpet as the sun worked its way across the sky. Slowly he hammered on the keys.

Humans tell stories. It's what we do. It is the song of our existence, the engine of our souls. This will never change. However, the "how" of telling stories is always evolving. From the silver-tongued ballad-eer crooning, to revelers sated and huddled by their fires after a feast in the great hall, to the young woman on the train with her smart-phone seeking respite from the drudge of her commute, the channels have shifted, though this has in no way lessened our shared need for the well-told story, the voice of the bard. The mode and method of sharing of our tales has evolved, and now so, too, must I, Bruno Tannenbaum. That is why I've decided to start a consulting service for the food, wine and restaurant industry, one based on the latest advances in technology . . .

He wrote in fits and starts until he'd managed a full page, after which he reread what he'd written. It was flowery gibber-ish. *Damn!* He was losing confidence. He paced the room, striv-ing to channel his more businesslike sensibilities, and he acci-dentally kicked at the pile of dirty clothes from the night before, sending a small key chain tumbling out of his jeans pocket and across the carpet. And then he suddenly remembered the wine locker. How could he have forgotten? *Oh, what a cruel master is vodka!*

Invigorated, he abandoned the business plan, showered, dressed and went out to catch a bus. Chicago River Wine Storage lay not along the river, but the less-than-pristine Chicago Sanitary and Ship Canal. Still, this was where the well-heeled stored their surplus vino. He entered the warehouse with visions of uncovering classic vintages of Margaux or maybe some ancient Rieslings that had the rich and slightly oily quality they acquired with age.

It took a moment for his head to adjust to the pressure as the door of the facility sucked shut behind him. The place was sealed, and a symphony of whirring fans and coolers kept air moving and temperatures constant. A slightly bored but nicely dressed young fellow was cleaning glasses at the tasting bar. He looked up and alarm crossed his features.

"Hello, uh, Mr. Tannenbaum . . ."

Bruno vaguely recalled the man's face and also a series of image fragments from an auction he'd crashed here a good six months prior . . . blue blazers, open bar, a short, sequined cocktail dress revealing a vista of silky thigh, a stumble and fall, broken glass . . . that made him realize he must have performed some sort of transgression on his last visit.

"I'm, uh, not supposed to pour for you. I'm sorry, but the owners . . ."

Bruno merely proffered his key and grinned. The man took it, punched numbers into a computer and then sighed.

"Well. Looks like you're on the list."

Bruno snatched the key and whistled as he entered the warehouse, feeling the pressure on his eardrums as the door closed behind him. "Aleksei, you're a gem," he whispered as he eyed the rows of lockers stretched out before him.

The lockers near the front were smallish, no larger than broom closets. He checked the number on the key chain: 168. He had a ways to go.

The place was dark, with a few pale fluorescent lamps buzzing and flickering in the rafters. There was a scuffle in the shadows and he paused and squinted down an aisle looking for its source, likely one of the notoriously oversized rats one found near the canal. He felt out of place, as if he were being watched, perhaps by the security cameras mounted in the rafters. He imagined the treasures that were hidden in these lockers. Bottles in their hundreds of thousands, and worth a fortune. It made him feel small. Humble. And thirsty.

He found his row and was pleased to see that it was a hallway with doors spaced farther apart indicating rooms large enough to hold dozens, if not hundreds, of cases. Door 164, 165, 166, 167 . . . his pulse quickened. He mumbled a quick prayer to Bacchus before slipping the key in the dead-bolt lock. He twisted, pushed.

It was a small, plain room with a wooden barrel fashioned into a table in the center, half-empty wine racks along the walls and an open filing cabinet filled with packing supplies. A fan whirred above the door, a single ribbon of plastic wagging from the grille. There were a number of empty boxes and also foam shipping containers. He picked up a clipboard with an inventory list from a shelf and whistled through his teeth, noting the quality of the producers.

Then a collection of translucent brownish bottles on the bottom row of the nearest rack caught his attention. At first he thought that they were cheap brown glass, but as he bent and plucked one, reading the dusty, yellowed label, his hand began to tremble. It was a '63 Château d'Yquem. The glass was clear, but the wine was the color of maple syrup, which, for perhaps this particular wine only, is a good thing. He cradled the bottle to his chest like one of his daughters when they were infants and drew a ragged breath that ended in a sentimental sob of joy.

A Chateau d'Yquem is a Saunternes, which begins its life as a sweet white wine and turns all manner of miraculous earthen hues. It's made from rotten grapes, but it's a special rot of the kind they have in France, which also does wonderful things to their breads, cheeses and cured meats, not to mention their wines. Bruno loved Sauternes because, like him, they never followed the rules. In a world where red wines are king, sweetness is considered bourgeois, clarity and color stability are marks of character, d'Yquems are the antithesis of all of these traits. They are paradoxes. Like a working-class gourmet food writer who is broke, loves expensive wines and lives on his mother's couch.

Bruno set the bottle gently down and retrieved its neighbor from the lower shelf. Another d'Yquem . . . this one a '64. *Holy mother of God!* It was a flight, six bottles in all! He set them next to each other and rubbed his hands. Were they poorly handled and spoiled? Or was at least one of them drinkable still?

They were doubtless worth a fortune together, but given his streak of bad luck, he deserved a taste, didn't he? Hadn't Aleksei said he could have some for himself? He fished in his pockets until he found the silver corkscrew Aleksei had given him and he twisted it into the cork of the '63, which was alarmingly soft.

"Don't be vinegar, don't be vinegar, don't be vinegar," he whispered as he prepared to pull. He grabbed a dusty glass from a shelf, then tugged the cork out. It was more of a slurp than a pop, and for a moment he was concerned about the seal. But when he poured the gold-brown liquid and breathed in the layers of confection, citrus, honey and vanilla that rolled from the glass he knew he was in for a life-altering experience. He seized the stem of the glass, so certain of the coming bliss that he didn't hear the scuff of shoes on concrete behind him.

He was actually laughing out loud as he raised and tipped the glass, and the amber elixir was almost to his lips when his headache was reawakened with a skull-rattling thump before everything turned completely dark.

*   *   *

It was hard to say how much time had passed when Bruno awoke, his cheek pressed to the cold floor. The pain in his head no longer radiated from the center of his being as it had from the hangover: it now had a locus . . . a bloody knot at his hairline, which he fondled gingerly. He scanned the floor as he wiggled his toes to make sure he still had feeling in his extremities.

Objects came into focus. Shards from a broken wineglass were scattered across the floor. He stared at a puddle of d'Yquem—such a waste! He half considered licking it off of the cement, but he settled for a sniff . . . traces of honey.

It seemed pointless to get up, so he lay with his face on the floor for a long time. That's when he noticed a dark object under the filing cabinet where the lowest drawer had been yanked out. He crawled over and reached beneath the cabinet, feeling something soft. He pulled it out; it was a blue bandanna tied in a knot. He worked the knot out and unwrapped it to find a single cork with a wax cap on one end and indistinguishable scribbling on the sides. He couldn't discern anything about it other than that it was very old and the color of the stains indicated a red wine. He tucked it into his pocket and pushed himself off of the floor.

The assailant hadn't taken everything. The d'Yquems were gone, and there were a few other blank spaces on the shelves that hadn't been there before. There was no telling the total value of what was missing, but it was certainly a substantial sum. However, something told Bruno there was more to it than simple greed. There were several smashed bottles, one of the racks was overturned and drawers had been completely removed from the filing cabinet. It seemed like the intruder had been looking for something else. Something he hadn't found.

Bruno pieced together the label of one of the broken bottles—it was an old Burgundy, and there were several others like it on the shelves. He took out his little black notebook and tried to focus long enough to scribble down the name of the producer and the date. Despite the massive headache, he was feeling somewhat writerly. This, after all, was the stuff of spy novels.

Bruno walked unsteadily back into the front of the warehouse. The man behind the bar noted his uneasy gait.

"Tap into something good back there, Mr. Tannenbaum?"

"You might say that," Bruno mumbled. *Fucking smart-ass*. He staggered toward the door, the whole world threatening to spin on him. Then he paused in the threshold. He felt blood leaking from his right temple and he dabbed it facing away from the attendant. "Did my friend perchance leave already?"

"The guy with the accent? Scar on his jaw?"

"Um . . . yes. That's him."

"Yeah, maybe twenty minutes ago. Didn't look too happy. You say anything to piss him off?"

"Evidently."

"Hey, you want me to call you a cab or something?"

Bruno shook his head and plunged into the afternoon sunlight.

*　　*　　*

Morton Cohen had various talents, chief among them being his mental catalog of wine labels and vintages as well as his ability to patch cuts with alacrity in the corner of a boxing ring. Bruno was in need of both of these skills at the moment, so he caught the Pink Line out to Fifty-fourth and Cermak in Cicero, where Morty had a small, cluttered shop that was hard to define. In addition to random antiques, coins and stamps, he also bought and sold rare wines and cigars, both authentic as well as quality fakes.

When Bruno stumbled into the store, Morty leapt from his stool at the end of the counter, where he was in the process of applying forged labels to bare Burgundy bottles that were likely filled by wines he'd made in his garage from grape concentrate that he ordered from the Lodi Valley in California. Morty spotted the bloody welt in Bruno's hairline, as he was accustomed to searching for such things. He was a sort of cut-rate surgeon, willing to give free stitches in exchange for some tidbit of information he could use in the seedier levels of the pawn trade.

"Jesus, what happened to you?" Morty asked around the stump of an unlit cigar as he proffered his stool and slipped into the back room for his first-aid kit.

"I fell."

Morty returned to attend to Bruno. He was a short gnome of a man who had to look up as he worked on Bruno sitting on the stool. He had large white eyebrows and glasses propped up on a spotted, bald scalp that gleamed in the dim light. He wore a strange and permanent grin through which he was able to talk without losing his grip on the cigar stump.

"Bullshit. Somebody conked you on the head." Morty fished a cotton swab and some alcohol out of the kit, dabbing Bruno's brow and making the writer wince. "At least it looks like you won't need stitches."

Though Bruno's head was aching, his ears ringing, he managed to shift gears now from medical services to gathering intelligence. He knew that to get the information he wanted without giving away his hand, he had to play his cards right. His aim was to validate the authenticity of the cork in his pocket and also get a read on anyone who might be looking to pawn some of the missing bottles. Bruno suspected the cork was either extremely valuable or a good fake. Either way, it was a clue to a bigger story. The assailant had been looking for something special in that locker, and Bruno had been in the way.

But he had to be careful. Morty was coy with the truth, and getting information from him was always a game.

"Listen, Morty, what could I get for a '63 d'Yquem?"

"Depending on the condition . . . if I could authenticate the label . . . four to seven hundred a bottle."

Bruno moaned.

"Where would you get a d'Yquem?"

"I had it in my hands . . ."

"You're trying to tell me someone knocked you on your head and took your d'Yquem?"

"It was a vertical. Six, maybe seven bottles. I was at a friend's locker . . ."

"I'd slug somebody on the head for that kind of stash."

"But something tells me that's not what he was after. The bottles were there for the taking, but when I woke up, the place was tossed," Bruno mused. He felt Morty's attention fixing on the scenario as he applied an adhesive bandage. It was time to up the ante. He reached into his inside breast pocket and pulled out the cork. "What do you make of this?"

Morty seized it and held it up to the light, squinting. "Hmmm. Burgundy. It's old. Wax. Probably thirties . . . or a '43. Right there. Look at that. And does that look like a *J* or a *T* to you?"

Bruno shrugged. Morty studied him carefully before rifling through a bookshelf behind the counter, finally retrieving a thick catalog with yellowed paper. He slammed it down in a spiral of dust and leafed through the pages, muttering to himself. "It's definitely a *T*. There it is. Clement Trevallier. They're still around. Near Pommard . . . town called Les Cloches. Smack in the middle of the best vineyards."

"Sure, I've heard of 'em. I used to live around there. They make some pretty good juice."

"Damn right they do. Sylvie Trevallier, the owner . . . she doesn't mess around. I hear she's a real piece of work. Won't talk to the press. Doesn't go in for fancy glass or labels. Real stubborn, micromanager-type . . . directs all the operations herself. But year after year she makes stuff that stands toe-to-toe with the big boys. In any case . . . this '43 . . . it's a fake."

"Why do you say that?"

Morty spun the book around and tapped the page. In the inventory of labels there was no '43 listed. The listings jumped right from the '42 to the '44. Bruno's heart leapt.

"No '43? Why not?"

"Occupation. Nazis. Story goes they shipped all the good stuff to the party leaders in Berlin. Some of it turned up again . . . but not the Trevallier. One of the lost vintages." Morty paced, holding the cork, his eyes sparkling. His grin was as unreadable as ever around the cigar stub. He slipped his glasses down onto his nose and squinted at the cork more closely. "It's a damn good fake, though. I'll give you a buck fifty for it."

Bruno could use another hundred and fifty dollars. But why would Morty offer so much for a fake?

"No, thanks."

"Okay, two hundred," Morty said with a hint of annoyance.

Bruno tried not to smile. He recognized by his friend's tone that Morty thought the cork was authentic. "What are you going to use it for . . . a good luck charm?"

Bruno held out his palm and Morty reluctantly relinquished the cork. "I could use a little luck."

"Well, I tell you what. Maybe it isn't a fake. You find yourself one of those little guys still in the bottle, then you've really got yourself something. Find a case and you could buy yourself a nice bungalow in Belmont."

Morty winked. If it was real, then that meant that somewhere, out there, a vintage of wine assumed lost to the Nazis, maybe just a case or maybe even a single bottle, had survived the occupation. Had this cork been pulled from the last bottle? Or did more exist out there somewhere? And why was this under a file cabinet in a warehouse in Chicago? These questions coaxed the return of Bruno's headache. *Some good luck charm.*

Suddenly it no longer seemed so magical. After all, it was just a cork. The legendary lost wine that was once sealed beneath its pulpy texture was long gone. Like everything in Bruno's life, it was now a dusty reminder of past glories.

"Thanks for the patchwork," Bruno said, slapping Morty on the back as he headed for the door. He put the cork in his pocket, ready to forget about it. More immediate on his mind was Carmen's parent-teacher conference and his chance to finally present Anna with his new business plan.

SEVEN

A Revelation

One can hide, within the humble pirozhki, a message. It is at the cook's discretion to stuff them with wild mushrooms, giblets, sweetbreads, fresh apricots or bitter chocolate. And the guest is only required to bring a sense of wonder and a willingness to entertain surprise.
—BRUNO TANNENBAUM, "A WALK THROUGH LITTLE WARSAW,"
CHICAGO SUN-TIMES

Bruno sat in the passenger seat while Anna drove. She was briefing him on Carmen's classroom performance in preparation for the conference while he was distracted, wondering if he'd left the girls with all the ingredients they'd need to make pirozhki.

"She's gotten three 'whoops' notes in recent weeks for talking during class."

"I wish they had 'whoops' notes back in my day." Bruno chuckled, hitching his hips uncomfortably in his seat at the memory of the polished wooden paddle his middle school principal kept in the top drawer, holes drilled into the surface to reduce wind resistance and also to produce a terrifying whistling sound.

"Her reading scores are a touch below grade level on the standardized tests," Anna said through her teeth. Bruno refused to be alarmed. He was enjoying the clear evidence that his child was . . . well . . . an actual child rather than an animatronic pawn in the growing national pastime of competitive child-rearing.

"Wouldn't worry about it," Bruno said. "Did you see that stuff they want her to read on those practice tests? I couldn't choke it down, either."

Anna sighed. Bruno knew his laissez-faire attitude frustrated her. But he also felt that life was far too short to start making it a contest in the third grade. Carmen was smart, funny, she had a few good friends and a healthy appetite, and that counted for a whole lot more than grades in Bruno's mind.

As he gazed out at the passing neighborhoods, his thoughts kept returning to the cork in his pocket. He had tasted a Trevallier only once in his life, and it had been a spiritual experience. He was working in France as a vineyard laborer, and was with a group of other workers at a small restaurant off the village *place* in Puligny Montrachet, a dingy little hole of a joint that served an excellent cassoulet. One of the men, trying to impress a girlfriend, demanded the best bottle of wine in the house, and the owner very proudly brought up a '76 Trevallier and dusted it off. The normally raucous crew sipped the wine in reverent awe. Bruno held the glass under his nose and swirled as layer upon layer of aromas unfurled for him, and he recognized the full potential, depth and complexity of a single glass of wine for, perhaps, the first time.

As they pulled into the parking lot and got out of the car, Anna reminded him to take off his cap before going inside.

She frowned at the bandage on his forehead but didn't ask. She reached up and straightened the collar of his lapel, biting her lower lip.

"What's the matter?" he asked.

"I'm just worried Carmen might have behavior issues."

Bruno wanted to dismiss her concerns with a laugh, but instead he swallowed his reply and took Anna's shoulders, offered a reassuring squeeze. "She's a feisty girl. Which will serve her well in life. But let's see what Mrs. Jackson has to say first." Anna drew a deep breath and they went inside.

Mrs. Jackson had lots to say, all of it good. They sat across from the teacher at Carmen's little worktable, Bruno engulfing the tiny chair. "Carmen's a very social girl. We just need to make sure she focuses when she has to. But she's a delightful student," Mrs. Jackson said. Bruno felt Anna exhale with relief. They leafed through Carmen's folder of work. One of the assignments had been to write a "how-to," in which she had described the process of making a chilled English pea velouté, and Bruno blushed with pride. Anna didn't. The last thing she needed was another gourmand in the family. The next essay was about the person Carmen most admired in the world, and it was, deservingly so, her mother. Anna brushed away a tear and Bruno touched her knee under the tiny table. Anna took his fingers and gave them a squeeze, the automatic, unthinking reaction of a longtime couple. Now Bruno wanted to cry.

"Well, that was a relief," Anna said as they were leaving.

*   *   *

Thirty minutes later, Bruno was standing next to Anna, carefully wiping dishes and carrying them, one by one, to the cupboards. The girls had trashed the kitchen, but they'd also left a plate of pirozhki on the flour-dusted, dough-splattered counter, and while Anna initially sighed at the mess, she also smiled to herself, and Bruno could tell that she was still quite pleased with the results of the conference. Bruno munched through the pirozhki. Carmen had opted for a sweet cheese filling, while Claire chose wild mushrooms and rice with a hint of dill. He had uncorked a bottle of very good champagne that he brought in anticipation of a positive conference experience, and Anna had even accepted a generous pour, although Bruno soon pulled ahead of her by three glasses.

Anna hummed as she scrubbed a fork and doused it in cold running water, absently fingering the tines. Bruno watched her in profile and found himself startled, as always, by how striking she looked, so close to him but so unreachable.

How could he fuck this whole thing up? Aside from James Beard, who was a largely decent fellow, Bruno's other literary heroes, Henry Miller and William S. Burroughs, were impulsive and completely self-absorbed bastards. What he was beginning to realize, though, was that some heroes punched a clock. Some heroes dragged their asses through the maddening crowds to a cubicle in a sterile downtown high-rise with little complaint. They held down steady gigs and paid the bills and sent their kids to college and fired up the grill on the weekends, sizzling a tenderloin with a decent dry rub and uncapping a cheap lager beer, maybe two. Other heroes did it all on their own, after their lout of a husband came home late one too many nights without explanation, discovered the next morning snoring up a storm on the couch with a slip of paper bearing a number written in a feminine hand, half-dialed phone on his belly, the annoyance of the looping operator's message not even rousing him. Some heroes woke up at five to catch up on emails from their job and then make breakfast for their daughters, driving them to two different schools before heading to work. They passed over a promotion they really wanted, despite the fact that they could have used the money because they couldn't rely on their husbands to do even the simple things, because the miserable wretch traveled for "research" purposes but was actually blowing away royalty checks that should have been augmenting the girls' college funds. Some heroes worked out on a stair machine at lunch and drank smoothies at their desks hoping to counteract the sedentary lifestyle of an office job, hoping to hang on to a sliver of youth so that they could maybe meet someone new even though they didn't really have a social life, so what was the point? Some heroes picked up their daughters from after-school programs and then fixed dinner and helped them with their homework before collapsing exhausted into bed wishing that they'd made smarter mating choices—as if you could choose such things— but then they had these two glorious, lovely daughters who were a joy and a delight even if they fought too much and the teenage years made one of them a headstrong, unpredictable bundle of overconfidence and anxiety but she was still a good girl, a very good girl. Some heroes still loved their husbands and were willing to forgive them to a point, even if they were exasperating schemers who probably didn't deserve it, and not a day went by when they didn't second-guess their decision to kick him out until he grew up, which would likely never happen, though one still held out hope. Some heroes didn't feel so heroic at all, but rather like speeding, overloaded trains hurtling downhill and threatening to wreck at any moment, hurting the ones they loved the most.

Anna polished a plate and sipped from her champagne when she felt Bruno's stare across the room. He drifted over and she could feel him close. It was so nice and comfortable to just have the big, cuddly bulk of him standing there like a favorite mangled teddy bear that happened to be actual size. *The miserable shit . . .* if only he could just do a better job of keeping his pants zipped. If only he'd step up and put his daughters . . . not even Anna, but just his daughters . . . ahead of whatever it was he was trying to do with his life . . .

But then, he tried, didn't he? He made some lovely (and expensive) dinners and he showed up with his groceries (though she would have preferred money), wearing unwashed clothes like some favorite eccentric, homeless, genius uncle, and Carmen leapt into his arms and Claire drifted down and glowed and everyone was so happy to have him there, even Anna.

Now she looked over at him and he winked and smiled with a familiar, desirous glint. She knew that he physically, honestly wanted her and would spend the night if given half a chance. It felt good to be wanted in that way even after all this time, after all the lines drawn in the sand and then recrossed and redrawn. In that way he was forgiving. He never held it against her. She was *the one,* he'd told her so often, and she knew he meant it.

"Thanks for coming tonight," she said to break the silence. "It meant a lot to have you there."

"Wouldn't have missed it."

She saw him smile out of the corner of her eye. *Don't you get any ideas.* She studied him, his unruly hair, the bandage across his temple that he hadn't explained well ("tripped, coffee table"), the glaze from his champagne buzz. And somewhere behind his amorous intentions she could see something else, something he wanted to tell her. "So, how's the book coming?" she asked finally.

"Great!" he said.

"Good. I'm glad." He was lying. She could tell by the smallest twitch of his eyebrow. "Everything else going okay?"

"Well . . . I've been wanting to talk about something . . ."

Uh-oh. He turned to her. She was nervous.

He led her over to the kitchen table, making a show of pulling out her chair. She braced herself for one of his schemes as he sat across from her. He fished into his pocket and pulled out a wad of cash and coins. "This," he said proudly, pushing the money over to her, "is for you."

She straightened the bills as she counted. Close to seven hundred dollars. "Where did this come from?"

He retrieved a check stub from *Gourmet* and carefully unfolded it, laying it in front of her and patting it. It was for a thousand dollars. Double-entry accounting was hardwired into her being, and before she could think she asked, "Where's the rest of it?"

He was silent.

"You spent it on groceries, didn't you? And how much was that bottle you brought tonight?"

"We had to celebrate the good news about Carmen, and . . . "

"And what?"

He was bouncing in his chair now. This couldn't be good. He fished around his pockets . . . his jacket and jeans were his filing system . . . until he produced a slip of paper. He handed it over and produced another pile of cash from a different pocket.

"What is this?"

"A business plan."

"For what?"

"My new business. I'm starting a consultancy and a blog."

"A blog?" she asked, trying to contain her skepticism. Bruno could barely use an ATM—how the hell was he going to run a blog? She swallowed and said as calmly as possible, "You don't own a computer."

"Claire's got one, hasn't she?"

"And what's this?" She gestured to the second wad of money.

"Start-up capital. Not all of it. I'm looking for other investors."

"Where did it come from?"

He shrugged. She was suspicious. She couldn't help raising her voice. She could see him measuring his words. "It's from my severance check, and you can have some of it, but I'll need to set some aside . . ."

"Severance check?"

"So, this consulting business . . . do you know how much value I could add to a new restaurant? Just a few simple sugges- tions and I could boost the chance of a favorable review every time a critic walks into the joint. I could help them with word of mouth. For just a few hours of my time I could increase their chances of success in the first few months . . . exponentially! Do you know how much I could charge?"

"Severance check? You got fired?"

"Um . . . yeah, I'm not at the *Times* anymore . . ."

"Bruno, what the hell? What the fucking hell? Haven't I been telling you that I need help with the bills?" She was losing it, and she didn't like it when this happened. She tried to keep her voice below the level of a shriek, for the girls' sake. It wasn't working.

"But I have this plan," he said, tapping the wrinkled paper. He shrank back in his chair as she stood up.

"That's not a plan, Bruno. It's a fucking grocery list!" She grabbed the paper and flipped it over to where he had written the shopping list for the pirozhki. "Jesus, it's like having another child around here! It's worse than another teenager . . . Claire and Carmen have got it way more together than you could ever imagine. Look at yourself! Look at this!"

Adrenaline surged. She knew that when it subsided, if she allowed, she'd cry with her blanket over her head. But not until the girls were asleep. Not with Bruno here. She wouldn't let him see that. So she just stood in front of him and shook the paper and he hunkered down like a dog that had just shit on the rug.

"You can keep the money," he said, pushing it across the table to her. But then he licked his lips nervously and plucked a pair of hundreds off of the pile, tucking them into the inside pocket of his blazer. Anna returned to the sink, dumping the rest of her champagne down the drain.

*   *   *

Minutes later Bruno was lying on Claire's bed, ostensibly helping her with an essay, hands laced behind his head, trying not to think about what a mess his life had become.

Claire sat at her desk, laptop open, fingers hovering over the keyboard. After a long moment of inaction, she sighed and leaned back.

"I just can't figure out where to start."

"I know the feeling."

Claire flopped down next to him. They sighed together.

"You and Mom had quite the row."

"You heard that?" Bruno winced.

"Hard not to. So you lost your job?"

"Uh-huh."

"It was kind of a crappy gig, wasn't it?"

"I guess."

"Cheer up. You still have the book, right? How's it coming, anyway?"

"Ah, fine." He grimaced. He hated lying to his daughter.

"What's it about?"

He swallowed. Did he continue the charade? Or did he 'fess up and admit that, in addition to his newfound unemployment, he had an entire drawerful of false starts? It was to be a book about wine. About the meaning of wine in his life. But the problem was that wine was one of the things that had likely mucked up his life.

"Come on, Dad, you can tell me. Don't be so secretive. I won't tell anyone. Is it another one of those food-sex books, like *Twenty Recipes*?"

"That's *food-romance*."

"Yeah, right. Wink, wink. So tell me what this big secret book is about. I want to know."

"Well . . ." Bruno knew that though this sounded like idle conversation, it was an important moment. Claire was a teenager, practically an adult. She'd soon be driving two tons of steel and hot metal filled with combustible fuel. Her peers were likely copulating, drinking and doing the things teenagers do. In a pair of years she'd be able to vote for president or die for her country (though not drink wine). She was smart, witty. And she probably still loved him.

Bruno could easily squander her trust as he had that of her mother. The thought of it conjured a pain in his chest, or maybe it was heartburn from the pirozhki. Should he lie and say that the book was going well? Or should he confess that his career was in the tank with no prospect of resurfacing? That he was beginning to see himself through Anna's eyes, and it wasn't pretty? He'd been on a roll in his twenties and thirties that led to the slow downhill slide of his forties and now he'd hit bottom. A part of him wanted to admit this all to her. He wanted his daughter to console him. Motivate him. Inspire him. He released a long sigh.

"Dad?"

Bruno struggled to draw breath, the ache in his chest growing nearly unbearable. He reached up and undid his collar and then pressed his hand against his ribs.

He felt the cork in his blazer pocket. An idea struck him. *This was it!* His heart pounded. He suddenly saw a way forward for his book. The cork . . . the cork was the key!

"Actually," he said, barely realizing he'd reached a decision, "can you keep a secret?"

"Sure. I'm not a blab like Carmen."

He sat up and pulled the cork out of his pocket. He held it in the lamplight. Claire leaned forward and studied it. She frowned, unimpressed.

"What's that?"

"A cork."

"So?"

"The bottle that it came from supposedly doesn't exist. Some say the entire vintage was stolen by the Nazis. Whatever the case, no trace of it has ever been found. But this cork . . . if it's real . . . suggests that it's still out there somewhere."

"What if it's a fake?"

"Morty just offered me two hundred bucks for it. Trust me, it's real."

"So what do you think happened to it?"

"Well, that part of France was occupied. The vineyard was crawling with German soldiers. Somebody either stole it, or it was hidden away. And now it's turned up again. And . . . I'm going to go look for it."

"That's cool. So it's kind of like a treasure hunt." Claire

brushed her hair out of her face and looked at him, a hint of childish awe in her eyes. She scooted next to him like she used to when she was little and he would make up stories about fairy castles (and the sumptuous banquets that went on inside them). "What if you don't find it?"

"Even if I don't find the wine, there's still a story there."

"The journey *is* the destination, right?"

"Exactly. Wow. You're the one who should be a writer."

"I thought about that, but that's where Mom draws the line. She doesn't like that chef thing at all, but she really hates that writer thing. She said that if I was a cook, at the very least I'd be able to eat and feed my family."

"Ouch."

"Yeah. Anyway, I like your story idea. What does your agent think?"

"Harley says they're going to go crazy for it in New York." Bruno couldn't help adding that little exaggeration. But he was sure this idea would sell. He'd never been so sure about anything before.

EIGHT

Of Flames and Courage

Don't allow anyone to tell you that you can't cook. I know, dear reader, that you may be intimidated. You might be afraid of failure. And fail you shall. Often. There are those who claim a superior palate. Maybe they've summered in Florence and own stainless-steel appliances. They have kitchen gardens and wine cellars, which are fine, though hardly required. All you truly need to learn to cook: a pan, a flame, good ingredients, an open heart, a dash of tenacity and a pinch of courage. The rest will take care of itself.

—Bruno Tannenbaum, from the foreword to *Twenty Recipes for Love*

Harley Collins stood behind his desk staring through the glass wall of his office. It was eleven o'clock, but he was thinking about lunch. Lunch at an expensive restaurant. Harley didn't have time for cooking. He was a salesman, and he was always working a deal. He burned long hours. He didn't have time to stock a kitchen or shop for groceries. No time for relationships. He didn't have a family. He made sacrifices for this job. For his clients. And he deserved the occasional reward.

But there was one problem. Expensive lunches were, well, expensive. And sitting in the chair across his desk was his former client Bruno Tannenbaum. Bruno once had a career. But, like many writer-types with appetites larger than their talent and work ethic, he crashed hard after his first bestseller and hadn't written a word since. Harley held out hopes that he'd eventually shake his slump and crank out, at the very least, a solid follow-up to *Twenty Recipes for Love*. So he'd endured Bruno, entertained his presence, and even took him to lunch from time to time, as the fading gourmand always seemed to conveniently show up just before the noon hour—and before he knew it, Harley would be spending two hundred dollars at Everest. But that wasn't going to happen today. Today, after listening to Tannenbaum's latest pitch, Harley was ready to cut the man loose. He issued a forced sigh and tried to sound sympathetic.

"Bruno . . . how shall I say this . . . they're never going to go for this in New York."

"What the hell are you talking about, Harley, this is big . . ." Bruno leaned forward.

"It's just too risky. Where would you even start?"

"I've been doing research. Trevallier's granddaughter is still in the business. I go to France and interview her about the old man. Then I follow the clues. I dig up the best little bistros along the way. I'll stop at the big chateaus, the small producers, taste from the barrel."

"The story's great, if there's even a shred of truth to what you're telling me. That's not the problem," Harley said. He faced Bruno now, hands in his pockets, head cocked. Bruno slumped in his chair. He looked like a partially deflated, bearded balloon in a bad tweed sport coat. *He's really letting himself go,* Harley thought.

"Then what's the problem?"

"Frankly, you're done, Bruno. And I hate to say this, but it's true. You crashed too many auctions. You've slept with too many tasting-room girls. You now live with your mother. And I guess that's all well and good, but you committed the granddaddy of all writerly sins: you quit writing. I haven't seen a manuscript in ten years. I could sell that story just fine, Bruno. But not with you attached. You've got nothing."

"I've still got readers."

"I heard from Grovnick. I know the column got axed. You're just another washed-up restaurant critic—"

"It's *food writer*, not *critic*. There's a difference. Look at this," Bruno said, shaking with anger now and rising out of his chair. He stalked over to the wall of shelves lining one entire side of the office, lined with crisp first editions. He plucked out a thin hardcover. The dust jacket gleamed in the light from the window. The spine read *A Season Among the Vines*. The byline: *Bruno Tannenbaum.* He flipped it over. There, in black-and-white, in baggy, wine-stained cargo trousers and a flannel shirt, leaning on a vine stake, with a fuller beard and milder paunch, stood a much younger version of himself. He wore a beret at a rakish angle as he smiled at the photographer. "Look at this. This is a hell of a book."

Harley took it. He paced, examining the cover. It really was a good book. A critical, if not commercial, success. Had Bruno continued to publish, perhaps it could have been rereleased in a new edition. But now it was remaindered. A memory. Destined for secondhand shops or library rummage sales. "This was twenty years ago, Bruno. You're a dinosaur now."

"I'm still that same writer. That's a classic. I wrote it. And I can do it again." Bruno said the words, but Harley could tell by the waver in his voice that he didn't really mean them.

"Well, it didn't sell. *Twenty Recipes for Love*—now, that sold. Write up a proposal for a sequel to that puppy and maybe we'll talk. But this . . ." Harley grabbed the Trevallier cork Bruno had set on his desk and flipped it in the air, catching it. "This little idea of yours would take a huge advance. Travel and research expenses. Nobody in New York is going to take that kind of risk on you. Not anymore."

"Harley, please, I need this . . ."

Harley shook his head. It was sad. He hated to do it, but sometimes people needed to hear the truth. Bruno stood with his arms at his sides, his jowls in a pout. *God, he is so frumpy.* Harley had heard all of the stories . . . the women, the affairs. But how could anyone find this lump of poor wardrobe choices even remotely appealing? Fucking artists. And the hardworking agent in a good suit? He's scorned. There was a part of Harley that was enjoying this. Another part of him felt sorry for Bruno. But not sorry enough to ask him to lunch. He strode to the shelf and plucked a paperback volume so new it smelled of bleached pulp: *A Buyer's Guide to the Wines of Tuscany,* and next to a map of the region stood a well-groomed, tanned, middle-aged man in a pale suit raising a toast, presumably to the reader. The byline read *Parker Thomas.* "Take that. Read it. Maybe you'll learn something."

Bruno took the book and glanced at it, holding it at arm's length and cocking his head away as if the book bore some stench he couldn't abide. Then he tossed it on the table and grinned at Harley with enough defiance and contempt that the agent saw a brief flash of the Bruno of old. "So that's what it's about, eh, Harley? You don't want me to upstage your superstar."

"Upstage? Hell, Bruno, I'd love for you to write a bestseller. Parker Thomas is what wine readers want nowadays. They can't get enough of him. They don't want some crusty philosopher brooding about lost vintages. They want someone optimistic. They want the future. Super Tuscans. Global brands. Agro-tourism. Someone to give them the confidence to walk into a store and buy a bottle of wine."

"I don't score wines, Harley, I tell stories."

"It's a consumer economy. Books are consumer products. So is wine. Scores sell. And nobody does it better than Parker. Go ahead. Take it. Read it. Learn something. Save your stories for tucking in your kids at night."

"Go fuck yourself, Harley."

Bruno snatched the cork out of Harley's hand, whirled on his heel and stormed out the door, slamming it hard enough to rattle the autographed photo of Julia Child hanging on the wall. A small part of Harley was rooting for Bruno. Maybe this little dose of reality would be enough to send him back to his antique typewriter with a fire in his belly. But the rest of Harley was glad to be rid of him once and for all. It was like the relief he felt after dumping a clingy girlfriend.

Then the Thomas book caught his eye. He put his phone on speaker and punched in the number, throwing his feet up on the desk and leaning back. It rang.

"Y'allo?"

"Hey, Park, how's it going?"

"Good, good. What's up, Harley?"

"Making us money, my friend."

"You're the man."

"Hey, guess who was just in my office. Think *washed-up*."

"Richard Nixon?"

"Close. Bruno Tannenbaum."

"Hey, don't pick on poor Bruno."

"I showed him your new book and told him to do his homework."

"And he didn't beat you to death with a lamb shank?"

"He didn't like it, but what else can I do? It's like he's stuck in 1988."

"You kinda gotta feel for him."

"Yeah, well. Hey, listen . . . he actually had a crazy idea, but let me know what you think of this . . ."

Harley picked up the copy of *Season* and flipped through it as he relayed the story. When he paused to clear his throat, he thought he could hear the scribbling of pen on paper coming from Parker's end of the line.

NINE

Street Food

Great meals don't require tablecloths or silverware. There isn't always time. Even so, everything passing one's lips should be an experience. Whether you're in Cleveland or Kolkata, a good meal can be had in a pinch. A decent hunk of cheese and fresh bread can carry you from Chicago to Paris as you munch on the El to Wrigley Field. If you must go fast, go local. The Chicago-style hot dog, for example, is a creation to be found nowhere else and is vastly superior to fast foods created in some corporate laboratory.

—Bruno Tannenbaum, "The Chicago Way,"
Chicago Sun-Times

All writers face rejection, though how they handle it varies greatly. For some it fuels a furious and defiant return to the page. Others row slowly back toward the keyboard on a brooding sea of doubt. One classic response, of course, involves alcohol.

And so Bruno made straight for Gus's, on Chicago's North

Side a few blocks from Wrigley Field. The owner, a retired pitcher, was the closest thing Bruno had to a mentor, and the closest thing Bruno's father had had to a hero. Gus's was filled with baseball memorabilia, including a glass-encased Ernie Banks jersey on the back wall. The bar top was vinyl and they had only the cheapest brands on tap. It was a place without pretension, and the straight-talking bartender always had a few words of wisdom.

Bruno took a seat and patiently waited for Gus, who was wiping glasses and watching the ball game on an old picture-tube television above the bar. It was the bottom of the eighth and the Cubs were losing by seven.

Bruno caught Gus's eye and ordered a "beer and a bump," which was a mug of lager poured over the top of a shot of whiskey, to settle his nerves. He was here to contemplate his future.

"Hey, Gus, what would you do if someone told you that you were washed up?"

"I'd open a bar," Gus replied, stone-faced, holding a mug in his huge paws and wiping it with a stained apron. His nose had been flattened after beaning one too many left-handed batters and the opposing dugout rushed the mound. He wore a military buzz cut and a permanent lump of chaw bulged under his lip.

"I don't have enough money to open a bar."

Gus wiped another mug. He liked to think things through before he spoke, a quality Bruno both lacked and admired. Gus leaned with one elbow on the counter, watching the Cubs' third baseman strike out.

"You're not washed up, Bruno. You're just psyching yourself out." He regarded the writer with tired eyes.

"What was it like . . . when you gave up pitching?"

"I woke up one day and I couldn't keep the ball down. I threw wild. I lost speed. The fans started to turn on me."

"So did you just quit . . . cold turkey?"

"Naw. I went back to Iowa. Played in the minors. I thought I might shake out of the slump. But it didn't happen. I tried best I could, but my arm was just worn out. They didn't have the fancy surgery they got now, otherwise I could have had another year or two. So I cashed in my chips and opened this joint."

"But what does a writer do, when he's got no edge left to his pitch anymore?"

"With baseball it's physical. It's got to end. There's just no way around it. Your body gets old. But what you do . . ." Gus leaned closer and fixed Bruno with his knowing gaze, filled with the hard-worn wisdom won from cheap motels and minor league ballparks on both ends of an all-too-short career as a reliever for the unluckiest team in baseball. He tapped his temple with a thumb. "What you do . . . it's all in here," he said, now thumping his thumb against his heart, "and in here."

Gus paused then, staring out the front window for a long time.

"What I'm saying is . . . and you probably don't want to hear this . . . is that you got no fucking excuses."

Bruno met Gus's hard stare and looked away. The man was right. What excuse did he have? Maybe that's why Anna was always so exasperated. After all, he'd been talking about his book for ten years. Only the night before he'd been telling Claire about how confident he was in this new story. It had dropped in his lap, and instead of chasing it he was sulking in a bar. Maybe Anna had rejected his consulting business idea. Maybe Harley hadn't believed he could deliver the new book. But he didn't need their permission to write. He explained all this to Gus.

"Sounds to me like you only got two strikes and you're ready to just up and walk away from the plate."

"So what should I do?"

"Swing for the fence like you got nothing to lose."

"You're one of the wisest guys I know," Bruno said, finishing off his beer and slapping the counter.

"Atta boy, Bruno!"

"I've got a book to write, Gus!"

"Damn right you do!"

"Also, can I borrow a couple grand?"

"No fucking way. Pay your bar tab and then we'll talk."

Bruno laughed and straightened his cap as he headed out into the street, marching toward the El to hop the Pink Line to Morty's shop.

*　*　*

Morty stood on a stool dusting empty trophy bottles on the top shelf when Bruno rattled the chimes on the door. He locked it behind him and flipped the *Open* sign to *Closed*, stalking to the counter.

Morty came down, smiling broadly.

"Hey, Tannenbaum, I been meaning to get ahold of you. I called the paper, but they said—"

"Yeah, yeah."

"Say, you still got that cork? I wanted to apologize. I don't think I was straight with you. I definitely think it's real, and I should offer you some decent cash for it. Five hundred sound good?"

"You have a buyer or something?"

"I'm sure I'll find someone."

"Maybe a big guy with an accent and a scar?"

Morty fidgeted.

"He's been here, hasn't he? What do you know about him?"

"In my business, I don't just hand over information about customers."

"Bullshit, Morty, information is your main product line."

"It could get dangerous."

"Don't I know it?" Bruno pointed to the bandage on his forehead.

"Don't you think it's worth some compensation, then?"

"I'll make it worth your while." They eyed one another. It was a chess match they'd been through a number of times over the years. Morty usually wound up with the upper hand.

"You know the old rule about friends and money."

"If I turned up a Trevallier from the war . . . one of the missing ones . . . what could you sell it for?"

"You kidding me? A shit-ton."

"What about a case?" Bruno leveled his eyes at his friend and he could see greed reflected back as Morty nervously licked his lips.

"I'd get my usual commission?"

"Of course." Bruno thrust out his hand.

There was a pause. "Okay," he said, cautiously shaking Bruno's hand. "There's this guy comes in yesterday. Just like you say . . . tall, scar. Had an overcoat on . . . bit too much for this weather, in my opinion. And he was asking about war vintages."

"You didn't tell him about the cork, did you?"

"I told him I'd just seen something he might be interested in."

"Morty!"

"That's all I said, I swear. And that's when I started calling you. I figured I'd give you a fair price and then turn it over to him. Everybody makes out. But you'd been fired."

"He leave any contact info?"

"Said to call him at the Palmer House. Room 317."

Bruno jotted it down in his notebook and made for the door. Morty followed him like a small dog yapping at his heels. Bruno was starting to feel like he'd gotten the upper hand this time around.

"Hey, why don't you let me do the negotiation for that cork? We'll split it. I think I could get three grand out of him, easy."

"I'm not going to sell it."

"Bruno . . . that's cash money. Think about it."

"What else do you know about him?"

"Well, he asked where he could ship a few cases overseas . . . discreetly."

"That's probably the juice from the wine locker."

"I gave him a few suggestions."

"Anything else? Think."

"Oh, yeah . . . while he's here, his phone rings. He answered. Sounded like he was speaking Russian or Polish or something. I could hear a woman's voice on the other end."

"Okay. Thanks, Morty."

"Be careful, Bruno. If you get clumsy, we're both screwed."

*   *   *

Bruno found this detective work both exhilarating and somewhat frightening. He stopped for a Chicago-style hot dog to bolster his conviction, and it worked marvelously. It reminded him that the details were what mattered: a poppy-seed bun steamed to perfection and sport peppers elevated the humble dog to the level of regional cuisine. He needed a full belly to be able to think on his feet, and this little meal prepared him for an evening assault on the Hilton.

One might not expect a food writer to excel at espionage, but over the years Bruno had crashed small-town festivals and bacchanals, weddings, auctions and even state dinners. He'd mastered the art of swiping name tags from sign-in tables and adopting a new persona. So when he spotted a conference sign-in table in the lobby he studied the names and selected one that read *Dr. Piotr Piotrowska.*

"Here is me . . ." he said, holding the badge up for the woman checking in guests. "Am late for lecture!" He slipped down the hall and then ducked into the service elevator and pinned the name tag to his lapel, wondering what sort of doctor he should be. He couldn't help but imagine what they were serving at the convention, the sustenance of the hot dog already starting to wear off.

Room 317 was, of course, locked. But a cleaning cart stood next to it with the sounds of vacuuming coming from the neighboring room. Bruno plucked a fresh bathrobe from a stack on the cart. He changed quickly in a vestibule, stuffing his clothes behind the ice machine and melting a few cubes in his hands to wet down his hair.

He popped out again and stood before 317 with his best forlorn pout. When the maid emerged from the next room, he sighed.

"I just had a swim and I'm afraid I've locked myself out," he said. He suddenly hoped that the Palmer House had a pool.

The maid simply shrugged. She glanced up and down the hall and, seeing no one, she slipped her master key into the slot. Bruno feigned embarrassment and gratitude, though what really concerned him was the thought of finding the large thug with the scar inside.

The room was hot and stuffy. He let the door close gently behind him, and he heard the sound of running water coming from the bathroom. Then a deep baritone singing, some sort of anthem, confirmed that the man was in the shower. Bruno spoke some German and French, and could get by well enough in Italian, Spanish and Yiddish, but he was lost when it came to Slavic languages. The singing sounded Russian, but whatever the case, it was a robust baritone that produced it: the man sounded large.

Bruno gulped, his heart in his throat. He was tempted to dash out, but he gathered himself and minced on trembling feet into the room.

It was spare. A small suitcase lay open on one of the beds. Socks, shorts, slacks were folded in crisp piles inside. A wristwatch sat on the nightstand.

The singing stopped and Bruno froze, eyeing the door. But then it started again and he rifled through the suitcase. Lifting up a clean white shirt, he found a pistol in a holster. Seizing it would give him the upper hand. He could interrogate the thug, or at least escape unscathed in the case of an altercation.

But Bruno could no more wield a pistol than he could balance a checkbook. If the thug were to see it gripped awkwardly in the writer's hand, he'd easily be able to overpower him and beat him senseless with the handle, or worse. So Bruno covered it up again and tiptoed over to the desk. Best for the fellow not to know someone had been here.

The room was pristine. Nothing interesting jumped out at him. He grew more nervous. The shower was due to end. He rifled through the wastebasket and the drawers.

Then he spied a blazer hanging on the bathroom door. He tiptoed over. He felt his heart thumping against his ribs so loud that the man in the shower had to be able to hear it.

He gingerly checked the inside pockets of the blazer and there found a pin and a slip of paper. The message bore a few lines written on it in Cyrillic, a few numbers, plus, written in curvy script, *'43 Trevallier*.

Fucking Morty, Bruno thought.

Bruno quickly transcribed the note on the hotel's courtesy paper, hoping he wasn't making some error that rendered the information useless. The pin had a red cross with a strange bat-wing logo. Bruno slid it into his pocket, hoping the man wouldn't miss it. Then he returned the original note to the jacket pocket.

Relieved, he headed for the door, but stopped when he spied the minibar.

He hesitated. He deserved a treat, didn't he?

He tiptoed back over, opened the small refrigerator and found a split of passable California Chardonnay. Just as he was about to grab it, he heard the water in the shower turn off.

He froze.

The sound of the curtain dragging along the shower rod.

He seized the bottle and made for the door, Chardonnay clutched to his chest.

He heard the bathroom door open just as he was gently allowing the hotel door to click into place behind him.

Breathless, he made it back to the vestibule where he'd hidden his clothes. His hands shook as he dressed.

*   *   *

Visiting Aleksei the next morning didn't help to settle Bruno's nerves. He needed help with the translation. He found his friend in his corner booth at the Samovar, with his shirtsleeves rolled up, painting a porcelain tea set. Bruno sat across from him nervously while Aleksei gently set a cup down and frowned as he studied the note.

"Well, it's definitely Russian," Aleksei confirmed. Aside from the mention of the Trevallier, the rest of the transcription seemed to be information on an Air France flight. "Yuri, call the airline and check the flight numbers," Aleksei said, and the large bartender appeared at his elbow.

"Flight is leaving tomorrow morning," Yuri said after patiently wading through the menus and then speaking to an actual human to confirm. This story was becoming Bruno's entire future, and the Russian fellow was a step ahead.

But what was worse was the pin. Aleksei turned it over and over in his hands, whistling through his teeth. "This is the insignia of the Spetsnaz," he said. Russian special forces. Aleksei told him that this specific unit operated with deadly efficiency in the Second Chechen War.

"I don't understand . . . So the Russian government is after rare wine?"

"Many of the former soldiers are employed as bodyguards and chauffeurs for the Russian elite . . . oligarchs, industrialists and crime bosses. They're the ones more likely to care about rare wines. My suspicion is that this fellow is a henchman in the employ of some wealthy collector."

"And I led him right to your locker."

"No matter . . . Sometimes these repossessions can cause more trouble than they're worth. But perhaps there is also an opportunity in it for you."

"Perhaps," Bruno said, though his hopes had clouded over. How could he find the Trevallier and write a book about it if some well-funded collector and the Russian equivalent of a Navy SEAL were also after it?

"Bruno," Aleksei warned, "this guy could probably kill you with his little toe. Be careful."

TEN

A Sour Apple

One must thank the Hapsburg Empire for the gift of stru-
del. The stew of ethnicities comprised of their imperial
subjects blended the cuisines of the Ottoman Turks with
Jewish, Alsatian, French, Dutch, Moravian, Slavic and Pol-
ish traditions. Eastern baklava met German restraint in
Vienna, forming a perfect pastry of subtle complexity to
serve with good coffee: an excellent choice for when you
need to have a serious conversation.

—BRUNO TANNENBAUM, *TWENTY RECIPES FOR LOVE*

Aleksei's warning and Bruno's financial inability to pursue
the story of the cork kept him awake late into the night. As a
food journalist, he was supposed to dream of sauce reductions,
pastries, craft cocktails or barrel tastings, not pursuit by a Russian super-soldier. He finally drifted into a heavy slumber until
Anna called and roused him at noon the next day to ask him if
he could pick up the girls because things were going to shit at
the office. She of course knew that he had nothing better to do.

He could tell by the sound of her voice that she was still angry with him.

All of this weighed on Bruno to the point of distraction. In times of such stress it's always best to focus on the very next step, which—of course—should involve food. So he stopped at the grocer's to inspect the produce. A small basket of gnarly, blighted apples caught his attention, so sad next to their gleaming, waxed and flavorless cousins. He took a bite of one and smiled at the acidic tang. They were Belle de Boskoops, perfect for baking and especially tasty in strudel. Anna loved strudel. He imagined her coming home from a bad day at work to the smell of apples baking in brown sugar. He would enlist the girls to help him make her some. He also picked up sultanas, fresh cinnamon and some good bread flour.

A little later Bruno was sinking his teeth through an apple as he leaned against the schoolyard fence at Claire's high school, holding a paper sack of groceries in one arm as he waited for his oldest daughter to emerge from the stream of students disgorged through the school's metal detectors

He caught sight of a familiar flash of coppery hair in a gaggle of girls walking his way and then Claire was standing before him in surprise. He was pleased that she showed no hint of annoyance or embarrassment. She'd gone through a phase when she was horrified by the mere proximity of parents. But now she was confident and unabashed.

"Daddy, what are you doing here?" she asked, hugging her books as she waved goodbye to her friends.

"Your mom's got to catch up at the office and I happened to be available."

"Okay, cool!" Her smile warmed his heart. He tossed her an apple and she looked knowingly at its blotchy green skin with a blush of orange russet. "So, we gonna bake something?"

"Strudel for your mom."

"Fun!"

They followed a street lined with brownstones and leafy trees that buckled the sidewalks with their swollen roots. They chatted as they walked. They'd become better friends since his and Anna's separation, though he sometimes suspected that Claire felt sorry for him. You've reached a new low when you earn the pity of your teenage daughter.

"Have a good day?" he asked.

"Yeah, great," she said, but she read something in his furrowed brow. "Dad, what's bothering you?"

"Is it that obvious?"

"Um, yeah."

They walked to Carmen's school a few blocks away. She was in choir practice for another twenty minutes, so they hung out on the playground. Claire sat on a swing and drifted slowly back and forth, gusts of spring wind pushing her. A lone sparrow pecked in the gravel under her feet as Bruno drew a deep breath.

"Claire, I haven't been writing."

"But your book . . ."

"I'm stuck. I get two, maybe three pages in and then I get bogged down."

"But you've been working so hard."

"No. Not really. Sulking, mostly." Bruno sat on the swing next to her, the chains creaking.

"But what about that cork . . . ?"

"The cork is the key to everything. It's like some kind of sign. I've been playing around at being a writer for a long time now. I've been stubborn even though it clearly hasn't worked out. And now all of a sudden there's this great story just sitting in front of me. And I think that if I can take a shot at telling it right, then everything would have been worthwhile. I could make it up to you. To your mom."

"You're psyching yourself out, right?"

"Exactly. I'm afraid to get started. And then there's a . . . er . . . problem. Researching this lost vintage is going to require funding."

"But Harley said they were excited about it in New York . . ."

"Harley said *no*."

"That douchebag . . ."

"Claire!"

"Well, I never liked him. Anyway, I'm sorry, Daddy. That really sucks. What about Mom?"

"You heard our last financial discussion. I don't think she's in any mood to entertain more of my schemes."

"You could explain it to her the way you've explained it to me." She gave him a reassuring, sympathetic smile and he wondered who the adult was. Then she asked him for a push and he got up and gave her a running shove, dashing underneath her before she dropped again.

"Underdog!" She laughed and began to pump her legs to push the swing as high as it could go. The chains creaked and she was like a little girl again, and his heart ached over all the time he'd spent away and misbehaving when he should have been home pushing his daughter on a swing before she became too old for it. Ten years he'd been wasting his time.

Claire shrieked and hurtled through the air, leaping off the swing. She landed in the gravel and fell onto her backside. She stood up, laughing, and brushed off her jeans. Then she walked up to Bruno and hooked his arm. The bell rang and they walked toward the front door of the school.

"Why don't you just let me talk to Mom about it? Maybe she could float you a loan," Claire said as they craned their necks to see if they could pick Carmen out of the rush of students.

"I've gotten you into enough hot water with your mother over that whole culinary school thing. Maybe it's best you just keep out of this one."

"Can't I just talk to her? Girl-to-girl?"

"You'd do that for me?"

"Of course." She smiled. "Why wouldn't I?"

Bruno couldn't think of how best to answer that.

Carmen came bounding out the front door and squealed when she saw them. She raced toward them and looped her arms in both of theirs, and the three of them walked home together. Moments like these always saddled Bruno with the sweet and sad knowledge of how life just tended to slip away. When was the last time the three of them had walked home from school? He couldn't remember.

He cheered himself with the thought that they'd all soon be kneading air into the dough until it felt like something alive, as the metal of the warming oven ticked. With any luck, Ella Fitzgerald would be crooning on the kitchen radio.

ELEVEN

Something for the Road

A well-made sandwich is an act of love. Whether it's Mom cutting the crusts off a PB&J and tucking it into a paper sack or fixing yourself a monster corned beef and Swiss with sauerkraut, aioli and tomato, plus a poached egg for good measure as a pick-me-up after a nasty lover's spat, there is always a subtext to this sacred wizardry one finds between two slices of bread. When Hillel the Elder first documented three thousand years ago the Passover tradition of wrapping lamb and herbs in soft matzo, did he know he'd set into motion a revolution of portable cuisine?
—Bruno Tannenbaum, "A Natural History of the Sandwich," Chicago Sun-Times

Two days later, Bruno was lingering over breakfast while Greta fussed preparing sundries for his flight to Paris, the first stop in his quest to track down the Trevallier. He tried not to watch as she wrapped a pair of sandwiches in waxed paper and tied them with kitchen twine, making a neat little bow. He wanted to be surprised. This was a gift of the highest order, one of the ways his mother conveyed her love for him. He couldn't recall her ever actually using those three little words, but then there is no more clear and effective way to express your feelings for another soul than preparing them something wonderful to eat with your own hands.

She filled a sack with edibles, including an entire baguette and an expensive bit of Fragnière Gruyère. His mouth began to water as he considered shaving off a slice or two on the El train en route to O'Hare.

"Did you pack a warm sweater? It might get cold at night."

"Yes, Ma."

"That suitcase looks too small."

"I'll be fine." She blushed and frowned. Greta hated flying, despite never having been on a plane. Her folks came over on the boat in the mid-thirties for obvious reasons when she was only three years old. She'd grown up with no love for either the Germans or the Vichys, which was how her parents had referred to the French. Still, she did like to brag to her pinochle clutch whenever her son was in Paris or Berlin.

"What if they don't let you take your lunch on board?"

"Stop worrying, Ma."

"Those security people might confiscate it."

"I don't think they're on the lookout for terrorist sandwiches."

"I better pack you some hard-boiled eggs just in case."

Bruno took the Blue Line to O'Hare and grew giddy. He loved to travel. And he was going back to France! If he had a spiritual home, it was most certainly Burgundy. He reflected on his good fortune. Claire had apparently spoken with Anna about funding Bruno's research for the Trevallier, and though his estranged wife was understandably reluctant, Claire's enthu-

siasm had won the day and somehow she had convinced Anna to
trust him with a loan. There were, of course, conditions. Bruno
was to provide an itemized list of receipts so that Anna (ever
the accountant) could properly track the tax write-offs. He was
also to report on his progress. Finally, he was to refrain from
mentioning anything to Greta, Carmen or anyone else about
the loan. Claire had explained all of these rules to him carefully,
and he listened intently. Claire was to continue as emissary in
the whole affair. Indeed, she was the one who had delivered
the cash, nearly six thousand dollars, to Greta's apartment in a
plain envelope. Opening it was exhilarating. He felt like a spy in
a Cold War novel. Bruno purchased a ticket to Paris first thing
the next morning before Anna had time to change her mind.
He also wanted to hurry because the Russian had a head start.
And also, if he acted fast, he could catch one of his favorite wine
events, a large, hedonistic party or "bacchanal" that took place
this time every year. The wine town of Beaune would be his
first stop, and he'd find a way to connect with Sylvie Trevallier
there. Then it would be simply a matter of following the clues
wherever they led.

Now at the terminal, Bruno carried his small wicker suitcase
in one hand and clutched a laden paper bag from his mother's
deli in the other. Greta's fears proved unfounded, and though
TSA sent his plastic-wrapped baguette through the X-ray
machine a second time, he made it to the plane with his lunch
intact.

While finding his seat, Bruno, being a largish fellow, elicit-
ed a look of horror from the woman in the aisle seat who was
holding a baby when he asked if he could scoot into the middle
spot. A teenage girl with a nose ring and black lipstick was
pinned between his shoulder and the window and was likewise

none too pleased to be spending eight hours squashed next to him.

"Don't worry, I don't bite," he announced.

But he was quick to make friends using Greta's ingredients to good effect, and by the end of the flight he had made sandwiches for his entire row as well as the folks across the aisle. The young mother even entrusted him with the baby while she stretched and used the restroom, and the child fell asleep, a dozing bundle of heat pressed to his chest, her breath sweet against his beard. His eyes grew misty at the nearly forgotten memory of holding his own daughters in this way.

At Charles De Gaulle Airport, Bruno found a postcard featuring the famously bored gargoyle on Notre Dame and he scratched a summary of the flight to Anna. In the past he'd sent frequent postcards during his travels on book tours and while writing articles for *Wine Spectator* and the like. Claire thought it would be a good way for him to report his progress to Anna. She had first suggested that he report on his journey via direct messages on Twitter, but Bruno had looked at her as if she were speaking another language.

"When you get back, we're going to have to work on your integrated marketing strategy," Claire said, exasperated.

"Where do you get such absurd notions?"

"In school. We had a class on it."

"So that's why they've dropped Latin?"

He bought stamps and a *carnet* of Métro tickets from a tobacco stand. He had a few hours until his train left for Dijon from the Gare de Lyon, so he made quick stops at Place de la Concorde and then Abbesses to have a coffee and a beignet at his favorite café across the plaza from the Bateau-Lavoir, where Picasso had once lived. The tables on the cobbled plaza were empty save one, where a pale woman with haphazard brown hair scribbled into a notebook. She was younger than Bruno, and something about the way she wore her hair pulled back made him think of Anna at that age. He recalled vividly the very moment he'd first spotted his wife.

It had been his first big review, a traditional and uninspiring Chicago steakhouse, though he was still tickled by the blank expense check publications issued to reviewers in those days, one of them burning inside his jacket pocket. The hostess had just seated him when he spotted Anna on the far side of the room, lit by a hanging Tiffany lamp, leaning over a table and laughing easily with an elderly couple. Their eyes met briefly and she smiled, though he was afraid he'd imagined it. She was beautiful without trying, her skin pale, her cheeks flushed, her unruly curls haphazardly pulled into a noncompliant bun, the depth of her green eyes making him dizzy. Other servers criss-crossed in front of her and Bruno closed his eyes, leaned back his head and whispered, *Let her serve me, let her serve me, let her serve me.*

And suddenly, there she was, a hand on his shoulder, the closest thing he'd ever experienced to an answered prayer: "Sir, are you okay?"

Bruno opened his eyes and gazed at her openmouthed, issuing a sort of gurgle. She furrowed her brow in concern and pushed up her sleeves like she was considering the Heimlich, but he snapped out of it.

"I'm fine," Bruno said finally, and then she offered a smile at his awkwardness, the corners of her eyes pinched with mirth, and he was floored.

"Can I get you something to start?"

"Um . . ." Bruno stammered. This was unlike him. He was

generally gregarious and never shy when it came to women. But with Anna, his tongue was tied. "Do you take these?" he blurted, thrusting the magazine check forward. He wasn't supposed to tip his hand as a critic, but at least they'd be sure to take extra care with his food.

"Of course," she said. "So you want some time to look at the menu?"

Bruno nodded stupidly.

Between her visits he ate ravenously and tried to plan something clever to say. But for perhaps the first time in his life he was at a loss for words. Every time she reappeared he was mute. He grew so frustrated that after she brought the final bill he pounded the table with his fist, drawing attention from the other diners.

He realized while leaving that he'd forgotten to leave a tip on the check. He of course didn't have any cash, so he skulked back into the restaurant and wrote a poem on a bar napkin:

> *Words lie unused on the floor*
> *Frightened to the shadows by your radiant grace*
> *The sweet remembrance of this little defeat*
> *A lovely regret I'll carry*
> *As long as I breathe*

He signed it and left his telephone number, passing it to the bartender for delivery, certain that if it even reached her it would be immediately discarded. Surely she'd had this effect on customers often.

"Never," she said three weeks later, when she actually did call him. "Actually it's the sweetest thing anyone has ever done for me."

Bruno stared into his coffee for a long time. The woman at

the café was now gone. He still had time before his train left, so he took the Métro to Censier-Daubenton and hurried on to the market on Rue Mouffetard. He stood at the end of the narrow street, which was blossoming with colorful stalls and awnings, momentarily overwhelmed by the churn of pedestrians with cloth bags and shopping trolleys with protruding baguettes and sausages. A dozen distinct smells accosted him at once and he felt the urge to kneel and genuflect, thinking that this was what it must be like for the devout when they enter a church or synagogue. Because his mother's family leaned Catholic and his father's halfheartedly practiced Judaism, Bruno's parents had compromised by generally avoiding religion. They worshipped instead through food. He'd inherited the religion of the table and felt that God dwelt there, and in street markets like this one.

It took him twenty minutes for an initial reconnaissance before he finally purchased one perfect tomato and a cucumber with character. He picked up a baguette, an aged, ample *saucisson de laguiole* and some goat cheese of indeterminate origin, a sample sliver of which brought him close to tears. He asked the *fromager* to lop off a square of butter onto some waxed paper, and his chores were complete, his stomach rumbling merrily. He purchased a cheap paring knife from a kitchen vendor and headed back to the Métro.

He bought his ticket at the Gare de Lyon, opting to pay the extra thirty euros for first class, figuring he was due a little splurge. He could budget more carefully toward the end of the trip.

*   *   *

Bruno heard the station announcement, thinking at first it was part of his dream. But when he choked mid-snore and cracked an eye he saw that they'd arrived. He leapt from his seat and slipped through closing doors. The train rattled away, leaving him standing dazed on a concrete pad with weeds growing in the cracks. The station was deserted save for a large, lone man on a bench in a long dark coat and hat reading a newspaper. A cat lazed in a patch of sun between the far rails, clearly unconcerned about the prospect of traffic.

From the station, Beaune looked like a sleepy town of little consequence, but to Bruno and anyone else who lived for the grape's elixir it was the center of the known universe.

He was parched, so he ordered a Fanta at the Hôtel de France across from the station. For some reason the orange soda always tasted better in Europe than it did in the States.

The town had barely outgrown its medieval footprint. He crossed the ring road and passed between a pair of houses that had been producing wine since before France's first revolution. Thinking about the cobwebby magic stacked in their ancient cellars, he suddenly felt insignificant in his own little quest.

He found a small hotel with a vacancy that was built right into the old, crumbling city walls. It was a series of small towers of rough-hewn stone, confining but tastefully appointed with a delightful little courtyard beyond the lobby where he could take his coffee in the morning. His mood lightened considerably when the young woman at the desk smiled at him and complimented him on his French. Her name was Lisette, and she had a sunny, unadorned demeanor that made him think of a wholesome Burgundian farm lass. She insisted on carrying his suitcase to his room at the top of the hotel's single tower, hefting it up the steep, narrow staircase that wound up into the darkness. Her skirt was very short, and he admired the striations of muscles in her thighs and calves for a moment before tearing his gaze away.

She arrived at the top landing and unlocked the door with a rusty, ancient key and revealed a chamber with bare stone walls, a small writing table and a plush, massive bed. She set down his suitcase and began the quick tour, not even breathing hard, while Bruno leaned against the wall panting and mopping his forehead with his bandanna.

She threw open the shutters to expose a hazy vista overlooking the Côte-d'Or. There was a bottle of a simple white AOC Bourgogne on the table by the window with two glasses. "Shall I open this?" she asked with a smile.

"Of course," he said, imagining that this may be one of those romantic moments about which he sometimes wrote. But when she only overturned one glass he realized that she had no plans to join him, and he felt silly for having hoped otherwise.

She left and the room reacquired some of its medieval gloom without her presence. He sat sipping his wine and arranging his things on the desk: a stack of black hardcover notebooks next to a row of newly sharpened pencils, a photocopied bundle of research materials on the occupation from the Harold Washington Library in Chicago and a few volumes that included *Parker Thomas's Guide to Burgundy,* which he had to admit was a useful index of the vineyards and producers of the region.

So, here he was, in Burgundy, the magical kingdom of the vine. If the world of viticulture and enology had a sun around which all other places revolved, this would be it. He was inspired to write in a way he hadn't been in ages.

But after jotting down only a page of random observations from his brief time in Paris he drank most of the complimentary bottle of wine and fell into a deep sleep. He felt a warm ray of evening sun slipping through the window to bake his cheek and he awoke suddenly, panicked at the waning day. This was, after

all, a research trip. He was here to interview the elusive propri-
etress of the Trevallier label and he knew next to nothing about
her other than the fact that she rarely, if ever, spoke to journalists.

As he headed out, evening sun lit the empty streets near the
city walls. Beaune drew its share of tourists, but it still was a
working town, with *négociants,* coopers, laboratories, winery
equipment suppliers and the like, a fact Bruno loved about the
city. As he turned on the Rue des Tonneliers, he saw two men
rolling freshly coopered oak barrels out of a workshop and to
the curb, where they hoisted them into the back of a truck. He
smelled the vanilla bite of the new wood as he passed. *Tonneliers*
means "barrelmakers." He knew he could have visited the town
in the 1400s and witnessed the same activity.

He paused to ask one of the men if they knew anything about
Mme. Trevallier. One shrugged and the other, without looking,
made the universal French gesture for craziness, putting his
index finger to his ear and twisting back and forth like a drill.
He waited a moment for elaboration, but they were clearly busy,
so he bade them *bonsoir* and went on his way.

He next inquired at a *fromager* down the street. She was
wrapping up the cheeses in her display case for the evening, and
Bruno was distracted by the pungent, fruity aroma of the half
wheel of Morbier in her hand. She must have heard his stomach
rumble, because she shared a generous slice. He held it up to the
light to admire the rich gold with its ash stripe down the middle.
It melted sweet against his tongue.

The woman was less helpful on the matter of Mme. Trevallier.
She'd never met her, though she'd heard that she was an absentee
landlord living the good life in Paris. "Have you seen the price of
her wines? That woman's never worked a day in her life."

A group of young men in mud-spattered rubber boots two

blocks farther along were about as helpful as the *fromager*. Bruno
asked them if they were vignerons and they laughed and said
that they installed septic systems. But one of them had worked
on the Trevallier estate.

"The place is really run-down. And that woman is crazy . . .
an old crone with wild gray hair and cheap costume jewelry.
They say she's a genius when it comes to wine, but also a tight-
wad. I'd stay away, if I were you. There are plenty of estates that
have more class and charm, and at a better price."

Bruno was dismayed that investigative work was getting him
nowhere and producing such a poor assessment of this elusive,
magical wine. But as the streetlamps popped on he realized it
was time for a meal and his spirits brightened. He chose a small
restaurant and sat at an outdoor table on a street corner with
a view of the Place Carnot, where a vintage merry-go-round
turned slowly, the music faintly audible over the sound of conversation. He ordered a plate of *gougères* and took some time
before choosing a Volnay Premier Cru from a producer he'd
never heard of. It was delightful, light, clear and floral, but with
a hint of the cellar and farmyard, a tad too brown in the glass
under the streetlight. At La Marseillaise he might have been
underwhelmed . . . another random bottle of very good Burgundy. But here it took on mystical qualities. The walls of these
houses that surrounded him had stared across the hills for how
many hundreds of vintages? This rustic Pinot Noir was the perfect compliment.

The *gougères,* small puffs of *choux* pastry with local cheeses
mixed in the dough, were especially light, and they disintegrated
against the roof of his mouth. He finished with a salad of mixed
greens served with the classic egg poached in red wine sauce,
oeufs en meurette.

His belly full, he wrote down what he'd learned about Mme. Trevallier, and then swayed from the table, gifting the remaining half of his bottle to an attractive young couple. He bowed to the woman, doffing his cap and winking.

He then went into the back and asked to speak to the chef. The fellow was gruff, eying the Cubs cap with suspicion, but the quality of Bruno's French usually won people over quickly.

"Can you tell me anything about Madame Trevallier?"

"Sylvie? What do you want to know? Just drink her wine and you'll understand that she's got impeccable taste and she doesn't suffer bullshit."

The chef waved the writer away, and Bruno felt he might want to tread very carefully when it came to his approach to this Trevallier woman. But careful wasn't his style, so he decided on a full-frontal assault instead. In the morning he'd muster as much of his clumsy charm as possible and see where that got him.

He wandered the city center and absorbed the burble of restaurant conversation, the popping of corks and clink of glasses, the sound of tires on the cobbles. The air was thick and warm, and he felt a few drops of rain from somewhere in the darkness above. He knew that Burgundian weather was fickle, and a flash storm could appear out of nowhere, dropping rain in buckets. It was part of the risk of growing Pinot and Chardonnay in a continental climate.

As he circled his way back toward his hotel on the emptier streets near the old city walls, he picked up the sound of footsteps behind him. He glanced over his shoulder and spotted a figure in a dark coat and hat slipping into the shadows between the streetlamps.

He turned onto the next street, not recognizing the street corner. It was darker here, and he again heard the *click, click, click* on the cobbles behind him. His pulse quickened. Instinctively he felt for the lump on his forehead, the dry, scabby skin at his hairline from the thumping he'd received in the wine storage unit.

Was he in danger? He looked up at the shuttered windows. They were all dark save one, where the blue light of a television flickered between the slats in the shutter. He wondered if he should shout. There was one streetlamp ahead, and it buzzed and suddenly flickered out, bathing the entire stretch in darkness. On impulse he slipped into a tight gap between two houses, his belly wedged against the stone side of the building. He remembered now the quick glimpse of a figure in a dark coat and hat at the train station earlier in the day. Why hadn't he been more alert on this trip? He recalled the Russian thug and Aleksei's warning about mysterious parties interested in this vintage. Why wouldn't they also be here?

The footsteps grew louder, and indignation swelled within him. The wine was giving him courage. Here he was in one of the loveliest towns on earth and he was allowing a specter to torment him.

Just as the figure drew abreast of him, he leapt out of the narrow alley. At that moment the temperamental streetlight clicked back on and a shriek rose in the narrow canyon of apartments.

No thug stood before him now, but instead a matronly woman in a trench coat and rain hat. She was carrying an umbrella and she whacked Bruno's knee. He stumbled and put up his hands in protest, apologizing profusely in English. The woman didn't back down. Evidently thugs and muggers weren't tolerated in Beaune.

She struck Bruno again on the legs and shoulder with her umbrella. Lights came on overhead and he heard the creak of a shutter being thrown open. The woman marched away a few steps but returned to deliver one final whack on Bruno's ear for good measure.

"*Merde! Je ne tolère pas les criminels,*" the woman was shrieking. Bruno heard laughter from above.

"*Ramper dans votre trou, vermine!*" the woman shouted, jabbing the umbrella at Bruno and then striding away without looking back. Bruno bent to massage his sore knee and watched the woman in admiration as she strode away. Above him a shutter creaked and slammed shut, and he was beginning to wonder if he was cut out for adventure of any sort. He thought that he might need a glass of sherry to steel his nerves before bed. He decided it was time to stop fooling around. Tomorrow he would march on Les Cloches.

TWELVE

Grand Vintage

Anyone who tries to tell you that love, passion or lust are solely the provinces of youth has never stumbled across an aged bottle in the depths of the cellar. While it may be covered in dust and the label faded, one need only pull the cork to learn that the more mature wine has advantages of depth, complexity and wisdom. Wine reminds us that, like matters of the heart, inclusion of the dimension of time has an additive rather than diminishing effect.

—BRUNO TANNENBAUM, *TWENTY RECIPES FOR LOVE*

The truck jolted over a rut in the road, rattling the empty grape lugs and almost tossing Bruno from the flatbed. The old, gray-whiskered dog riding next to him panted in amusement. He was obviously more used to the broken roads of these ancient Burgundian wine towns than the writer, who tightened his grip on the edge of the bed.

Bruno stared across the tidy rows of vines edged with the golden light of morning, each leaf wearing the tint of possibility. It was morning in Burgundy, and he was here, at the beginning of the grand adventure that would be his next book. He was nervous, excited, afraid. Ahead of him lay the story of a lifetime. Tonight was the bacchanal. And beyond that, anything could happen. The magic he'd sensed as a much younger man on his first journey here hung now in the haze above these tidy vineyards.

The wines in the Côte-d'Or were managed with more precision than anywhere else in the world. It was a by-product, perhaps, of the fact that a single row of these vines could provide the income for an entire winemaking family. Everything about the landscape, from the gradual eastward slope of the hillsides, to the villages clustered in shallow draws and the crumbling stone walls demarking the vineyard blocks, reminded him that he was in his beloved Bourgogne. They passed the sign marking the beginning of the Route des Grands Crus and then another denoting the first village, Pommard.

The truck's cab had no back window, so Bruno poked his head inside. "What do you know of Madame Trevallier?" he asked the driver.

"Reclusive. Ruthless," the man said after a moment of thought. He was a laconic farmer. He added, "Icy, humorless and brilliant." Bruno nodded. He was forewarned. How was he ever going to get any information out of this woman?

Bruno banged on the side of the truck, and it slowed by a church so he could jump off. He leapt to the ground by the memorial to "the children of Pommard" who gave their lives for France in the Great War. He slapped the truck again, waving thanks to the driver in the mirror. The names on the cold stone read like a wine list of the great producers. How many great wines were never made by these young men? How many promising young vignerons were trod into the mud between trenches?

He followed the pitted road west out of town, climbing a gentle slope. He passed the rusted hulk of a truck and then a crumbling building, suddenly struck by the notion that this ramshackle village produced luxury products few could afford. If anyplace was a polar opposite of the Napa Valley, it was Pommard. Wine and its economics and production formed an unfathomable puzzle. The more he learned, the less he understood. He was a child humbled before the mystery of the fermented grape. One could memorize scores, buy futures or even strive to become a "Master of Wine," but in Bruno's mind such pursuits missed a fundamental truth about the stuff: It isn't some refined substance to be analyzed or studied and ranked on a scale of seventy to one hundred. It's a story. A form of communication, meant for facilitating a conversation across a table and through the ages. A time stamp of geology and weather, of wars and domestic strife. Of human folly and hubris and passion and sublime appreciation for the great mystery that sends pale green shoots out toward the warm spring sun, conjures its fruit by the ton and then dies back to a dried woody skeleton every fall, every vine, every drop a tiny homage to the Big Bang, the celestial orbit and the miracle of cellular division.

Bruno was feeling more writerly than he had in months, maybe years, and he whistled as he climbed the switchbacks up the slope. A dragonfly paced him for part of the walk, hovering just past his shoulder like a guardian angel.

The estate he sought was a lone enclave of pitted stone buildings that stood beyond the village and in stark contrast to the more prosperous wine houses in Beaune, with their iron crests and elaborate tasting rooms. He'd heard much about Mme. Trevallier now, and it was not without a little trepidation that he sought her out. He had gained only a vague picture of her in his head from his conversations, but what he knew was that she was eccentric, capable and aloof. And she refused to talk to the press.

Bruno, in short, had his work cut out for him, and he fully expected to return to town with his tail between his legs. Anna had proved that he was little match for a formidable woman.

The sun rose higher and he was beginning to sweat, so he removed his sport coat and folded it over his arm, sitting on a stone wall mopping his brow with a bandanna before climbing farther. He was whistling the prelude to *Carmen* when the buildings came into view. There was nothing to announce the winery save faded, stenciled lettering on the mail drop in the stone fence: *Trevallier*. He entered the gate to find himself in a courtyard with a simple plain barn and buildings, tractors, a forklift and huge steel doors that opened to a vaulted cellar set back into the hillside. There were few contemporary adornments of any sort, and the scene could have materialized out of a photo from the 1940s.

Two field hands worked on a tractor while a handsome if slightly underfed peasant woman rinsed barrels on a concrete pad. She may have been his own age, perhaps a tad older, with the healthy weathering of someone who spends her life mostly out of doors. She wore work clothes and a bandanna tied back around her hair. He figured she must be seasonal help, and he expected to encounter a Polish accent, maybe Moldovan, as he approached her. It was very much like Bruno to fall temporarily in love with the very first woman he saw on any given day (Lisette hadn't been at the desk when he left his hotel that morning), but something about this hired woman appealed to him. Maybe he should skip his attempted interview with Sylvie Trevallier and spend the morning with her instead.

*   *   *

Sylvie rinsed a barrel, purple stain spreading on the concrete pad in front of the cave, when the bearded man came into view. Her first impression, when she viewed him through the rainbow arc in the cloud of mist rising from the stream of her pressure washer, was that of a frumpy salesman, perhaps a new account representative from the tank manufacturer in Beaune or the glassware producer in Chalon-sur-Saône. There was something familiar about him, as if he'd attempted a lame pass at her some years ago when such things still regularly happened to her. He was unshaven, with bloodshot eyes, mussed hair and a rumpled sport coat thrown over his shoulder. *He won't last long in this business,* she thought.

He leaned against the wall and waited for her to finish. Ordinarily she'd be annoyed by this stranger's appraisal of her, but there was something inexplicably charming about the way he whistled and politely pretended not to be watching while still sneaking glances her way. She gritted her teeth and finished the task at hand, then finally paused and straightened up, back aching. She'd been working since before sunrise and she'd lost count of the number of barrels. Each one weighed sixty kilograms and they seemed to get heavier each year.

Across the yard, Claude pulled his head out of the engine of the temperamental Bobard tractor. He was shirtless, his muscled shoulders covered in grease and sweat, and Sylvie had a momentary twinge of lust as he flexed and gripped his wrench, gesturing toward the salesman with his chin and a questioning look in his eyes, asking her if he should chase the fellow off.

Sylvie shook her head. Claude had grown too protective since they'd become lovers, and even though he was half her age he was beginning to act like he owned the place. She was going to

have to end their relationship soon before it grew too complicated. This made her a little sad; Claude was a reliable morning
fuck, if a tad unimaginative in bed.

She approached the salesman, drawing off her bandanna and
shaking out her hair, and he blushed slightly. She liked that she
still had this disarming effect.

As the salesman began to talk, he struck her on two accounts:
he was American, although he didn't look like a tourist, and his
French was quite good. He held her gaze, though she could
tell by the sparkle in his eye that he was struggling mightily
to not size her from head to toe, and she allowed herself to be
flattered. In the background Claude flexed and craned his neck
curiously.

"Excuse me, miss, where might I find Madame Trevallier?"

Sylvie wiped her brow and tipped her head toward the cave.
"This way, follow me."

This wine cave was an actual cave . . . dark, damp and
musty . . . not the sort of marbled, tiled or otherwise adorned
grotto that one finds so often in the modern Disneyfication of the
wine industry. There were mosses and lichens by the door and
then a damp, musty darkness farther in, relieved only by dim
yellow bulbs that hung in metal cages overhead above the stacks
of barrels.

Bruno followed her to a dingy office at the rear of the cave
with fluorescent light and rusting metal furniture. She cleared
stacks of papers from two folding chairs, taking one for herself
and gesturing for him to sit. Recognition dawned on his features.
She liked that he was surprised.

"This is my office. I'm Sylvie Trevallier," she said. She paused
and let the realization settle on him.

"Oh, excuse me, Madame Trevallier, I didn't . . ."

She waved him off. "Don't worry. Most people are surprised
by the fact that I'm just a farmer who couldn't afford to drink
her own wine."

The man smiled. It was then, as she scanned the row of notebooks, manuals for machinery, press clippings, a few wine compendiums and some crime novels on a shelf above his head, that
the flash of recognition she'd felt earlier when she first spotted
him came into focus. This was no salesman. This was an older
version of the American writer who'd spent a year traipsing
about the slopes of Hautes-Côtes de Beaune in the early nineties.
The book was one of her favorites, and she'd read it several times
over the years. He had talent. Or at least he did when he'd written that book.

"So, Mr. Tannenbaum, how can I help you?" She smiled. He
was clearly shocked that she knew his name.

"I'm flattered by your recognition . . ."

"You used to work in the vineyards of Michel Leroux? You're
that American writer."

"That was a long time ago."

"I miss Michel," she said, rising from the chair and taking the
dog-eared copy of his novel from the shelf above his shoulder.
She handed it to him and he flipped it over, smiling at the younger version of himself on the back cover. "It's a wonderful book,"
she said, folding her arms and leaning on the desk. "But just so
you know, I don't speak to journalists or wine critics."

"I'm not a wine critic, nor much of a journalist. I'm just a
writer."

"All the same, I don't grant interviews."

"I'm not looking for a byline, just some information."

"I don't like questions."

"How about just one? Then I'll leave you alone."

She pondered this, standing to pace and running her fingers through her hair. She thought about the barrels that needed cleaning. "Okay, one," she said, finally.

"Is this real?" he asked, proffering a cork from his pocket. She looked at it, sighed deeply, and then took it, rotating it slowly and squinting at it in the fluorescent light. She needed reading glasses, but she'd been avoiding a visit to her optometrist in Beaune.

She opened a drawer in the metal desk and pulled out one to compare. It was a '51, and the lettering matched. "It's one of ours. Or a very good copy. But I'm not an expert."

"I did check with an expert. He thinks it's real."

"So?"

"You notice the date?"

She looked again and then raised her eyebrows. She turned on the desk lamp and studied it while he waited.

"Where did you get this?"

"In a locker in Chicago."

"Then it's a fake."

"Are you sure?"

"You've had your question," she said, tying her bandanna back on her head. Bruno stood up and followed her out of the office.

"I know that during the occupation, the Nazis shipped the '43 vintage back to Germany, starting with the best, the Grand Crus, the Premier Crus . . ."

"I'm sure you can read all about that in some book."

"Your grandfather lived through this. He saw it happen. There must have been stories. Did he ever talk about it?"

"I'm not going to help you hunt treasure." She walked faster. She was disappointed in him. She had wanted to like him, but like all of the other journalists, he seemed more interested in the family history. The legendary vintages. She just wanted to make the best wines within her ability and allow them to speak for themselves. Wasn't that enough? Evidently not. The writer was still at her heels.

"The '43 was the best of the war vintages, wasn't it? I studied the weather charts. And many of the other Pommard vintages turned up later at auctions. Some of them undoubtedly recovered from the Nazis. But never a Trevallier . . . Why?"

"Most of the men were away at war. Or in hiding. Or fighting with *la Résistance*. Many vintages weren't even produced, or the women and children brought in the harvest. Anyway, this is a private family matter," she said, emerging from the cave and squinting at the light, frustrated with herself for talking too much.

"What I'm wondering . . ." Bruno said, but then he was stopped short as Claude suddenly appeared and applied a strong hand to the man's shoulder, pulling him away from Sylvie. Then Sylvie turned around and walked up to the American, placing her finger in his chest.

"Let me ask you a question," she said, waving Claude away. He reluctantly sulked back to his tractor.

"Okay, shoot."

"How much would a bottle of my grandfather's '43 fetch at an auction?"

"A lot."

"How much is a lot?"

"Ten thousand. Maybe more, if it were authenticated."

Sylvie smiled dryly and turned to scan the vine-laden hillsides. "My grandfather would not like that. He was a simple farmer. And to him, all wine was *vin ordinaire,* everyday wine. The thought of a bottle of his wine fetching a fortune would not please him."

Bruno looked sheepishly down at his shoes.

"And you want to know about the stories I heard of those times? They were not romantic tales of adventure or resistance. They were stories of hunger. Of starving families. Of fear. The SS or the *Milice française* coming to your door in the middle of the night. No . . . my grandfather's wine now worth a fortune because of that . . . he would not like that. And neither do I."

The American met her eyes with a gaze filled both with respect and determination. He held up the cork. "I'm going to find out if this is real. And if it is, I'm going to find the wine."

"I can't stop you from looking. But I won't help you."

"Okay. Fair enough," he said. He flipped the cork in the air and tucked it in his pocket. "Thank you for your time." He nodded at her and turned for the road. Her instincts screamed to let him walk away. Intriguing men always disappointed her. This was the one lesson she'd drawn from her failed marriage. But Bruno was almost through the gate when she let slip a call for him to stop. "Are you going to the bacchanal?"

"Wouldn't miss it." He smiled.

"Wait a moment."

She disappeared into the cave and then returned in a moment with a dusty bottle. It was a '73 Premier Cru, with a yellowed label and cobwebs around the cork.

"Take this," she said with a smile. "It will cause a stir."

Bruno studied the label, astounded. "I couldn't . . ."

"It's a gift. Because you wrote a lovely book."

He grinned and touched his forehead with the end of the bottle in salute, and then he walked away, whistling. Sylvie watched him for only a moment before returning to her work.

THIRTEEN

A Bacchanal

When you make that hard choice to end an affair, and you so rend your soul in the process that you feel as if you will never love again, I have a secret restorative: your own personal bacchanal. Press a pound of foie gras into a terrine, then slice an entire black truffle, paper-thin, layering it on top. Add another pound of foie gras and glaze with a dash of brandy. Cook rare for 30 minutes at 190 degrees, pour off the juices and chill overnight. Eat it in slices the following day with a bottle of the best Volnay you can find and some day-old farmer's bread. After a fortnight of celibacy you'll have trouble conjuring your former lover's visage in your mind's eye, and after six weeks you'll be eager to embark on your next romantic voyage.

—BRUNO TANNENBAUM, *TWENTY RECIPES FOR LOVE*

Bruno walked the edge of the long, curving drive to the manor, past manicured shrubbery and bubbling fountains. Headlights splashed the trees as an odd collection of cars, ranging from long black Mercedes, Citroën field trucks and battered old Renaults, streamed past him.

When he reached the chateau, he paused to take in the scene. White-gloved attendants stood on either side of the door with trays of clean glasses. Guests filed past, each plucking a glass to balance the bottles of wine held in the opposite hands. A parade of passengers disembarked as smartly dressed valets slipped into the driver's seats of Jaguars and Opels alike, speeding them off toward some distant lot amid a cloud of racing fuel or oil smoke.

A pair of farmers arrived in coveralls and berets, each with a dusty bottle under his arm that had to contain some undiscovered elixir. Next came a gull-wing Mercedes and a pair of long legs followed by the hem of a shimmering cocktail dress. The woman stood and slipped her arm into one offered by a young man in a sleek suit tailored to fit in such a way as Bruno had never been able to emulate even back when he had money and fewer inches on his waistline. Next were two gray-bearded men, one in tweed and the other in a black turtleneck: professors, surely. A pair of grand dames in flowing gowns followed by a stout, red-cheeked woman with two children in tow. Then field hands in plaid and jeans.

Bruno hefted the rare Trevallier and ambled down to the queue at the door. The Bacchanal de Trouvé Silence was one of the more egalitarian and eclectic of Burgundy's grand wine fetes. Like Les Trois Glorieuses, the Trouvé was ostensibly for charitable purposes, with all proceeds going to a school for the deaf in Dijon. Unmarked, unlabeled barrels of first-growth wines contributed by producers and vineyards across the spectrum, from the most storied Grand Crus to the lesser appellation wines. There was no advertising or promotion of any sort. Guests simply knew to arrive on the evening of the first Monday in May at the

Château de Landreville. Who actually organized the event and what relation it had to the estate, which belonged to a reclusive telecommunications magnate who was rarely if ever seen in the Côte-d'Or, nobody seemed to exactly know. The fete sprang out of the ether like a spring mushroom in the nearby Morvan forest.

There was no guest list, and, as the barrels were unmarked, no possibility of prestige for the winemakers involved. The lots were judged by guests who tasted directly from the barrel and, if moved, simply marked a hash on the side in chalk. The barrels with the most hash marks at the end of the night were auctioned first at a somber (and hungover) event the following day, and tended to fetch the highest bids, though given the unvetted and inebriated quality of the judges, nobody took the competition too seriously.

Most interesting to Bruno about the Trouvé was the tradition of bringing one's favorite wine from his or her collection, and the best flavors of the evening tended to come from the bottle and not the barrel. The food was always sumptuous and plentiful, and its provenance was as mysterious as the party's elusive host.

Feeling a tad guilty that his estranged wife was underwriting his attendance to this exercise in overindulgence, Bruno decided to compose a postcard update in his mind as he waited in line:

My dearest Anna:

We are separated by class, station, political affiliation. We are separated by gender. By disposition. Nationality. Some of us are eccentric. Some of us beautiful . . .

Bruno caught a flash of silky brown hair in the light of a foyer chandelier. A tall, youngish woman with high cheekbones and scarlet lips chatted with a friend, both of them in slight cocktail dresses. Bruno couldn't help but stare, and when the woman glanced back over her shoulder and caught the intensity of his gaze, she frowned and turned away, annoyed.

> . . . and others among us are by turns invisible or conspicuous.

Bruno retrieved a glass from a waiter at the door and he flicked the bow of it with a fingernail to make it ring. The queue now wound through the grand house toward a double-wide staircase that descended in a spiral to the cellar. As he shuffled toward the stairs, above the reverent whispers of the guests and the sliding of shoes on marble, he heard a dull roar that grew louder as he descended. Laughter and conversation blended with chamber music.

> Even when we stand shoulder to shoulder, there are walls between us. But our existence is made bearable by those few glories unique to our species: music, art, carnival, the well-laden table.

Rounding the last spiral, he was met with a blast of warm, rich, living air, a mixture of sweat, spilled wine, damp stone and oak. The cellar stretched as far as he could see in all directions. Clusters of barrels stacked six high loomed in the dim light, and threaded between them was a sea of undulating bodies, arms protruding with proffered bottles, the occasional smash of broken glass, the clink and ringing of a thousand toasts like bells in a church of some wild and accidental religion.

> And in this writer's humble opinion . . . singular among such glories . . . is wine.

Bruno was swept into the throng. He felt a tug on his glass as if from a fish on a line and suddenly he saw it sparkling with a pale elixir. He held it up to the dim candlelit chandeliers to make out the slight gold-brown that told him it was likely an aged and weathered Chablis, which a swig confirmed. He hadn't even seen who his benefactor was. He elbowed through the mass and suddenly found a tiny elderly woman with a flushed face in his path. She handed him a plate with slices of truffles and a terrine of foie gras laid on lettuce. He seized it and thanked her by kissing both her cheeks while she returned the favor with a bear hug of his midsection. He spun, finding himself suddenly face-to-face with the shining-haired woman with the scarlet lips whom he'd earlier spotted and ogled.

"Are you following me?" she asked, her hostility not lessening her attractiveness in any way.

"I was about to ask you the same," he replied. When she rolled her eyes, he whipped the plate under her nose. "Have you tried the truffles?"

The human face is a miraculous work of biological engineering, and this young woman's was that and even more. What always amazed Bruno, as a writer and observer, was the subtlety of expression. The woman's pruned and lovely eyebrows shifted ever so slightly, indicating first curiosity, and then, as she plucked and placed a translucent wafer of truffle on her glistening tongue, her throat pulsing in a swallow, the face almost magically morphed into an expression of ecstasy. She was rolling her eyes again, but in passion now rather than condescension, and Bruno savored every trip of this emotional journey, pressed close as he was so that he could feel her breath on his ear as she spoke, the rest of the crowd a blur as it surged around them.

"So, what did you bring?" she asked, gesturing to his bottle with her elbow as she slipped another slice of truffle on her tongue.

"Oh, I almost forgot."

He raised the bottle and she gasped in awe at the label.

"Would you like to try some?"

She nodded.

Bruno wedged the bottle between his knees and wrestled it open with the corkscrew Aleksei had given him in Chicago, the one with the ill-fated accountant as the former owner. Then he held the bottle above his head and circled to be in a position to pour into the young woman's glass. There was a bustle and murmur in the mass around them.

Bruno poured a splash into the woman's glass as well as his own. They clinked and sipped the rare Trevallier.

Wine writers, critics, collectors and a thousand bloggers have intricate systems of evaluation and classification, and entire vocabularies of descriptors for wine. Butter, hazelnut, dark cherry, forest floor, tobacco, meringue. To Bruno, though, such words couldn't convey the power of wine. He was interested, rather, in the effect that it has to transform people in a split second.

The young woman sipped, swallowed and pondered. Her hazel eyes glistened. She dropped her hand to his arm, and even through his jacket sleeve, Bruno felt the electricity of her touch. Her eyes bored not into his, but through him entirely, and he knew from the flavors on his own palate what she was experiencing. It was the story of a thousand angles of sunlight dappling clusters through the manicured leaves, a hundred mornings of fog slipping down the hillsides into the stream bottoms, of the ghosts of long-vanished oceans, of uplift and erosion and the steady alluvial sculpting that created these very few hillsides where the beautiful and finicky little fruits grow so well.

All of this . . . in a sip.

Adjectives and descriptors couldn't possibly convey the feeling of her light touch on Bruno's arm, her lips parted so slightly, and her gaze borne back through the millions of years of geology and all of human history encapsulated in that lone sip.

"I'm about to weep." She shuddered. "Where did you get this?"

"From a good friend."

"My name is Annette," she said, hooking his arm and pulling him close. Where before she couldn't get away from him fast enough, now she wanted to stake a claim.

A wiry Englishman in a navy blazer and colorful cravat suddenly appeared at Bruno's other elbow, drawn in by the label. "I have to try this."

Bruno poured. The Englishman swirled, sniffed, pondered a moment without expression. He said very simply, "This is the most extraordinary thing I've ever tasted." Then he suddenly began belting out an absurd rendition of "La Marseillaise" in his Cockney accent.

The crowd had taken note by now, and Bruno was twirling, pouring, embracing, laughing, working them like a conductor, waving the bottle of Trevallier like a magic wand, pouring splashes in dozens of glasses with the occasional reminder for himself of the mastery by this family of a magnificent little slice of French hillside.

Across the room, a small cluster of vignerons stood apart, leaning on a stack of barrels mumbling to each other beneath the fray. They were used to quiet hours among the vines or in cellars, spending most of the time inside their own heads while performing the thousand menial and repetitive tasks that making wine requires. While they understood the reason for all the fuss, many were still puzzled and even amused by it, and they were just as likely to be sipping a bottle of Kronenbourg beer or maybe even a half glass of homemade calvados or *marc* better suited for removing paint than human consumption, though the perfect antidote for a day of hard work. For them wine was mostly about scrubbing tanks and barrels.

Among this group in their threadbare denim, translucent plaid and frayed wool, with muddy rubber boots and only a splash of cologne or perfume or the quick application of a dampened comb showing any forethought for the evening's festivities, stood Sylvie Trevallier. She'd just made arrangements with Yves Jobert of Bouchard to borrow his bladder press next year, as he usually finished his Chardonnay a day or two before she crushed hers. The press was much larger and might shave hours off of what was already an incredibly long day.

Out of the corner of her eye, she noticed the swirl in the crowd, like a maelstrom spotted on the surface of some gaseous planet. And at its epicenter stood Bruno, looking quite different from the frumpy salesman she'd assumed him to be earlier in the day. Here he stood as the bard bowing in triumph to his audience, laughing, whispering in ears, embracing the adulation of his fans.

She caught his eye, and he, hers. He stared at her across the vast room. He raised his glass to her, and she lifted her own Kronenbourg in response. She felt herself blush for a moment in a way that she couldn't distinctly remember doing since her second year at the *lycée*. It was at once unsettling but also kind of nice. She felt a momentary flutter at the base of her stomach that she instinctively shrugged off. She turned to Yves, suddenly remembering that she wanted to ask him about buying used barrels, since he considered them spent after only three years, while she preferred the subtlety and character to be found in the second half of a barrel's life. When she again glanced over in Bruno's direction, he had disappeared and she was surprised to find herself disappointed.

*　　*　　*

Bruno needed air. He staggered out into the gardens, breathing deeply the rich dark of the countryside. He was tipsy. He'd tasted his way through twelve of the barrels and sipped from a myriad of shared bottles.

He found himself in a sort of maze with fanciful figures hiding in the shadows. One was trimmed in the shape of a satyr, and the next a large, bearded figure of Bacchus not too dissimilar from himself, had he been able to transform some of his paunch into muscle.

Ahead a broad pool shimmered in the darkness, its surface rippling a reflection of stars and the crescent moon, a fountain pushing a dark column of water skyward in the center. An upright figure stood at the edge, staring across the water to the Morvan forest beyond. Something about the smart cut of his jacket suggested refinement, and Bruno wondered if it might be the chateau's enigmatic owner. But when he approached and the man turned he was shocked to meet the plastic grin of Parker Thomas.

"Bruno, it's been so long! How are you?"

"Imagine finding you here."

"Thought I'd kick off the grand tour with the Trouvé this year. Rhinegau next, then Tuscany, Piedmont. Finally Moscow, of all places. Imagine that! You should check it out." He handed over a card for someone named Nikolai at *Red Square Wine Adventures* and Bruno studied it dubiously.

"Need to fill your quota of scores? Have you finished handing out all your nineties for the year yet?" Bruno snapped. The mention of Moscow made him suspicious. Was Thomas connected to the Russian in the hotel room? Bruno was a pacifist, though he wondered if anyone would notice if he drowned Thomas in the pool right now.

"You're such a stick-in-the-mud, Bruno."

They stood a moment in silence. Thomas sucked back the last of his glass, paused, then shook his head.

"Excellent. Simply excellent."

"Would you give it an eighty-five?"

Thomas pondered a moment. "Probably a ninety-one. But then I'm a little buzzed. And, of course, there's this setting." He gestured out across the water. "It's bound to color my perception. Hard to trust your palate in such a setting."

Bruno huffed.

"Believe it or not, I try to be precise about these things."

"So you taste sample bottles at home from a brown paper bag and spit it in the sink like you're doing some sixth-grade science project? That's not what wine's all about."

"That's where you're wrong, Bruno. That's precisely what wine's all about. I'm simply providing a service to consumers. People buy wine. It's why this all exists. It's a product. I'm not some artiste who pretends to be a poet. The wine industry is a *business*. A very *lucrative* business. It produces a product that people *enjoy*. I help them do that. How does that make me the bad guy?"

"Half the people down in that cellar are farmers. They buy their wine in bulk, filling cider jugs or stone jars. They drink it with meals at weddings. Wine to them is a place. It's a set of values. It's their lives. They've been doing it that way for a thousand years. You can't reduce that down to mere supply and demand."

"That's a quaint observation. But it belongs in the *National Geographic*, not in my column. Say . . . not to change the subject . . . but I hear you're working on another book. Is that why you're here?"

"Where'd you hear that?" Bruno asked, hit with the sudden wave of panic and nausea that all writers feel when they suspect someone could beat them to the story. As much of a hack as Thomas was, he did have ability. His prose was passable. He had a nose for a story. He had readers. He was good on talk shows.

"Isn't every writer always working on a new book? So what's it about?"

Bruno snorted. He was certain that Harley had shared his idea.

"Well, I don't mean to pry. Hey, so what did you bring?" Thomas asked, gesturing to the bottle protruding from Bruno's coat pocket. Still fuming, Bruno pulled it out and dribbled a bit into the critic's glass, saving the last dozen drips for his own. He reluctantly clinked glasses and then swirled, sniffed and sipped in the darkness. Thomas began pacing.

"Good heavens. Holy shit! What is that?"

He came at Bruno with his cell phone and used it to illuminate the label. Then he let out a low whistle.

"How did you get your hands on that?"

"Sylvie Trevallier gave it to me," Bruno offered, not without great satisfaction.

"You talked to Sylvie?"

"Sure."

"Anything on the record?"

"Some."

"That's a major coup. I've tried before. She doesn't talk to wine writers."

"No, Parker, she doesn't talk to wine *critics*."

Bruno could see the artificially whitened teeth of Thomas's ear-to-ear grin in the moonlight as the critic sniffed the traces of the '73 Trevallier in his glass. "You know, Bruno, you're an asshole. But I like you anyway."

Thomas slapped him on the shoulder and walked away, leaving him standing on the edge of the pool. Bruno picked up a flat stone from the footpath and tried to skip it on the sheer surface, but instead it plunged in, sending out a circle of rings that slowly closed in on each other until they disappeared.

*   *   *

Back inside, the crowd had thinned. The chamber quartet was replaced by the accordion and fiddle of a *groupe folklorique*. A short farmer in overalls was dancing to the sad tune with a much taller, elegantly gowned woman with silver hair, his head pressed against her breasts, her arm resting on his shoulders, grasping a bottle of Beaujolais. There were other couplings hinted at by movements in the shadows in the tight, dark alleys between stacked wine barrels. People were flushed, joyful and tired, conversing with their arms draped over strangers, leaning on one another, glasses held against the light. It was a mass of people knit steadily closer together with every sip.

Bruno wandered through the coagulation, enjoying the sights, making a mental catalog. Perhaps there was an article for the *Sun-Times* in this. Maybe he could talk Ernie into buying a stringer piece for the travel section.

He suddenly felt lithe hands encircling his arm, and Annette from earlier was holding him and guiding him toward a group of her friends, her cheek pressed to his shoulder. Someone served him a cool, clean pour of a bracing white that must have been Aligoté, and he found himself looking at a lovely group of young people.

"Why didn't you tell me you were a famous writer?" Annette was saying in his ear.

"I think *famous* may be an exaggeration."

"Nonsense, everyone here knows who you are."

She smiled up at him and he wanted to bend to kiss her. He considered leading her back out into the topiary. *Have you seen the gazebo? No? Let me show you . . .*

"I've read your book," said a young man with a trim mustache and tortoiseshell glasses that Bruno suspected were merely an affectation. "I'm a writer, too, you know . . ."

Bruno enjoyed the attention but was beginning to tire of the chatter when he spotted Sylvie leaning against the far wall, talking with another vigneron, her hands stuffed in the pockets of her jeans. He thought he noticed her glancing his way, and suddenly Annette felt like a great weight on his arm.

He half reluctantly broke away, though the feeling of Annette's fingers on the inside of his arm and the softness of her breasts through the rumpled fabric of his blazer lingered. He vaguely heard her calling to him as he weaved through the crowd, but he didn't look back.

He reached Sylvie as she was sipping on a glass of *marc*. He could smell the pungent alcohol on her breath. She smiled wryly.

"So, how's the famous writer?"

"It's nice to know that some people still remember."

"That lot was in the nursery when your book came out. It must be flattering that they know who you are."

"I suppose."

"And you can still charm the ladies. Who was that gorgeous creature?"

"Annette? She's just a kid."

"Tonight, of all nights, is a time to sample a little of that *vin nouveau,* is it not?"

"Actually," Bruno said, swaying a little closer, "I prefer the complexity and character that comes with a little age . . ."

"What a terrible line." She laughed. "Do you have any more?"

"Quite a few, actually."

*   *   *

Sylvie was aware that it was clichéd and maybe even old-fashioned to smoke in bed after making love, but it was a ritual she nevertheless enjoyed. Since she'd started her tryst with Claude she'd gotten up to four or five cigarettes on some days, and she was beginning to worry that it might affect her health.

Bruno's appetites seemed, surprisingly, as robust as the more athletic Claude's, though the pauses between were longer and more enjoyable. Claude liked to turn on the television and watch the shopping channel after a quick fuck, which was fine with her because this was actually more mentally stimulating than attempting a conversation with the young man. But Bruno punctuated the silence between deep drags on the cigarette with the most absurd and charming banter. The man had no shame. He couldn't possibly be sincere . . . or could he?

She heard the paper of the cigarette burn as she sucked and then expelled a stream of smoke toward the ceiling. Bruno pulled the sheet off of her shoulder and kissed her collarbone, his whiskers tickling her neck. She breathed in deeply. He pulled the sheet down farther to reveal one breast and he kissed it gently.

"You're a remarkable creature," he said, and she smiled around another drag of the cigarette. It couldn't be true, but she still enjoyed it. Her ex-husband had once lauded her breasts when she lamented that they may be too insubstantial. He'd called them *guilleret*, "perky," but that buoyancy was long gone. "Absolutely gorgeous," Bruno purred now, pulling the sheet down lower and kissing her stomach just above her navel.

"Such talk," she said, crushing out her cigarette and lacing her fingers behind her head to watch the shifting cloud of smoke that hung below the ceiling. "Please continue."

Bruno propped his head on his elbow and stared up at her. "What's it like, being the best in the world at what you do?" He gave the sheet a tug, pulling it lower.

"I'm no Aubert de Villaine, Bruno. Trevallier is not Romanée-Conti. I'm a farmer's daughter with a mountain of debt."

"But surely you have to admit that your reputation, the reputation of Trevallier, is unassailable. It's almost mythic. By anyone's definition, you're a success."

"In that part of my life . . . perhaps."

"And the other parts?"

"Well. When it comes to finances, I don't always make the wisest choices. I cling too much to tradition, and those that embrace the more modern practices are passing me by. I'm stubborn, opting for quality over cash. I don't have many close friends. I work too much for that. And my marriage was something of a disaster."

"Was that really your fault?"

"Maybe. You see, my insides don't work the way they should

for a French country girl. Michel, my former husband, didn't appreciate that the noble line of his genetic material would end with him. He has three children now with his second wife. All girls, the fact of which I imagine still causes him some consternation."

"Good. Still . . . is that really your fault?"

"Who else's? Also, I'm a bit of a tyrant, really."

Bruno laughed.

"No, it's true. Ask my employees. I'm in charge. My ideal man would be someone to occasionally fuck, make small talk when I feel like it and stay quiet when I don't. And then he could make me breakfast, keep the house in order, help with the entertaining and then generally stay out of the way until I have some other chore for him. I have no patience to tolerate ambition outside of my own. Of course, I'd expect him to pitch in with the work or at least pay his own share. What male ego would be really happy with that sort of arrangement?"

Bruno frowned and shrugged. "Sounds like you need to date more writers."

"I'm no prize, Bruno. When we separated, Michel said I was too bitter to be capable of love."

"Too bitter? What rubbish. I'd say you're perfectly balanced." He kissed her stomach below her navel, and slowly worked his way down. She felt his breath against her skin.

"Ridiculous," she said, her smile broadening as she closed her eyes and tilted her head back. "What else?"

"So complex. I taste strong acidity. Soft tannic structure. A hint of sweetness. Gorgeous mouthfeel . . ." As he worked his way lower, his muttering became incomprehensible right at the point where words no longer mattered.

*   *   *

When Sylvie awoke the next morning, the bed was empty. All that remained of Bruno was a not-insubstantial impression on the mattress next to her and a few brownish-gray hairs on the pillow. She stood and stretched with a mixture of relief and disappointment. But then the aroma of breakfast drifted in from the kitchen, along with the operatic humming of Bruno's voice, and both emotions were replaced with a sense of satisfaction. She recognized the tune as an *opéra-bouffe* by Offenbach, though she couldn't recall the exact name. She smiled because it had been ages since a man had spent the entire night in her bed, and she somehow had slept well despite Bruno's occasional snore. With Claude, it was always a quick morning screw, and by her last years of marriage to Michel they'd been living in separate cities.

She threw open the windows and let the cool air wash over her bare skin. She couldn't find her silk robe usually draped on her chair so she pulled on a soft wool sweater and tights. She combed her hair with her fingers and tucked it under a cap, avoiding the mirror, fearing the woman she might see would look a good twenty years older than she was feeling right now.

The wood floors of the old stone house creaked under her feet, but Bruno was busy at the stove with his back to her. He danced as he tossed a pan full of wild mushrooms, garlic, onion and something else she couldn't quite place but smelled wonderful. He didn't notice her until she laughed at her pink robe wrapped around him.

This made him spin and he spotted her leaning against the doorjamb. He winked and smiled and continued the circle, reaching to crack eggs, two at a time, into a bowl in a fluid motion.

He whisked briskly and in moments was sliding omelets onto plates next to slices of butter-softened bread. The surprise ingredients were a pesto he'd made of diced *noisettes,* Saint-Nectaire cheese, oil and basil. They sat on stools at the rough slab of granite that formed an island in the kitchen, eating in comfortable silence.

"You didn't ask me any more about my grandfather," she said after a pause.

"I thought you were finished answering questions."

She chewed slowly, measuring how best to respond. Bruno's questions had stirred something inside of her and the evening before, after she'd finished her work and showered and was waiting to head to the bacchanal, she'd carried a glass of wine to a storage closet in the back of the great cellar. She sat on the cold floor rummaging through a box of her grandfather's things. She found his ledgers and notebooks. He had recorded the weather and sugars, and he made notes on the tannic structure of the wines by the very unscientific method of chewing a mouthful of grapes until only the seeds were left, then mashing them into a pulp and noting their bitterness, rating them on a scale of "green" to "woody."

What surprised her most was a bundle of letters written to and from her grandmother that she hadn't read before. They contained more detailed accounts of the day-to-day operations, the comings and goings of family and workers, what was prepared for meals and also descriptions of the family's struggles during the war years. It reminded Sylvie how intimately involved her grandmother was in the business compared to how little recognition she received. She knew that the information would be helpful to Bruno and the only reasons to keep it from him were pride and spite.

She began talking between bites and without looking at him. "After your visit yesterday I spent some time in the family archives, which consists of a pair of soggy cardboard boxes in the cellar. I sat on the floor until my ass froze and I lost feeling in my legs. So many memories . . ."

Without looking, she could feel that Bruno had stopped eating and was watching her carefully.

"I learned a few things that might interest you." A quick glance told her that Bruno now studied her with surprise, an incipient smile somewhere inside his beard. "There was one Nazi officer whose name was frequently mentioned in my grandmother's letters. Von Speck. They called him the *weinführer,* and all of the region's producers were accountable to him. My grandmother also mentioned a neighbor boy who was young enough that he stayed behind when the other men left. He still lives here and if you speak to him it may help you on your quest."

"I don't know how I can repay you," Bruno said.

"You might consider last night a down payment," she said, blushing. "He's an old man now. His name is Gérard and this time of morning you'll find him in his vines . . . the first three rows in Les Charmots just to the east of the village." She rose quickly and carried her plate to the sink. "It was delicious, thank you. Now you should go and speak to Gérard before it gets hot and he's finished for the day."

"Would you like me to bring something back for lunch?"

"I have a busy day, Bruno," she said, as dismissively as possible, though there was a tug in her chest that was heavy with regret. A large part of her would love to have him stay around for a few days, maybe a week. If he insisted, she'd allow him to stay another night.

"Of course, I don't want to be a bother," he said cheerfully, and her heart sank just a little. But no matter . . . there was work to do. "Let me clean up and you can get started," he said, kissing her on the back of the neck and taking the soap and dish rag from her hands. She stood on her toes and kissed him on the cheekbone above where his beard ended and smiled, turning and heading to her room to put on her work clothes.

Later, as she tightened the oil filter in the Bobard and inspected the work that Claude had done the day before, Bruno ambled out, showered and trimmed. He'd evidently found her iron and pressed his shirt. His jacket was hooked on a finger and thrown over his shoulder. He whistled Debussy while alternately watching her work and scanning the hillsides, squinting at the sunlight streaming through the dissipating mist.

"Thank you for a lovely evening. And morning," he said.

"Thanks for the *petit déj*," she said without looking up from her work.

"I hope to see you again."

She responded to this with a slight nod, a quick glance and a sliver of a smile. He beamed back in return.

As he left through the east gate she watched his head above the stone wall until it disappeared. She surprised herself by the fact that she didn't want him to leave. As charming as he seemed, though, she knew him for the type who would have disappointed her in the end. And the ease with which he had breezed in and out of her life only confirmed that fact, justifying the coolness with which she had dismissed him.

When she could no longer see him, she returned to the tractor. As she suspected, one of the bolts on the compressor was loose. If something was to be fixed properly, she had to do it herself.

FOURTEEN

Breaking Bread

In the places where humans eat and live the best, freshly baked bread is a religion. Leavened or otherwise, as a crust or wrapped around a shawarma, a steamed and chewy bao hiding a quail's egg or merely the fragrance cushioning the morning air of every side street in France— its qualities are sacred and its gift for creating community unparalleled. In this chapter, I will detail some of the more spiritual properties of this miraculous substance, and instruct the reader in a few techniques through which it can be employed in the meeting of strangers and fending off of loneliness and other such malaises.

—BRUNO TANNENBAUM, *TWENTY RECIPES FOR LOVE*

As Bruno left the Trevallier estate, he grew suddenly sad. He stopped and leaned on a rock wall, enjoying warmth from stones that had already absorbed the morning sun. Despite the lovely day and the promising turn of events, he was morose. He wasn't exactly sure if it was self-pity at being so far from his family or leaving such a captivating woman behind. For the moment he was absolutely in love with Sylvie Trevallier. This morning he'd woken up ahead of Sylvie and had taken her cell phone from her nightstand while she slept and written down the number with a marker on the palm of his hand before placing it back exactly where he'd found it. Like a teenager, he was afraid that she wouldn't give it to him had he asked. Whether it was actual depth of emotion or just temporary infatuation was not immediately obvious to him. He had to admit that he'd imagined staying on longer, perhaps quite a bit longer. He could cook, clean the house, generally help out in exchange for a small room in the garret in which he could write, and maybe an occasional place beside Sylvie in bed. He guiltily recognized that he'd recently had the same plan for Anna. And he was technically still married to her, even if she had kicked him out. To fantasize about a new life with this Frenchwoman on the first stop on a trip that Anna was financing certainly ranked as a betrayal. A sense of duty drove him onward. He had discoveries to make, fresh leads to chase.

As for Sylvie, beneath the carefully cultivated frosty reputation was an enigmatic and fascinating woman. Her laugh was glorious and full-voiced when she chose to employ it. She was an enthusiastic lover and wickedly funny. And then add the fact that she made some of the most brilliant wines he'd ever tasted. It was obvious to him that she was the driving force behind everything that happened at the estate. She was no mere figurehead. With what he knew already, he could write a crackerjack profile. She might even become a central figure in his book.

As he walked upslope from the village, the church bell chimed the hour behind him with echoes passing in waves overhead and rolling out across the vineyards. Bruno had never truly expected to return to the Côte de Beaune. It seemed so impossibly far away when he'd been on his mother's couch or hunched in his cubicle in the *Sun-Times* offices. Now he was here, he'd just made love to a very prominent and mysterious woman, tasted unfathomable wines and was walking over stones and soil that were singular on the planet. Life certainly was full of surprises, delightful and otherwise.

It was early in the season, and there were few people in the vines. Every so often he came across a van or car pulled into the edge of the vine alongside the road, with a hunched figure at work along manicured rows.

He reached the end of the block known as Les Charmots, and as Sylvie had described, there was an old Renault parked in the gravel and an ancient man in a tweed cap squatting between rows fifty meters upslope.

When Bruno reached him, the vigneron touched his cap and slowly pushed himself upright, releasing a clutch of young sucker shoots from his hands.

"Lovely morning." Bruno smiled, finding that he was now not only speaking in French but even thinking in the language as well.

"Good morning. I saw you at the bacchanal last night."

"I'm Bruno." He extended his hand, and the old man took it, his firm grip dry and papery.

"I am Gérard."

The old man walked slowly upslope and Bruno followed.

"How long have you lived here?"

"I've never lived anywhere else."

"You've always been a vigneron?"

"These two rows belong to me. The next three, my brother. Before that, it was my father and grandfather. The Proulx family has always made wine."

"Ah. I know your name well. Your wine, it's excellent."

The old man stopped and shook his head, pointing at the ridge above, where the stony soil was more white than golden. "There, that is excellent. They say it is marginal the higher you go, but don't believe it. That belongs to the Trevalliers. They are the best."

"Did you know Clement Trevallier?"

"Of course. He was a warm and generous man. And humble. So precise. A perfectionist. Everything that is done today, the research that comes from the wine institute: it's all what Clement was doing already. He knew it all by feel, by instinct."

"I was speaking to Sylvie, his granddaughter, about him."

"Ah," said Gérard with surprise, squinting to get a better focus on him. Sylvie did not speak to just anyone.

"She shared with me some of her family's stories. From the war. You must remember the war?"

Gérard didn't respond and instead resumed walking.

"Can I ask some questions about it?" Given Gérard's silence, Bruno wondered if he'd played his hand too suddenly. He could tell that the old man was deciding whether or not he wanted to answer. His eyes grew glassy as they stared back across the years. He paused and knelt down slowly, and Bruno could almost hear the man's knees creak. One by one, he plucked suckers off a vine trunk, gnarled and twisted with age. After a minute, he grabbed a post and slowly pulled himself up. They walked farther in silence. Then the old man stopped and knelt again in slow motion, breathing heavily with exertion. He patted a knotted trunk down low on a bulge in the wood the size of a melon that hovered just centimeters above the yellow dirt. This indicated the graft, where a trunk of one varietal had been spliced to the rootstock of another to create a strange alliance that allowed a vineyard its best chance of survival. In this case it had granted this vine at least a century in Burgundy's unpredictable climate.

"The Americans saved us twice," Gérard said. Bruno squatted next to him, holding his breath, watching the man's hands, as gnarled as the old vine they caressed. "The first time was from the root louse. You see the rootstock here?" He patted below the knot. "It's American. *Vitis riparia*. There was a time when all of the vineyards of France began to die. My grandfather remembered it. Nobody knew the reason. Everywhere. In the valleys of the Rhône and Loire. In the Bordeaux Arrondissment. All the vines were dying. Vignerons burned their vineyards in desperation, replanting. The new vines died, too. Families went hungry. Men lost their minds. Hung themselves in their barns. They finally identified the louse, but they didn't know what to do about it.

"Then two Americans came with an answer. They were from a place called Missouri. It was their idea to graft our vines onto American roots, which could resist the louse. And it worked. This simple technique saved all of our great vineyards. The roots of every vine in France are now American. Imagine that! There is a statue dedicated to those men in Montpellier. If you're ever there, you should see it.

"That was the first time they came here to Pommard to help us," Gérard said, rising again and walking on. "The second time was when we saw their trucks coming up the road. Earlier that morning, the Germans had fled. They'd packed up and left. They'd been here for so long, and we'd moved so carefully out of fear, out of terror, and suddenly the buildings they'd occupied were empty. The Nazi flags gone from the windows. It was like they'd never been here. I was a boy of twelve, and I went sprinting down to the Route de Beaune, my legs feeling light and wobbling as if I hadn't run in years. I remember laughing. Unrestrained laughter. And the Americans were streaming through the village, laughing with us. Our girls kissed them and they blushed. These fellows had frightened the Nazis away. Without firing a single shot. That was the second time." Gerard stopped. "So, you're American?"

Bruno nodded.

"Then go ahead, ask me your questions."

"I'm looking for a vintage Trevallier. A specific '43 that hasn't been seen since the war."

"I've heard the stories."

"Are they true?"

Gérard shrugged. "Who knows? The Nazis took what they wanted in those days. They say Clement was working for *la Résistance française*, and he went underground. But he still managed his vines, working them in the dark of the night by candlelight while other vineyards were overgrown and untended. Clement's vintages were always perfect, even during the occupation."

"Sylvie mentioned a name. Von Speck. Does that mean anything to you?"

Gérard nodded slowly, staring over the vines into the past. "He was not an unreasonable man. He oversaw the shipment of our wines to Germany. But he only took the best and most reputable wines. We put them in cases marked for Berlin and loaded them onto the trucks. I was a boy, but I worked with the others. So many of the older men were away. Von Speck, he made sure the workers had food. Others weren't so lucky. The officer, he was a connoisseur."

"How do you know that?"

"Because some of the wines . . . the best of the best . . . were not sent to Berlin. But we marked them for Naumburg, outside of Berlin, and sent them by train."

"Why Naumburg?"

There was an amused glint in his eye. "You know, they make wine in Naumburg. Good wines. Some of them are like those from Alsace. I suppose they appreciate good Pommard there as well. You see, Naumburg was where Von Speck was from."

As Bruno stopped and stood in contemplation while he watched Gérard labor uphill, he realized that he'd just uncovered the next stop on his journey.

* * *

Walking back to Beaune, Bruno skirted the highway and was nearly run down by drivers whose aggressiveness behind the wheel came in inverse proportion to the size of their cars, a distinctly European phenomenon.

Back at his hotel he greeted the lovely Lisette, who stood behind the counter. "You were out early this morning."

"Or late last night," he said with a wink.

"Oh, yes, the bacchanal." She blushed.

"Hey, I've got a question. I need to find someone named Von Speck who lives in Naumburg. Do you know how to work the Internet? Can you show me?"

"Of course," she said, leading him back into the tight little business office where there were stacks of receipts, telephone books and a wall of spare keys. It was close quarters, and she sat him down at the computer, then leaned over him and guided his hand on the mouse, reaching across his body to type. He felt her breath on his ear and heard her unconsciously grunt and groan as she explored blind alleys before finding a directory that listed names and addresses as if by magic. The Internet could be so handy, and Bruno made a note to learn more about it. "Here's a list. Just use the mouse to scroll and click here to print."

"You're brilliant!"

Bruno realized that during the whole operation he'd been pressed close to Lisette and he hadn't felt the slightest twinge of lust as he had the day before on the stairs. He printed out a dozen pages and then he thanked Lisette on his way back up to his room, thinking that while she was a beautiful woman now, she'd likely be even more so in ten years. This certainly was new thinking for Bruno. France was getting under his skin. France and Sylvie.

He sat for a moment at the desk enjoying the view of the hillsides and thumbing through the indexes of his research books for the name Von Speck, but didn't find it. He looked out the window back toward the distant villages of Pommard and Volnay, barely making out their church towers in the haze. Was he finished with France so early? Would he ever return?

His online research had turned up a dozen "Specks" in Naumburg, with only three dignified by the noble "Von" preface. He had also scribbled a plan of his next steps on the back of the list. It was actually more of a shopping list for what he planned to eat on the train, but adventure needs its provisions, does it not? He also jotted down timetables and train connections to Naumburg and a reminder to send another postcard to Anna.

He reluctantly left his hotel after having a coffee in the courtyard. As he passed Lisette at the counter he considered pausing to talk to her one last time, but then he saw the phone and also wanted to call Sylvie, whose cell number was starting to smudge and distort on his palm. He decided to do neither.

He took one last amble around the inner walls of the town, pausing by the unassuming door to the Marché aux Vins that he knew led down to an underground candlelit labyrinth filled with gorgeous wines. Next came the Hôtel-Dieu, with its multicolored roof tiles and elegant spires, a delicate manifestation of northern Renaissance architecture at its best.

He passed a shop window displaying a random assortment of wines, all of them fantastic. Wine, coincidentally, was the first item on his list. When he spotted a very good price on a bottle of white Mâcon, his taste buds tingled in anticipation of the bright tang of the Chardonnay, good Mâcon being the closest thing to biting into a fresh grape. It was the precise moment of harvest captured in a bottle.

Bruno entered the shop and a gray-haired man in an apron gave a conspiratorial wink when Bruno pointed at the bottle.

"Is a good price, no?"

Bruno nodded and pulled out the envelope of cash in his breast pocket, thumbing through. When the shopkeeper saw this he tried to sell Bruno three more bottles, including a rare Romanée-Conti, all of which Bruno reluctantly declined, proud of himself for exhibiting such self-control. He still felt a tad guilty about spending Anna's money on wine, but thirty euros for a Mâcon of this stature was a steal and a necessary purchase. He stuffed it into his suitcase with trembling hands. Why shouldn't he celebrate a little? After all, he was fast on the heels of the story of a lifetime.

A bottle of wine is one of the two absolute requirements for train travel. The other is bread, a *boule* of which Bruno picked up next at a *boulangerie* that was just beginning to shutter for the afternoon. He also secured a quarter wheel of Époisses cheese, which he had double-wrapped in waxed paper lest it be seized. Bruno had heard the rumors of zealous conductors confiscating this odoriferous variety.

The next train to Dijon arrived in an hour, so Bruno had a chance for one more café au lait at the Hotel de France while reading the timetable. Budgeting wasn't his strong suit, but he wondered how many wine regions he could afford to visit on his way to Naumburg. Given the fact that Germany and France both factored heavily in his story, he had very good reason to stop, say, in Champagne, where the vineyards had often served as battlefields between those nations. Then, of course, was the Rheingau, which also had excellent wines and had seen its share of conflict. He decided on Alsace, the region being the true political football pitch between France and Germany. Its inhabitants were French citizens (for the moment), spoke mostly French and made their wines in a French style, but they had German names, lived in German houses and used German bottles. Also, his mother's family had come from the region, and despite the circumstances of their flight he suspected that she still harbored hopes of someday returning. After recounting his last trip, Greta had become visibly emotional. Alsace it would be. He wondered how many bottles he could manage to carry home in his suitcase.

Bruno pondered how a continent he viewed largely as a culinary amusement park could have such a long, vile and recent history of atrocity. How could a place so steeped in great food cultures also be so full of pain and hatred? Why hadn't more people broken bread together, and could history have changed if they had? Bruno believed so, and he feverishly scribbled notes to this effect into his notebook.

The train arrived and as he headed to the platform he composed his next postcard in his mind:

Dear Anna, all over the world, people are unhappy in different ways.

He wrote as he scanned the vacant expressions and frowning faces of his fellow passengers. He found a compartment with an empty seat and almost passed because he'd have to sit opposite a dour, matronly woman who regarded him with disapproving annoyance. There were also two hungry-looking backpackers and a businessman chatting on a cell phone. But when Bruno remembered his bread and wine, he decided that his entire view of the world hinged on its ability to transform this unhappy collection of passengers.

When we are shrouded in our own concerns, we tend to withdraw into ourselves.

The older woman's bag occupied the free seat directly opposite her, and Bruno gestured to her to move it. She did so with a reluctant sigh. Bruno slumped into his seat and tried not to allow her disapproving gaze to impale him. He also tried to give her the benefit of the doubt. Maybe she was having a bad day, month, life . . . and perhaps this small comfort of extra train cabin territory was a reprieve from the thousand varied challenges of simple existence.

Bruno smiled at her. She declined to respond in kind.

But perhaps we should pause and remind ourselves that we are not alone in this world.

Bruno felt a hollowness in his stomach as they left the hills of the Côte-d'Or behind. A manic mix of panic and sadness that he might never be back this way again. The weight of that fear kept him staring out the window, and he eventually dozed without speaking to his seatmates. He awoke feeling a prick of responsibility for his traveling companions. They were making the journey together, fellow pilgrims, a cross-section of humanity not unlike those Chaucer had described gathered around the table at the Tabard Inn, and when nobody disembarked in Dijon he knew it was time to change the tenor in the cabin.

He ceremoniously flipped the window tray down and smoothed out his bandanna as a tablecloth. He pulled out the *boule*, flakes of crust scattering on the matron's black slacks. She brushed them off with a huff, but he could also see, out of the corner of his eye, her nostrils flare at the warm and nutty scent of the lovely bread. One of her eyebrows arched. He heard the stomach of one of the backpackers—an undernourished-looking young woman with dreadlocks—growl, and he knew he was, in his own small way, changing the world.

Anna, we are surrounded by humanity, awash in it. And it is our choice to either brood in the silent cocoon of our own troubles or to break bread with our fellow travelers.

Bruno sawed the bread with a pocketknife while the businessman pretended to read his newspaper and the backpacking couple looked on with open, famished stares. It was clear by the time he'd divided five slices that he intended to share. The dreadlock girl's stomach growled again, and everyone chuckled this time. Bruno's eyes met a friendly gaze, and suddenly, with the simple ragged slicing of his pocketknife, the cabin-mates were now a small family.

When Bruno produced the Époisses and began to remove the rind, there was an audible murmur of appreciation as its tart pungency filled the compartment. Somewhere between the odor of overripe fruit and smell of the body of someone you care

about, the variety can be offensive to the uninitiated. But the
cohabitants of this compartment all seemed to understand that
the salty-sweet taste of Époisses was well worth its bombastic
emanation. Bruno smear-sliced the cheese and the businessman
carefully folded his newspaper and smoothed it on his lap as a
makeshift table. The matron dug into her own purse and produced a small souvenir jar of Moutarde de Bourgogne. She ceremoniously gave the top a twist, sacrificing the vessel for the good
of the company.

Bruno responded by digging into his own bag and producing
the bottle of Mâcon. When he popped the cork, the backpackers applauded. But the matron won the duel with a final dig
through the bag at her feet after which she produced three proper souvenir wineglasses.

The food was distributed. The backpackers proffered a pair
of tin cups and they all drank the Mâcon until the bottle was
empty. A short while later, and from outside the car, it would
have seemed that the compartment held a raucous reunion of
old friends. Bruno told stories of his daughters, and, as the wine
loosened his tongue, shared the outline of his quest, which all
the travelers assured him was the foundation for a compelling
story and perhaps even a bestseller. The backpackers, who were
Australian and taking a year off post-university to do everything
they could think of to delay adulthood and employment, largely
through the use of credit cards, dashed off the train at the stop
in Mulhouse and returned breathless with bottle of Épernay
and some beignets from the station bakery. The matron was
on her way to Strasbourg to meet with her estranged sister to
settle affairs around the commitment of their mother, who was
suffering dementia, to institutional care. The businessman had
just completed a circuit of three trade shows and hadn't seen his

wife or two young sons in a month and was debating if he should take a junior position in his father's furniture repair businesses at a greatly reduced salary that would at least keep him close to home. When he revealed that his wife was expecting a baby girl the following November, good use was made of the Épernay, the golden sparkles creating an instant celebration.

By the time they reached Strasbourg, the cares and joys of the entire company were Bruno's own. They embraced upon departure. Bruno and the matron wept and they wished each other well. They knew the names of the siblings, parents, children of all in the group as wallet and cell phone photos were shared around, though Bruno realized as he walked through the station that they hadn't even learned each other's names, but it didn't matter. They were all fellow travelers on the surface of the same celestial orb. He felt more strongly than ever, with a belly full of bread, champagne and cheese, that every meal was meant to be a communion. He was warm and happy inside. He stopped at a *tabac* kiosk and purchased a phone card and a postcard.

He paused at a bench to jot down the postcard he'd been composing in his head, describing his new friends from the train and mourning the fact that he'd never see any of them again. He dropped the note in a post box. He knew that Anna would receive this little report three to seven days later, or longer, depending on the fickle gods of international mail. Or more likely Claire would be the one to intercept it since she always checked the mail first. And after it had been read and passed around, Claire would be the one to save it and pin it to her wall or stuff it into her collection box under her bed. She was as emotionally invested in his adventures as Anna, and Bruno was determined not to let them down.

He took out his phone card. He wanted desperately to call

home and hear Anna's and the girls' voices. But when he found
a phone, he noticed Sylvie's fading number on the palm of his
hand, and he dialed that instead.

* * *

"What do you want?"

"It's Bruno."

A pause. Then, "Did you leave something here?"

"My heart."

Unrestrained laughter, then, "*Merde,* Bruno. What is it you
Americans say? Bullshit!" She pronounced it *bool-sheet,* which
he found endearing.

"May I at least stop by to see you again on my way home?"

Another pause. "That would be fine. When?"

"Not sure. Whenever I finish my research."

"I've already told you everything I'm willing to share."

"That's not what it's about."

"Then just call me. Maybe I'll be here. Maybe I'll be too busy.
How did you get this number, anyway?"

"I looked it up on your phone while you slept."

"That's devious."

"Would you have given it if I had asked?"

"Definitely not."

"Then aren't you glad I'm devious?"

"Perhaps. Is that all?"

"That's all."

"*À la prochaine,* Bruno."

"Until next time, Sylvie."

FIFTEEN

Plum Cake

Phlaumenkuchen is a dish that understands its role. To those used to rich desserts that scream for attention, this German plum tart might seem out of balance… a tad too acidic, a bit dry, not enough refined sugar. But then the phlaumenkuchen has no desire to upstage the moment, and it is happy to accompany a coffee, or a touch of brandy, a glass of eiswein, not to mention casual conversation. It is a facilitator. A reason to visit Grandmother. An excuse to meet with a former lover for whom you still have feelings. To understand this is to realize the true understated glory of this humble cake.

—Bruno Tannenbaum, *Twenty Recipes for Love*

"Bruno! There's my favorite poet!" Marcy rushed him, engulfing him in a plush, sweaty hug. She was a thickset woman with a pink, expressive face, freckles and a mischievous sparkle in her eyes. She held Bruno at arm's length, sizing him up. "Let's have a look at you, then." She hooked her fingers in his belt with a mixture of alarm and disgust. "You've lost a few kilograms, what? Let's get a meal in you, and quickly!"

Marcy shouted to her waiter for a table and the day's menu. She disappeared into the kitchen, barking orders in her heavily accented French, and then emerged again to join Bruno with a plate of charcuterie and a bottle of local Pinot Blanc.

Marcy Cooper was an English expat, chef and owner of Petit Écureuil, a tiny bistro on the Rue des Tonneliers (there seems to be a "Barrelmaker Street" in every wine town) in Strasbourg, where Bruno was completing his tour of Alsace before moving on. She'd been a good friend since he'd first eaten there during a brief stint as an inspector for the *Michelin Guide*, a gig that didn't last long since giving Bruno a limitless expense account was like teaching a toddler to use matches.

"Tell me your troubles," Marcy commanded, leaning on her elbows while the waiter brought out bowls of her traditional cabbage soup, which featured slabs of bacon and salted pork, thinly sliced apples and Munster Alsacienne cheese. It had legendary restorative powers, which Bruno needed after a detour of several days on the Alsatian wine road, and it smelled like a farmhouse kitchen.

As Bruno unfurled his story, Marcy listened intently, her eyes flickering. She furrowed her brow and patted his shoulder when he described the implosion of his marriage (Marcy had been through a number of her own) and she refilled and clinked glasses when he talked about the Trevallier, somehow ending with Claire's intention of following in his culinary footsteps. Marcy cracked her knuckles, a tattoo of a bulb of garlic on the underside of her wrist poking out of her chef's whites. "Good for Claire! We need more strong girls in this business. I'll give her a

personal recommendation to LBC London. She can come work
for me and I'll teach her a thing or two."

She shouted for a second bottle of wine, followed by a pair
of expletive-laden commands to her sous chef, prepping for the
evening rush, and Bruno wondered if Claire really knew the sort
of life she was in for.

At that very moment, back in Chicago, Claire had just
received the postcard he'd written to Anna on the train. Instead
of sharing it with her mother, she spirited it up to her room and
read it several times over, searching it for signs of progress on
the book. His thoughts were coming together nicely, and it was
time that he started working on an outline. She knew that her
mother had doubts about his ability to ever finish a new manuscript, but Claire was counting on it. She wanted to attend culinary school, and if Bruno published again he'd have some influence and could use his connections and credibility to smooth
her admission to one of the more selective institutes. Anna,
though, would be devastated, and Claire was bracing herself
for the eventual confrontation. To Anna, forgoing a standard
four-year college degree was a waste, especially for a star student from a modest-household income that made her easy
scholarship bait. Passing up that opportunity was a risk, but
wasn't spending your life doing something you loved worth it?
Kitchens had always thrilled Claire, and she used to accompany
Bruno through the back doors of the best of them: the smells,
energy and noise stopping her in her tracks, the cooks and chefs
pausing to offer Bruno a greeting before jumping back to their
tasks. Everyone moved at such a brisk pace, rushing about with
a clear sense of purpose. The sounds were music to her. The
chopping and clatter of pots. The shouts and muffled slam of

the cooler door. The deliverymen slaloming around her with crates of raw goat's milk and fresh feta or chèvre, sealed cases of seafood rushed to the cooler, packaged like organs heading into a transplant operation. Claire figured that she'd entered as many restaurants through the loading dock as she had through the front door, and, unlike her father, she knew she wouldn't be happy as just an observer. Was she crazy? Her mom probably thought so. *Claire, honey, how can you possibly know what you love at sixteen?* Mom, how do you know at forty? *Honey, I just don't want you to have any regrets.* If I don't go for this, I'll always regret it. *We've spent years saving, and that won't even cover your first year of culinary school . . . I can't let you spend it all only to find out that you don't like it.* But Mom, I *know* that's what I *want* to do . . .

Claire had rehearsed the conversation over and over again, and in each case it didn't turn out well. Her mom was capable, reliable and composed . . . everything her father was not. But on this matter, Bruno was her only ally. It hurt because while both her parents loved her, her mother was the one hovering in the doorway each night, a faint smile on her lips as she watched her daughters drift to sleep. And Claire was determined to break her heart.

Postcard stowed, Claire went to the kitchen and took out a stockpot and some round steak that she proceeded to cube. She was making a simple *boeuf bourguignon* out of *Mastering the Art of French Cooking* by Julia Child, losing herself in the myriad details of the craft, trying to push the imagined argument out of her mind.

Back in Alsace, Bruno and Marcy shared a smoke on the street in front of the restaurant. "Well, I can't wait to read your next book," she said, crushing out the cigarette beneath her toe.

"It sounds wonderful. Oh, and your mate Parker Thomas is pretty excited about it, too."

"He's no mate. And when did you talk to Thomas?"

"Stopped by last week on his way from France to Germany. Seemed to know something about what you're up to. Well, back to the kitchen for me."

They embraced, but Bruno left with a sinking feeling that Parker Thomas was beating him to the punch. He'd been ambling through the Alsatian countryside for far too long, and it was with a renewed sense of urgency that he left the Vosges Mountains behind him and headed for the border. As he stalked across Marc Mimram's lovely pedestrian bridge into Germany, he was too flustered to enjoy the view or even notice the strapping figure in the unseasonably warm, dark coat shadowing him across the border as he headed for the train station.

*   *   *

Bruno spotted the four towers of the cathedral first and watched them grow in the darkening sky as his train squealed to a halt in Naumburg. It was late evening, and the town felt empty, which was probably why he noticed the footsteps in the darkness behind him now as he headed toward the city center. He pulled his head out of the stack of maps and pages he'd printed in Beaune and turned around slowly. Somewhere a small dog barked, and a gust tumbled a newspaper down the street.

He shrugged and squinted again at the pages in his hand, realizing that he should have studied them more carefully on the train. He wandered past a wine shop, but it was closed. He scanned the bottles in the window. He wasn't certain he'd ever tried Naumburg wine before, though he vaguely remembered a bottle of *sekt,* what the Germans called sparkling wines, on the shelves of his mother's deli. The quality of the glass and label paper in the window samples showed that the winemakers were proud of their product and invested in their presentation: a good sign, though it didn't always translate to good wines, and some wonderful wines were packaged quite poorly.

It was then that he noticed a reflection in the shop window from the street behind him, a fellow in a long dark coat and black hat pulled low over his face like the clichéd figure of a thug from a film noir. He turned to get a better look, but just as he did a city bus rumbled past and the man was gone. Bruno wasn't ordinarily given to bravery, but the fear of losing his story to someone else, whether it be Parker Thomas or some oligarch's henchman, suppressed concerns for personal safety as he trotted across the street. There was no one in sight, but then he spotted a narrow alley between buildings and decided to investigate.

Of course there was no light. Bruno reached into his pocket for the only weapon he carried . . . the silver eagle corkscrew Aleksei had given him. He folded it out and gripped the handle so that the spiral extended between his middle and index fingers. He held his breath and plunged into the tight alley, his suitcase brushing the stone walls on one side to help guide him. His eyes slowly adjusted, but still he couldn't see any farther than a few feet ahead. His foot slurped and then sucked as he stepped into something foul.

There was a shuffling sound ahead, and he froze.

"Thomas!" Bruno whisper-shouted into the darkness. He edged forward. "Thomas, is that you?"

His hand gripping the corkscrew began to shake in anger, or maybe angst, as he thought about losing this story to his rival. He took another step and heard more shuffling ahead.

"Thomas? Or whoever you are. This is my story. You hear me? So hands off!"

Another step. He could hear breathing now, a rapid snuffling. His heart pounded, adrenaline surging.

A large, dark shape loomed ahead of him now. He could barely make it out in the grayness. It was only a few feet away. It was the color of stone, and it had to be the man in the black coat. Too big, probably, for Thomas. But maybe it was the Spetsnaz henchman. There was a twittering in the shadows, and Bruno thought the man was now laughing at him, mocking him. It was a high-pitched, sniggering laugh.

Bruno had had enough. He always thought of himself as a poet and lover, and not a fighter. He hadn't been in a fight since a fifth-grade altercation with Mary Soblesky, who'd called him a "porky Jew-Kraut," after which Bruno rushed at her, only to be socked squarely in the nose.

The squeaky laughter continued.

"Fuck you, and hands off my story!" Bruno shouted, channeling his eleven-year-old self. He dropped his suitcase and swung forward with a punch, cocking back the other hand with the corkscrew in preparation to deliver the coup de grace, and he felt his hand crunch as it met something impossibly solid. And cold.

In such situations you hear people talk about experiencing a sequence of events in slow motion, but that's not quite what happened here. It all was over in an instant, and it was only on a careful deconstruction at the mouth of the alley as Bruno sat on his suitcase and sucked on his sore knuckles that he was able to piece together what had happened.

The massive, wall-like structure at which he had swung hadn't been a wall-like thug in a dark coat, but the actual wall-like wall of the bricked-over end of the alley.

The squeaking laughter hadn't been human, either, but instead a panicked rat that he had chased into the corner. It exploded between his legs with a squeal after Bruno struck the wall and shouted pained curses when his hand connected with the stone. Luckily it had been a feeble punch . . . otherwise he would have broken bones. His whole hand ached, and his knuckles were bleeding.

Bruno doubted whether he'd seen the man's reflection in the shop window at all. Perhaps the paranoia was getting to him. Maybe it was the guilt over the slowly dwindling bundle of Anna's cash he kept in his breast pocket that was nagging his conscience. Thinking of her pulled him out of his funk and he returned to the task at hand: finding Von Speck.

Naumburg wasn't so large a town that he couldn't locate the first address on his list after a pair of wrong turns and some quick directions from fellow pedestrians. But nobody answered the door and when he peeked in the window of the flat he saw there was no furniture. He crossed the name off his list.

The second Von Speck was a college student originally from Hamburg. But within the hour he found himself standing at his third door of the evening on the landing of a shabby, three-flat, half-timbered house. The third-floor buzzer had a handwritten tag in dignified but shaky script that read *H. Speck*.

He buzzed and waited. In the lower flat, a dog yipped. Bruno scanned the street in both directions, expecting to see his phantom pursuer again, but he was alone. He reprimanded himself for his delusion and buzzed again. He was worried. If he turned up no leads, then what would he do?

He buzzed one last time for good measure and was turning on his heel when the handle in the center of the heavy wooden door began to turn. It swung slowly inward and Bruno found himself facing a small, white-haired woman in a pressed flower-print dress looking up at him through thick glasses.

"Yes?" she asked, her voice cracking as if it hadn't been used in some time.

Bruno bowed ceremoniously, suddenly self-conscious of his German language skills despite having grown up speaking it at home with Greta. "Frau Speck?"

"Yes?" Magnified eyes blinking behind the thick lenses.

"I'm looking for a Herr Von Speck, who served in France during the war."

"My husband?"

"Yes, your husband. Is he available?"

"No. He is deceased."

Bruno took off his Cubs cap and held it against his chest. "I'm so sorry to hear that. Might I come in and ask you some questions about him?"

She thought for a moment. And then she began to slowly turn around with mincing shuffles as she ascended the steep stairs. "Of course," she said, "please follow me."

Bruno creaked up the steps after her and in a moment he found himself in a cozy apartment with faded wallpaper. Decorative plates hung on the walls and porcelain figurines stood at attention on shelves or arranged in a glass corner display case. He sat down at a polished walnut table and Hilda Von Speck lifted the crystal lid on a cake plate beneath which was a fresh *pflaumenkuchen*.

"I just made it this morning," she said. "Would you like some coffee?"

Of course Bruno would like coffee. He smiled as she set a plate before him, and he breathed in the rich fruit and felt the acids tickle his nose, his mouth already beginning to water. This reminded him of home, though Hilda's version of the open-faced cake featured a much more orderly arrangement of plum slices than his mother's, all of them uniform in size and hued purple like his bruised knuckles. His stomach grumbled. Hilda heard it and insisted that he eat a slice while she brought coffee on the stove to a boil.

He devoured it in three bites. He paused to admire the last piece of his slice only a moment, noting how the magenta juices had soaked into the crust, and smelling the hint of almond and something else he couldn't quite place.

Hilda didn't eat any herself, but she sat sipping coffee and watching him with pleasure as he gobbled his fourth slice, her hands folded in her lap, a sparkle in her eye, a pleased smile on her lips looking not unlike his mother's when she prepared something for him.

They chatted and he carefully steered the conversation toward the war, and it soon became clear that this was the correct Von Speck and he had found his next link in the chain he hoped would lead him to the elusive bottles. He felt the cork in his pocket as Hilda spoke, staring through the walls and across the years.

"Karl's family possessed a small farm on the Saale. That's where I stayed during the war. He was wounded when his car was struck by an artillery shell. I remember the day he came home. His leg was shattered and still hadn't healed. He was so thin. He had a cane, but still couldn't walk very far. The war was lost by then. We all knew it. We were hungry. The countryside was ruined. But he was optimistic. 'When the war ends, we can start over,' he always told me . . ." Her voice trailed off. Bruno cleared his throat.

"I understand he was an administrator?"

"Yes. This is true. *Militärverwaltung* in *Frankreich*, in the occupied zone. He wasn't a born soldier. He was older when he was drafted."

"And did he have a specialty in agriculture . . . in vineyards?"

"Why, yes. That's why he was selected for this job. His family estate had vineyards and he knew quite a lot about how they were grown and how wine was made. He was in charge of exports of farm products. Of wine, specifically. Good wine was so hard to come by in those days."

"And I understand that some of the wines, from his time in France, were shipped here, to Naumburg," Bruno said, trying to keep his voice from wavering. His pulse pounded in his throat now.

Hilda's eyes pulled back from across the years to focus on Bruno now, as if to ask who this man was asking so earnestly about what had happened so long ago. Surely she could sense how anxious he was. She must be able to see the desperation. The greed, perhaps.

She studied him for a long time. Her eyes were brown and cool. He could tell that she'd once been beautiful. And proud.

"Yes, that's true," she said, finally. "It came by train. They stored it in the cellars of his family's estate.

"Why there? Why not ship it to Berlin with the rest?"

Hilda bristled. "Karl was no thief, Mr. Tannenbaum. I always wanted to believe that he was keeping it safe. For what purpose, I don't know. Perhaps he meant to return it someday."

"He *meant* to return it? What happened?"

"He died that summer. His leg became infected. There was no medicine. It had to be amputated. He did not survive the operation." She dabbed her eyes now.

"I'm sorry," Bruno said, reaching across the table and placing his hand over hers. The faraway stare had returned.

"The Russians came. The Von Speck estate was *redistributed* under the Communists. But that was just a way of saying that everything of value was packed up and sent east. The Von Specks became just the Specks. Our estate became a collective and basically ceased to exist. All the wine, including that which had come from France, was loaded on a truck along with everything else. Forty years of the GDR and we lost everything. Everything except our dignity."

"And your family recipe for *phlaumenkuchen*. This is excellent," Bruno said, forking his last bite into his mouth.

Hilda beamed at him. "Oh, it's just a little something." She looked at him affectionately. "You know," she said, almost as an afterthought, "you should check the council house. They were Communists, but they were still German, and you can be sure that they kept records. If you stay in the *altstadt* tonight, you'll be close to the Goldenen Ganz. You should be able to find Heinz Blau there. He's the watchman at the council house. If you buy him enough beer he might even let you in without the hassle of paperwork." She grinned.

"Frau Speck," Bruno said with a conspiratorial wink, "it's quite a pleasant surprise to find that your talents not only encompass the baking of tarts, but extend to investigative journalism as well. By any chance do you happen to have more coffee?"

SIXTEEN

Beer

While wine holds the mystery and magic of weather and geography, beer, too, has something to offer. Beer is instant community, a reason to congregate. Whether it's Martin Luther in his backyard sipping home brew and philosophizing the origins of a new religion with Philipp Melanchthon or a North Side Chicago watering hole where union workers are planning a strike action around mugs of cheap German-style lager, beer has served to loosen tongues, free minds, incite revolutions and fuel a billion amorous encounters since the dawn of history.
—Bruno Tannenbaum, "100 Years of Windy City Beer," *Chicago Sun-Times*

The Goldenen Ganz, or Golden Goose, was a classic German *ratskeller*, a bar located below street level near or under the town hall. Truly institutionalized drinking. It was a comfortable, warm, humid cave, and Bruno saw its glow and heard singing as he walked across the cobbles of the marketplace. A cold wind whipped across the stones as he descended the stairs below street level and submerged into the warmth of inebriated companionship.

There were long rows of tables, a heavy wooden bar and thick timbers across the ceiling. A fire glowed in one corner and a group of men with red faces and suspenders were playing cards and drinking from half-liter mugs, occasionally bursting into song. Bruno took a seat at the bar. The bartender was a woman with a smoker's voice and a friendly wink. Hilda's plum tart had primed Bruno's appetite, and he now ordered the German equivalent of pub grub. His French friends disparaged German restaurants, but Bruno knew this was unfair, especially if you sought your cuisine at food stands, in butcher shops or in courthouse basements.

He ordered a plate of fried potatoes and a locally made knackwurst, or "crack sausage," which featured fatty veal and ground pork with garlic and spices overstuffed into a plump casing accompanied by a side of vinegar-soaked red cabbage. When he took a bite of the knackwurst, the skin popped and juices ran as soon as his teeth pierced the casing. The potatoes were crisp, butter-browned on the outside, and perfectly threaded with sautéed onions and a dusting of fresh parsley. Bruno wondered if there was a combination of comfort food anywhere in the world so well balanced and suited to the weary traveler. Perhaps only the Italian beef combo sandwich from Chicago's South Side could approach this.

With a half liter of *schwarzbier* at hand, Bruno immersed himself in the details of the meal. It relied on contrasts: the tang of vinegar in the cabbage against the soft pulp of the potatoes followed by the crunch and pop of flavor from the caraway and anise seeds. The pork sausage melted in his mouth, leaving a crunchy ring of the casing for the last swallow. This, in combination with the beer, lit the furnace inside him, and somewhere along the way he transformed from bone-tired traveler into a man on a mission. He suddenly remembered that he was supposed to be looking for someone. The crowd at the corner table began to thin, men putting on wool caps and hoisting coats over their shoulders. Bruno frantically asked the bartender for Heinz. She laughed and pointed to a man in the very corner of the last table. "He's always the last to surrender the breach," she said with a chuckle. "Perhaps you'll be the one to walk him home tonight to spare me the trouble?"

Heinz was just getting revved up, occupying the cornermost seat with a clay bottle of Sliwowitz, the Polish word for "fire water," or, more accurately, "you will regret this tomorrow."

Buno pushed his plate away and asked for a shot glass, heading to the corner to join the revelry, trying to think of some excuse for needing to see the archives in the morning without tipping his hand, not wanting to leave any more clues for either Thomas or the Russian stormtrooper.

But as it turned out, Bruno needed no excuse. He and Heinz were soon fast friends, arms around one another, singing *Ein Prosit! Ein Prosit!* and every other German drinking song Bruno could think of until they were the only two left in the *ratskeller*.

Heinz slouched soused on a bench, crowding Bruno next to the wall now, reaching for the Sliwowitz with an unsteady hand, his eyes growing ever more distant and glassy as he drank. Bruno tried to navigate toward the subject of the archives.

"Heinz, I'm working on a story about lost wine. Do you know Hilda Von Speck?"

"Of course. To Hilda!" They hoisted the liquor and toasted.

Bruno hoped that he could remain conscious. "She told me that some of his wine disappeared after the war . . ."

"The Communists," Heinz mumbled, wavering on the edge of sentience.

"Tell me more . . ."

"For all those years, we were their puppets." Heinz was practicing his broken, inebriated English now. He squeezed Bruno's shoulder—Bruno's status as an American elevated him in the old man's eyes. Living in the Soviet-controlled GDR and having relatives in the West made Heinz understand how much better people were treated on the other side of the Iron Curtain. He retained none of the nostalgia for communism sometimes found among the older generation in the former East Germany. "And what do we have to show for it? Forty years of looking over the wall while they prospered. You talk of the Von Speck estate. Their wines were wonderful. I remember my father bringing out a bottle at Christmas. It was special. The wines from the Rheingau . . . those we drank every day. But the Saale-Unstrut wines, they were special. They tasted like they belonged here. You have to drink a wine where it is grown to truly appreciate it. We've made wine here for more than a thousand years! But does anyone outside of Sachsen-Anhalt know about us? For so long we were cut off from the outside world. Because of them."

"It's not right," Bruno said, shaking his head.

"The bloody Communists!" Heinz pounded the table.

"Bloody Communists!" Bruno said, imitating Heinz. The glasses rattled. Out of the corner of his eye, Bruno saw the bartender roll her eyes and smile as she wiped off the counter. It was a speech, he suspected, she heard frequently.

"They ruined everything. They took over the wine production and set up collectives. The old family names were removed. Nobody took pride in what they made. They dumped it all into the same tanks. They amused us with parades and Olympic medals. Did you know that our little state of Thüringen has won more gold medals than any other place on earth? And why did they do this? So that we were distracted and they could rob us blind. And to think, I was drafted in 1945 at fifteen years of age to fight on the eastern front. So many of the boys froze to their rifles. They didn't even have bullets, but they died pointing them east anyway. I lost fingers to the cold."

Heinz held up his left hand, which featured three stubs that only reached to the second knuckle.

"We were told that we had to defend the Fatherland against the Soviets. That we must die for this. And then what happens? We became Soviet dogs! The Communists sold us out. The Russians came and took everything. Our potatoes. Our cabbages. Apples, strawberries, cucumbers. Our animals. They cut down our trees. Everything was loaded on trains and trucks and shipped east. If you want to know what happened to the Von Speck wine, there is your answer."

Bruno, seeing his chance, leaned close to Heinz and talked low, glancing around the room. "Do you keep records?"

Heinz leaned back in disbelief. For a moment, Bruno thought that he'd made a mistake.

"Records?" Heinz shouted. "Of course we kept records!"

"Do you think you could help me find them?"

"Will you write about this tragedy, about the thieving Communists, in your story?"

"Of course."

Heinz stood suddenly and began fumbling with an enormous ring of keys, jabbing the air with his finger and insisting, in his broken English, that he was now on a grave mission. "We go there now. Right now! Come, come!"

They stumbled across the empty *marktplatz,* Bruno hefting his suitcase in one hand and propping up Heinz with his other arm. They listed to one side and then tacked back onto course. Heinz sang a Hans Albers song: *Silbern klingt und springt die Heuer, heut' speel ick dat feine Oos!* Bruno knew the tune and he whistled along.

Whether it was from the alcohol or the drunken Heniz on his arm, Bruno was too preoccupied to notice the dark shape slipping along the edge of the marketplace, slowly pacing them.

The *rathaus,* a steep-roofed four-story building, squatted solidly on the end of the square. Every window bore a box of red flowers, shivering joylessly in the dark. The two men cut through an alley around to the back of the building and stopped at an overthick wooden door with massive iron hinges. Heinz fumbled with his keys until he found one that was up to the task, an iron affair that was as thick and long as his middle finger.

After considerable concentration, there was a click and the heavy door groaned inward. They descended a tight staircase and entered vaulted catacombs. Heinz flipped a switch and a few fluorescent lights buzzed and hummed as they slowly warmed, but they did little to dispel the chill and shadows.

Towering shelves stretched into the dark recesses of the chamber, and there was a small reception area with a metal desk and nameplate that read *Heinz Blau, Meister der Aufzeich-nungen.*

"Custodian of Records," Heinz said, touching the nameplate and pressing his other hand to his heart. Then with solemnity he added, "I perform my charge with honor and great pride."

After a moment of reflection, Heinz jabbed his finger in

the air again and said, "We go now, to thwart the Communist thieves!" with such enthusiasm that Bruno regretted that they were a good sixty years too late.

A low shelf in the front contained ledger books, and Heinz bent over, studying their spines intently before removing one.

Bruno heard a creak behind him, perhaps the wind blowing the huge door, but then it would have had to be quite a gale to accomplish that. Something dripped in a dark corner.

"Wheat. Pork. Mushrooms. Corn." Heinz shuffled through various ledgers until he found what he was looking for. "Ah, here it is: Fruit, berries and wine!"

He hefted a huge tome to the top shelf and flipped it open. The air was filled with the rich, dusty smell of history. Heinz traced lines across a ledger grid to steady his gaze, his tongue pinched in his lips and one eye closed as he concentrated. He grunted with the effort.

After several long moments he began nodding his head.

"Such wonderful, wonderful wines. Here we are: 1951 . . . 22,576 cases of Sylvaner. Shipped east as part of the agricultural exchange. Exchange! Bah. Such lies!"

"What about earlier?"

"Let me see." More groaning and one-eyed concentration. "Here we are: 15,754 boxes of Müller-Thurgau, each box containing twelve bottles of wine . . . Ah, this is strange . . ."

"What is it?"

"Very strange indeed."

"What, what?" Despite the chill, Bruno felt sweat on his brow. There was nothing like digging deep in the archives. It was almost as if he could anticipate that the moment of revelation was at hand.

But Heinz was starting to fade. His eyelids were heavy, and his speech slurred more. *Stay with me, Meister der Aufzeichnungen,* Bruno thought. "Please, is there anything more?"

"Three hundred and forty-two cases of ordinary red table wine."

"Red wine?"

"We produce mostly white wines. And this is such a small, unusual amount, of unspecified variety. Here, the other reds are labeled . . . Dornfelder, Spätburgunder . . . but nowhere else, no other years is there simply a 'red table wine.'"

"That has to be what I'm looking for. Can I find out more information?"

Heinz yawned.

"Please . . ."

"Aisle thirteen. There should be invoices. You look and I'll keep watch here." Heinz settled into his desk chair and was asleep in moments.

This, Bruno thought as he stepped back through the aisles laden with volumes and boxes of documents, *is research!* There would come a time when all research was digital and meant staring at glowing rectangles for hours on end. He sighed deeply. To think that all of this might someday be lost.

But after ten minutes of digging through boxes and flipping aimlessly through file folders, Bruno decided he'd been a tad too sentimental and he'd be more than happy with a good database. He unshelved and reshelved boxes. He dug through piles of invoices, receipts, ledgers. Sure, the Germans were good at keeping records, but much of them were inscrutable. The shelves towered three meters high, stuffed with boxes, and Bruno felt the impossibility of the task of finding the one shred of evidence that he needed.

He heard Heinz snoring from three aisles away and was tempted to try to rouse him, but decided to dig through another pair of boxes.

He selected one at random on a lower shelf and with a stroke of luck found a cluster of papers from 1946. A stack of folders labeled *Weinlieferungen* caught his eye, and he grinned.

Within moments he clutched a small square of carbon paper capturing the shipment of 342 cases of *rot landwein,* a designation that basically translates as "generic red wine," and unlike other regions suggested such low quality that you rarely saw it even used in Germany, let alone bottles that were exported.

The writing was in the archaic script that Bruno had seen in some of his mother's old family letters, hard to decipher. He was eager to enlist Heinz's help, and his hand trembled as he held the paper before him and walked down the aisle, amazed that the cork he'd found under a file cabinet in Chicago had led him to a *rathaus* cellar in the former East Germany.

He was so intent that he didn't see the advancing shadow rounding the corner at the end of the aisle. He bumped square into a large man in a dark fedora and long coat. It was not unlike running into the bricked-in end of the alley earlier in the evening, which had left his knuckles still smarting.

In the instant it took the fellow to rip the slip of paper out of his hand and shove him to the floor, sending him sprawling, Bruno caught a glimpse of the man's face. It was younger than he'd expected. He was pale, with light eyebrows, eyes that were a colorless gray and a long, thick scar that traced the edge of his square jaw.

Bruno hit the floor hard, slamming his head back onto the cold stone floor so that he saw stars with a crack that rattled his skull. He was still holding a corner of the slip of paper and the blossoming pain in his head was outweighed by the great sense of loss and a rising anger.

He stood and dizzily stumbled. He grabbed at the shelf to steady himself, pulling out several boxes in the process. The man studied the paper and then, purposeful but unhurried, walked briskly away. Bruno staggered after him, ready to grab the man's shoulders, but the man spun, long coat whirling in the dim light, and Bruno felt a pistol pressing against his stomach. He looked down and then up into the man's cold eyes. He slumped and raised his hands, defeated, as the man turned in the aisle toward the stairs.

Suddenly an earsplitting explosion shattered the air. There was a cloud of smoke and dust and a rain of shredded paper drifting from overhead.

Bruno and his attacker both ducked.

Heinz was now blocking the stairs, holding a massive antique rifle longer than he was tall with a bayonet affixed to the end. He cocked the bolt, unsteadily aiming for his next shot.

"Bruno, Bruno! The Communists have infiltrated the *Aufzeichnungen*! They slipped past me while I was distracted." He slammed the bolt home and pointed it at the man in the hat, whom Bruno had now dubbed "Scar."

Scar made to duck into the adjoining aisle, and Bruno stuck out his foot and tripped him, snatching the receipt in the process. Scar's gun skittered on the floor and Bruno toed it under a shelf as he tried to scramble back to his feet.

There was another explosion as a bullet slammed into a box precariously close to Bruno's head. Heinz grinned and cocked the rifle yet again, swaying in his stance. "Bruno, get going! I'll hold them off while you escape and tell the world of their crimes!"

Scar scampered down the aisle while Heinz lowered the bayonet and charged into the dark aisle after him.

"For the Fatherland! Prepare to taste my steel, Communist dogs!"

Bruno tucked the receipt in his pocket and made for the stairs, feeling a tad guilty about leaving Scar to Heinz's zealous bayonet, but then Bruno was sure now that this was the man who had clocked him on the noggin in Chicago and had been following him ever since. He was relieved that his paranoia was justified. The question remained: For whom was Scar working? Aleksei had mentioned an oligarch, so surely he could find out more. Whatever the case, Heinz's current condition meant that Bruno was as likely to end up on the receiving end of a bullet as Scar was, so now was no time for investigation.

After the musty air of the archives and the smell of gunpowder, the empty streets of Naumburg were a relief. He wanted to study his latest clue, but he could barely make out the script, though he recognized it as *altedeutsche schrift,* an almost indecipherable form of handwriting that was taught in schools until the forties. If his mother were here she could help him, and he half thought about calling her until he realized that Frau Speck was a lot like his mother. It was late evening, or more likely early morning, so he found a bench in the park around the corner from Frau Speck's flat and fell fast asleep despite the chill, with help from the Sliwowitz still circulating through his blood.

*   *   *

He was in the middle of a lovely dream in which he was lying naked next to Sylvie as she smoked, and they were talking about Heinz and laughing, when he was suddenly awakened by a little black schnauzer licking his face. The blue light of early morning filtered through the trees overhead.

"Shatzie! Get away from that filthy man!" a woman shrieked from the sidewalk as Bruno sat up. The dog glanced apologetically over her shoulder as she slunk after her owner.

"Shatzie, it's been fun. Don't forget to call," Bruno said in German.

Hilda was thrilled to see him. She ushered him in, correctly assuming that Bruno would be hungry, so she fixed *hopple popple,* a farmer breakfast featuring fried potatoes and eggs and whatever leftovers or extras you can find. Bruno stood at her shoulder watching. In this case the leftovers included small *champignon* mushrooms and two kinds of diced sausages, white asparagus and grated *rauchkäse,* smoked cheese.

Hilda made coffee, and while he ate she helped him translate the invoice from the archives. Not all of it made sense, but it did clearly indicate that the shipment of wine was headed to Moscow at the direction of someone named Constanoff. Bruno now felt he had enough details to warrant the purchase of a train ticket east. How convenient that Parker Thomas had given him a business card with some Moscow contacts when they were both back in Beaune. And also irksome to think that Thomas might already be there with several days' head start. How much did he know?

Hilda suggested Dresden as a first stop, and as he made to leave she blinked back tears, which were comically magnified by her thick glasses. Bruno smiled and hugged her. She was wizened and arthritic, but there was also strength in her embrace. Then as he was leaving he stopped and turned.

"You know," he said, "in France I was told that your husband was a kind and fair administrator, and he's remembered fondly despite the circumstances of the occupation."

"Thank you," she said, choking out the words between sobs.

It was impulsive and a total lie. Bruno didn't have sufficient evidence to exonerate the man, but then Hilda had fed him twice and reminded him of his mother. Would she have taken him in during the forties if she'd known he was half Jewish and a quarter French?

SEVENTEEN

Mămăliga

When it comes to affairs of the heart, there are two important categories of foods: those intended for seduction and those meant for restoration. Mămăliga, a Moldovan corn porridge that is boiled and served plain alongside a traditional fresh curdled ewe cheese like telemea, is certainly intended for the latter. After a harsh evening of hard words and too much wine, mămăliga, cooked in an iron pot to buttery perfection, can coat the very interior of your soul and set you on the path to recovery.

—BRUNO TANNENBAUM, *TWENTY RECIPES FOR LOVE*

Bruno wasted two days crisscrossing Germany and Poland, making his way east and spending too much on train tickets and eating from vending machines. He hadn't had a glass of wine or anything more substantial than seltzer water, and he was feeling dizzy—his constitution, his very soul, lacked nourishment. These languages puzzled him, and he made poor decisions. In the Ukraine he chose the wrong side of the tracks and wound

up in Moldova after dozing for four hours. It was in the countryside beyond Chişinău that he decided he needed to regain his
bearings before turning around for Moscow, and when he saw
some healthy but unkempt vine rows from the window of his
second-class car, he exited at the next station in search of a hearty
meal and a glass of local wine.

At first he regretted his impulsiveness. The town was ramshackle, with mud streets, houses with faded paint and sagging
roofs of rusted tin, straw or even cardboard, and nothing even
remotely resembling a restaurant. He stood in the center of the
main drag and smelled something foul, only to look down to see
he was standing in a mass of animal excrement. A young, toothless boy leading a goat on a frayed rope (or rather the goat led the
boy) ambled past and smiled at Bruno. Bruno listened to the fading sound of the goat's bell and hung his head, wondering how
many hours it would be to the next train. A mangy dog with
tufted fur, more like an underfed wolf than any recognizable
breed, trotted into the street. It caught sight of Bruno and then
scampered under a thatched fence.

Bruno scanned the dirt road, divots and potholes filled with
rainwater, the faint smell of failed plumbing and decay, the envelope of dwindling cash in his pocket weighing on him heavily
now. It had carried him here. To Moldova. The poorest country
in Europe. Chasing something . . . chasing what?

Bruno thought of Carmen, flour-dusted and whistling as
she kneaded dough for a flatbread, winking at him across the
kitchen island. He thought of Claire sitting cross-legged on
her bed texting her friends, his old postcards pinned to the wall
behind her making a map of places she might never be able to
go. He thought of Anna sitting at the dining room table late into
the night, the glow from her laptop lighting her features as she

worked through her spreadsheets, her weary head propped in one hand. What would they think of him now?

The absurdity of it overwhelmed him. He glanced at the sky, the sun covered by a layer of haze and wood smoke rising from the meager hovels of this wretched little town. He looked at the bleak road ahead. He couldn't take another step. What was the point? He set his suitcase down in the mud and sat on it, propping his elbow on his knee and his chin on his fist. He'd come far enough. He'd lost the will to continue.

It was then that he heard the faint sound of accordion music.

It came from beyond the rows of stone and plaster houses, rickety wooden fences and rusted wire chicken coops. He sniffed and wiped his nose on his sleeve, trying to locate the source of the happy noise.

And then, somewhere in this desolate village, there came another sound: the tinkle of laughter mingling with the chords of the accordion. It was the bright, hopeful sound of human existence. Next: a fiddle. Clarinet. Clapping of hands.

It drew closer.

From a side street, a lone accordionist emerged, rounding the corner, heading toward Bruno. The musician was dressed in a round embroidered hat with a tassel, a white blouse and colorful vest, billowy trousers and curled-toe shoes. He seemed to be an artifact, some kind of random gnomish figurine sold in a tourist stall, with a white beard and the widest, toothiest grin Bruno had ever seen.

Bruno watched in wonder as other musicians and now dancers emerged from the side street, in an eclectic mix of embroidered blouses and secondhand clothing. A man carrying a tambourine and wearing a pale blue tracksuit came spinning around the bend, his arm hooked in that of an elderly woman in a red brocade dress.

A line of churning, dancing revelers followed the musicians into the street, snaking their way toward Bruno. He now saw a large stone amphora inlaid with a grape and vine design, carried by two men who were pausing to pour what looked to be wine into jars and cups. Others carried bottles, and for a moment Bruno thought it was a wine festival, but then a woman in a veil and white dress spun around the corner, followed by a sheepish young man in a tie, and he understood the reason for the occasion.

It was a wedding party, and it surged around Bruno, parting around him like a wave of mirth and revelry. People clapped and sang and slapped Bruno on the back. When the man in the tracksuit and the elderly woman reached him, they hooked his arms between them and dragged him into the fray.

The river of people washed down the bleak street, illuminating everything now, and Bruno noticed things about the village that he hadn't before: colorful flags, bright blue paint on windowsills, red and black hens and window boxes of brilliant flowers.

He discovered that someone had tucked a flower behind his ear and pressed a cup of wine into his hand. It was dark, oxidized, heavy and tannic, like the Hungarian blends known as "bull's blood," though not quite as strong and sweet. It warmed him as it sloshed into his empty belly, and he soon found himself spinning with the bride on his arm.

They zigzagged up the street and then climbed a small hill where flowers were laid at the foot of a monument, a sooty, squared Stalinist statue of a peasant couple marching to the fields with scythes over their shoulders.

The party filed into an empty lot that had been transformed

into a lovely bower through flowered arbors, flags and tables laden with bowls of stewed lamb, pilaf, aubergines, cabbage rolls, fresh fruit, pastries and buns, and Bruno grinned so hard his cheeks hurt. He sampled everything, all of which made the jug wine come alive. His favorite dish was the fried *pelmeni,* small dumplings filled with minced lamb and pork that were flavored with cinnamon and mint, dusted with paprika and freshly made sour cream. The wedding party joined him at the table, eating directly from the large bowls with their hands, continuing to churn and spin, though it was clear that some sort of structured ceremony was beginning to emerge.

He was already composing a new postcard to Anna in his head as a small, graying man in an ill-fitting suit stood on a chair and began to speak to the revelers. Without grasping a word of the language, Bruno soon understood this to be the father of the bride. As the man spoke at length, both he and his daughter looked intently and openly into each other's tear-filled eyes, and in Bruno's head the words began to arrive:

> *Dear Anna, sometimes in life we take the indirect route. I thought I'd lost my way in Moldova, but when I left the train at some forgotten village on a whim, I found a wedding party. Or rather . . . the wedding party found me.*

Maybe it was the smiles, hugs and dancing, but Bruno was suddenly tempted to stay. With what he had in his pocket, maybe he could buy his own little cabin with a chicken coop and a feral dog to go with it. He could live here for at least as long as it took him to write a book, which at his current pace meant ten years or more.

He danced with both the bride and the groom, many of the dances separating the genders into groups. He was fortunately light-footed for a big man, and a small boy in a suit and tie was able to teach him many of the basic steps of a traditional dance where the men carried the bride on their shoulders and paraded her around the groom, who stood in the center with his arms folded, feigning arrogance and indifference though blushing underneath.

Few beyond this lost corner of the world have even heard of this village. Although the families earn their livings from the surrounding vineyards, no wine magazine has ever written about it. Still, it's never been so clear to me what wine means to our species.

An old man stood up to speak with Bruno in halting German, and after a brief chat Bruno was mistaken for a long-lost Austrian relative and invited to make a speech. He stepped onto a small wooden riser bordered with flowers. The father of the bride hugged him, squeezing Bruno until he was about to pop. Bruno raised his cup and spoke in German. Mostly he recited "Zum Einschlafen Zu Sagen," an old Rilke poem he'd memorized in college that had nothing to do with anything. Perhaps it was the rhyme and meter, but as he looked across the sea of faces there were smiles and eyes heavy with tears. The bride sobbed through a grin and her father was openly weeping. Bruno finished with a rambling story in English about his daughters and how much he missed his whole family cooking together, which had him in tears, and as he stepped down, the families cheered and the father embraced him once more, and they all resumed dancing.

The wedding ended with the bride seated in an ornately carved
chair with the musicians playing a lovely, slow tune while the
villagers laid flowers at her feet. I should have been taking
notes for the book, but I must admit at that moment all I could
think about was you . . . and our two remarkable daughters.

The rest of the afternoon and evening was a blur, save for a
spectacular sunset on the hillsides beyond the town.

He awoke on a mattress in a simple single-room house. Lying
next to him was the man in the blue tracksuit and a crown of
flowers who'd carried the tambourine, and an attractive woman
about his own age who wore entirely too much mascara and
was stuffed into a yellow dress that might have fit her better
twenty years earlier. On her other side was the clarinet player,
and a white-haired woman slumbered on a dining table. Bruno
vaguely remembered dancing with the woman next to him and
possibly kissing her briefly. He checked and was thankful that he
was fully clothed.

They all awoke together and stumbled about the house
in a polite, hungover silence, preparing a meal together. The
men sat in the doorway smoking while Bruno helped the old
woman boil some corn porridge for *mămăliga*. As he watched
her work he took notes this time, recording how much rock
salt she used and also how once the mixture solidified she used
a piece of thread to cut it rather than a knife. She carefully
lifted the slices into a pan and fried them in lard on the top of
the woodstove.

They ate the *mămăliga* quietly with a tart, fresh ewe cheese on
the side.

The woman in the yellow dress walked him to the train.
She was quite a talker, only pausing to drag on a cigarette until

the train arrived. He understood nothing she said, but her language was like a kind of music. They embraced and what Bruno expected to be a quick kiss actually came with a tobacco-flavored tongue that was not unpleasant. She slapped him on the butt as he ascended the stairs and the conductor winked at him.

That was Moldova.

EIGHTEEN

Lepeshka

I have always thought of Moscow as the City of Bread. While a baguette may protrude from every bag and backpack in Paris, it's the Russians who devour bread on a Tolstoyan scale. Whether it's the earthy black borodinsky loaves served with mountains of soft butter or my favorite, the lepeshka—Russian by way of Uzbekistan, round and indented in the center, sprinkled with sesame and a butter crust, dense and chewy, passed around the table in whole circles to be torn off in chunks—breaking bread in Russia is simultaneously a physical and spiritual act. Perhaps the most satisfying sensation in all of dining is the ripping of a chunk of lepeshka passed to you from the hands of your neighbor.
—BRUNO TANNENBAUM, "BAKING BEYOND THE IRON CURTAIN,"
CHICAGO SUN-TIMES

Bruno mailed his next postcard to Anna on his way back through Chişinău, and through some benevolence of the mail gods or maybe a bureaucratic accident, it appeared in her mailbox three days later. Anna had, on a whim, left her office early and accidentally intercepted the mail. This was a rarity. Fetching mail had always been Claire's job, a tradition that had persisted since she was four when she dragged a stool onto the stoop of the brownstone and climbed up to the box, playing the game of "Mail Munchkin" delivering royalty checks to Bruno and bills to Anna. Her mother had only collected the mail a few times since then, when Claire was bedridden with the flu or sleeping over at a friend's.

And on this day Anna would have left it in the box for Claire again, but she met the mailman at the steps. She admired his muscled, tan calves. He was much younger than she and attractive despite the silly shorts and uniform, or maybe because of them. When he smiled as he handed her the rubber-banded bundle, she blushed. She carried it in without thinking, and only when she set it on the counter did she realize that she probably should have just stuck it in the box herself and left it for Claire. It was one of the few remaining ways that her older daughter still acted like a little girl, and Anna worried that once Claire realized this she'd probably stop doing it. Wouldn't it be nice if she kept up the tradition until she left for college?

Anna unsnapped the rubber band, leafed through the stack, and the postcard from Moldova caught her attention. She'd seen plenty of Bruno's cards over the years, before his career imploded. The postcards were a tradition that she appreciated and it always made her think fondly of her estranged husband.

She knew of his harebrained scheme to scour Europe in pursuit of the story for his next book, a potential bestseller, or so he claimed. She hadn't quite believed him but she was hopeful. She could use a little financial help, especially with Claire starting college and Carmen in need of braces after her dentist recommended a visit to the orthodontist. Most likely, though, he was blowing whatever little money he had left. Classic Bruno.

She flipped the card over, not knowing what to expect. She hadn't heard a word from him since he'd left weeks ago. When she saw the date and the Moldovan postage stamp, her curiosity was piqued. Then she noticed that the card was addressed to her. She read it twice, and from the familiar tone and cadence it felt not like a single postcard, but one of a series. Where were the others? Were the mail systems in Eastern Europe so screwed up that this card made it through before all the rest? She was tempted to call Harley and get to the bottom of this, but then she remembered Claire's secret box of postcards. Mothers always know where such things are hidden.

And this was how Claire found Anna when she came home after visiting a friend: seated at the dining room table with the shoe box open, Bruno's postcards spread out on the tablecloth. She'd obviously been crying. Claire was furious, her voice the timbre of a shriek.

"What are you doing?"

"I found a postcard in the mail from your father, and I needed to figure it out."

"I get the mail."

"I got it today."

"Why are you going through my stuff?"

"Why is your father in Moldova?"

"That's none of your business."

"Actually, it is." She wearily plucked one of the postcards from the table, her forehead propped in her hand as she read, "'Dear Anna, sometimes in life we take the indirect route . . . In closing, I assure you that I'm now confident that enough of our funds remain for me to find the end of this strange and wonderful tale.'"

"Mom, that's—"

"*Our* funds? What does he mean, *our funds*?"

"He's doing research for his next book."

"I checked your college savings. It's gone. All of it."

"I loaned it to him."

"That was money *we* were saving for college. For you."

"It was *my* college savings and *I* loaned it to him. He's going to pay it back."

"What kind of father would steal from his daughter to finance some European bender?"

"He didn't steal it! I gave it to him."

"Even so, how dare he take money from you?"

"Well . . ."

"Claire?"

"I told him it was your money, and that you were supporting him. I thought that maybe it would show him that you still love him."

"What? Claire!"

"Do you still love each other?" Claire was crying now.

"That's not the point. You lied!"

"I had to . . . You know he wouldn't have accepted it otherwise. And you're overreacting. When he publishes his book, he'll pay it back and then some."

"Overreacting? He's not going to pay it back. You just threw away your future."

"He will pay it back. He's a good writer, Mom. He just needs us to have faith in him."

"I'd love to have faith in him, honey, but I've known him too long."

"Well, there's nothing we can do about it now."

"Yes, there is. We need to call him and make him come home before it's all gone."

"He won't listen to you."

"I'm not going to ask him, Claire. You are. And you're going to tell the truth about how you deceived us."

"I can't, Mom. He's doing important research!"

*   *   *

At that same moment, Bruno was standing with a raised shot glass at a polished rail in a Moscow hotel bar, his Cubs cap askew, his coat rumpled, swaying slightly on his feet in a cluster of stylishly dressed people smelling of perfume and cologne, including one lovely young woman named Svetlana who stood at Bruno's elbow. She wore a white cocktail dress that sparkled, her hair pulled in a tight ponytail, bright red lipstick anchoring her face, as the rest of the world seemed to shimmer and spin.

"*Budem zdorovy!*" Bruno shouted, hoisting his glass higher.

"*Budem!*" the young people rejoined.

They tossed back their vodka.

Bruno was celebrating. It had been a hard trip to Moscow, full of misread timetables, bad food and long stretches without a drop of alcohol. But he had made it, armed only with a loose translation of a sixty-year-old shipment invoice from Naumburg and the name of the man who had received it. The business card that Parker Thomas gave him at the bacchanal back in France had also come in handy . . . Bruno managed to get himself invited to a press junket given by a Moscow wine distributor, with a deluxe room thrown in. Now he was reveling in his good fortune. "I'm buying another, who wants another?" Bruno said, fishing a pile of wadded rubles from his pocket and scattering them on the bar. But his guests had started to disperse. Svetlana disappeared and Bruno's heart broke just a little.

Nikolai, the contact on Thomas's business card, appeared at his elbow, a short, stocky man with a trim beard and wearing a smart blue suit. "Mr. Tannenbaum, please, you are our guest," he said, scooping up the rubles and tucking them into Bruno's sport coat pocket while the bartender glared at him.

"I was just buying my friends a drink," Bruno slurred.

"Please come with me. Our presentation is about to begin."

Bruno nodded and plucked a bill out of his pocket, tossing it back on the bar. "'S for you," he said to the bartender as Nikolai dragged him toward the hotel's conference rooms.

"You know," Bruno said, waving generally at the conference center around him, with its nondescript corporate art, clean, sterile lines and overall uninspiring construction, "there's nothing Russian about this whole fucking place."

"Oh?"

"Yeah. We could be in the Marriott in Des Moines or Akron."

Nikolai shrugged and guided Bruno to a small side room with a projection screen and several dozen chairs arrayed facing a podium where a dignified fellow with a shock of white hair and an upturned nose was droning on in a proper English accent. The place looked to be set up for a time-share sales pitch. The moderator wore a blue blazer with a Sotheby's monogram on the breast pocket. The seats were half filled and a few people stood at the fringes nursing plates of cheese and pâté and sipping from Riedel glasses.

Bruno kicked a chair over despite Nikolai's best efforts to guide him, and the moderator paused and cleared his throat and heads turned to inspect the commotion. Bruno grinned and wiggled his fingers in a wave.

He broke away from Nikolai and helped himself to a plate of goodies. He studied the labels and had to do a double-take because he saw a bottle of Silver Oak and also a Margaux, both from the nineties. He poured himself a generous glass of the Margaux and tasted. He couldn't verify its authenticity by a single sip, but it certainly seemed like the real deal, as it was excellent. He whistled loudly, again interrupting the moderator as he found a seat in the back row.

The speaker, whose name Bruno would later learn was Nathan Hedges, RSA (Royal Society of Auctioneers), leveled an icy glare at him until he was settled. Bruno sank his teeth into a buttery slice of Edam and half listened as Hedges continued.

"Yes, well . . . again, welcome. We are grateful to all of you for joining us. You must be wondering why we've summoned the finest food and wine writers here to Moscow. I'm sure you've brought a great deal of skepticism to the notion of this city as a great wine destination. After all, there isn't a vineyard of note within a thousand kilometers. But in truth the hubris of the oil boom has led directly to the concentration of some of the most brilliant vintages right here within the city. There are also amazing collections dating back to the Soviet and even Czarist eras. While the modern Moscow sports an array of wine bars and haute cuisine establishments with brilliant lists of wines from across the globe—truly there are no favorites here—it is the collections that provide the pinnacle of the experience of wine in Moscow. Over the next several years, the contents of these collections will be made available at a series of exclusive auctions . . ."

Bruno tried to follow the thread, but the Margaux on top of the vodka made him sleepy. He dozed, then began to snore, but then an elbow in his side jolted him awake. He wasn't sure how long he'd been out, but he now found Parker Thomas sitting next to him while Hedges walked the audience through a series of slides of absurdly priced bottles and rare vintages.

"Hey, Bruno, glad you could make it," Thomas whispered. "What do you think of this whole thing?"

Bruno blinked at the screen and shrugged.

"Hey, is that a '47 Latour?" Parker said, pointing at the screen. After a moment the critic leaned over again. "Say, you didn't come all this way for this little dog-and-pony show, did you? Tell me, what are you really working on?"

"None of your fucking business."

Thomas laughed out loud, drawing another stern look from Hedges. He bumped Bruno's shoulder. "So secretive! I bet it's going to be good, whatever it is. Cheers!"

Thomas raised a glass and sipped. Then he gestured to the plate in his lap.

"You should try the caviar, it's out of sight."

Bruno managed to stay awake for the remainder of the presentation and then he made another trip to the snack table. Despite the rare wines, Bruno opted for the coffee to regain some of his faculties. He wasn't here to give this serious consideration. He merely wanted the free food and accommodations, the invitation merely to secure a home base in Moscow while he investigated the Trevallier. But he did understand that there were people here who might be able to point him in the right direction.

As the crowd thinned, he cornered Nikolai, who gestured to his coffee.

"Not trying the wines?"

"I need to clear my head."

"Of course. So what do you think of our little concept?"

"Elite wine tourism in Moscow? It'll take some pretty amazing bottles on the block to draw people here. Especially in the winter."

"I can assure you, we have such wines in storage. Quite a treasure trove, actually."

"Well," Bruno said, gesturing around the room, "you should get some serious ink. You have some heavy hitters here."

"I hope that's the case. You write for the *Sun-Times*, correct?"

"Um . . . yes."

"And this is something you might cover?"

"Sure."

"I'd wanted to simply pay writers a few thousand euros each, but I understand from my colleague that this is not how things are done. So instead we have to put on this charade and provide free flights and hotel and caviar, theater tickets . . . and we're not even guaranteed a story. How much more efficient would it be if we could just hand over a nice, clean envelope, eh?" Nikolai said, winking.

"How nice indeed," Bruno said, wondering if it was worth the risk of taking the bribe even though he had been fired from the paper. "So these collections . . . how did you acquire them?"

"There've been a series of state auctions. Some of the oligarchs who perhaps strayed too far had their collections impounded by the state, for example."

"What about older collections . . . from the Soviet era?"

"Those exist, too."

Bruno thought of the name on the receipt he'd found in Naumburg.

"Like that fellow, what was his name, Constanoff?"

"Ah, the agricultural minister. Unfortunately, we've never tracked down the Constanoff collection. He was a fan of French wines, I understand. Interesting you should bring him up. How did you learn about him?"

"A Russian pal in Chicago. He owns a few restaurants and likes his vino."

"I see. Well, if you'll excuse me."

While Nikolai tended to other guests, Bruno worked the room a little more to learn what he could, and he was surprised that the name Constanoff was recognized by a few of the writers. Under the guise of agricultural minister in the fifties and sixties, he'd amassed quite a collection (on behalf of the people). The minister had been a survivor, one of the few members of the old guard to have made it through the purges, and was quietly put to pasture when Khrushchev was replaced, given a pension and a small apartment in Moscow and a humble and nondescript dacha on the Oka River. Rumors persisted that Constanoff had secreted away the prizes of his collection in the cottage, though no evidence was found there after his death.

Bruno felt that he was beginning to sober, though it was clear many of his colleagues were quickly slipping the other way. Bruno spotted Nikolai across the room chatting with Hedges and looking at him. He tipped his coffee cup and the stout little man made his way over, pulling Bruno to a quiet corner.

"Mr. Constanoff collected wine for many years on behalf of the state. And as you know, state property was quickly and quietly auctioned off shortly after the collapse in the nineties. My colleague," Nikolai said, tipping his head toward Hedges, "believes that portions, if not all, of the collection were sold during the liquidation of state assets in the voucher period. However, no vouchers or any records have ever been found."

"Who would have known about those auctions?"

"The insiders. The Mafia. The oil barons. Some of the sales weren't exactly open to the public."

"Any speculation on what may have been in the collection?"

Nikolai's eyes brightened. He leaned closer to Bruno. "You wouldn't believe. Every classic you can think of. Imagine a 1928

Bordeaux, or how about a 1900? I even hear tell of some war vintages."

Bruno drew a breath. "How can I learn more?"

Nikolai scanned the room and scratched his beard. "There is one man. A collector's collector. I've always had my suspicions, though he would never talk to me. But to you . . . because of your reputation and because you're an outsider . . . he just may be willing to open up."

"I need to speak to him."

"That would be difficult. He is in Butyrka Prison."

"Do they allow visitors?"

Nikolai chuckled and patted Bruno on the shoulder. "Well, who knows? In the New Russia, anything is possible! You just need the right connections, plenty of cash and a clean envelope. Do a Web search on the name Anatoly Varushkin and you'll find out more than you need to know."

From across the room, Bruno caught sight of Thomas staring at them over the rim of his glass of Margaux.

*　　*　　*

Bruno's hotel room had a view of a bend in the Moskva River. He sat on his bed looking at the illuminated cityscape, waiting for Aleksei to pick up the phone. When Aleksei answered, he asked Bruno to describe the scene and then there was a long silence after Bruno did so. Bruno could picture him sitting in his corner booth, his eyes heavy-lidded and staring through the far wall of the restaurant.

"I wish I could see it," he said, finally.

"I think you'd like what they've done with the place."

"Someday, perhaps, I'll be able to return. So, what do you need, my friend?"

"I need information. I'm still on the trail of that wine."

"Are you getting close?"

"Very close. But I need some logistical help."

"Of course. I still have a few friends there."

"I would like to get into Butyrka Prison."

"Are you looking to contact tuberculosis? Forget it. You're in Moscow. The Third Rome! There are thousands of restaurants. Tens of thousands of beautiful women. Spend your time exploring the City of Golden Domes. In Butyrka there is only death and misery. I left Moscow to stay out of that place."

"I've come a long way. It's my only lead."

Bruno could hear the clink of a glass, and he knew that Aleksei was pouring himself tea from his samovar. He heard him swallow.

"Well," he said finally. "Suit yourself. I know someone. I'll make some calls. Oh, and do you have cash?"

"Some."

"Good. You will need it."

*　　*　　*

Bruno took a cab to Butyrka, or rather two blocks from the prison, because the driver would go no closer, despite the fact that Bruno had bought a lovely circle loaf of *lepeshka* from a street vendor and shared it with the driver, who talked in broken English about how expensive Moscow had become.

When he first rounded the corner and saw the prison, Bruno wasn't sure what was more depressing, the building's clinical red-brick façade or the fact that the surrounding tenements had windows overlooking the yard of the notorious prison.

Following the instructions he had been given, he knocked at a side door and an indifferent guard showed him to a bare room with block walls painted pale green and only a crude bench. He asked for his contact, a fellow named Khramov, and the guard simply turned and left, closing the door behind him.

He returned after an uncomfortably long time and led Bruno down antiseptic halls toward a small office. Khramov rose from behind an ugly metal desk and greeted him in English.

"So how is Aleksei? Does he prosper?" Khramov asked without any warmth in his voice, avoiding Bruno's gaze. He was the consummate bureaucrat, in a cheap white short-sleeved shirt, bad tie and large plastic-framed glasses.

"Aleksei's doing well. He's a restaurateur."

"Of course he is. Is his wife still a miserable cook?"

"She's learning."

Khramov issued a dry laugh. "Fortunately Aleksei knows how to diversify. Well, I understand you have an interest in seeing one of our guests. Mr. Varushkin. But I'm afraid he's in a very, very sensitive sector of our facility. It would be difficult to arrange."

Khramov cleared his throat. There was a long moment of silence and then he offered a wide, greasy smile.

Realizing that this was a signal, Bruno pulled a clean envelope of euros containing the larger part of his remaining balance of Anna's money. He set it on the desk and pushed it toward Khramov. The man tapped it gently, as if measuring the thickness of the stack.

"It will be difficult, but not impossible," he said.

He led Bruno down the narrow corridor of a classic cell block with pale institutional colors and a flat fluorescent lighting that made everyone look sick. Bruno couldn't help but feel a consumptive tickle in his throat, having been warned about tuberculosis so many times in the past few hours that he'd grown paranoid. They came to a secure portal and Khramov unceremoniously dipped his hand into the envelope of cash, pulling out a hundred-euro note and handing it to the guard, who unlocked a sliding iron grate of a door.

The cells here were small, lined with a dozen bunk beds and stuffed with inmates. Khramov noted Bruno's gaze.

"It's a bit tight. Especially during periods of . . . unrest. This block is a holding area. They're mostly awaiting trial or transfer. Sometimes we have to have them sleep in shifts. But we make do."

They passed another guard, and another hundred euros were handed out. They exited the building and crossed a bleak court-yard filled with small wire-fenced runs, like dog kennels. A grim stone building loomed ahead and then they passed another guard station and Khramov handed over another bill.

"Our system is very efficient, no?"

"I'd say the rules are pretty clear."

"This is the notorious second cell block of Butyrka. Where Isaac Babel met his fate. The place where Mayakovsky, Solz-henitsyn and Ginzburg wrote of horrors. You're a literary fellow yourself, or so I understand. Then you probably know how writ-ers like to exaggerate."

He paused at one cell, with three bunks, two of which were empty. A man lay on the third reading a newspaper. He looked over his shoulder with disinterest and went back to reading.

"It's more comfortable than the first cell block. We've painted and tidied things up after the whole Magnitsky affair, but other than that, it hasn't changed much. It was never so bad. Don't believe everything you read."

They wound through corridors, which grew dimmer and more damp, until they reached a door sided by another guard. Khramov peeked in his envelope and then looked at Bruno.

After a moment's hesitation, he gave the man one hundred euros and he opened the door to a bare white room with only a folding table and two chairs. The place was whitewashed, though old stains showed through the paint and an uneven fluorescent light flickered eerily.

A wiry man sat in one of the chairs, his hands cuffed together and his elbows on the table. He smoked, pulling both hands to his face as he dragged on his cigarette. He eyed Bruno and then nodded for him to sit. He had the bearing of a man used to giving orders, even in prison. The guard closed the door with a clang so that Bruno shuddered and then they were alone.

"Your first time in a Russian interrogation room?" the man asked, nodding toward the old stains on the wall. "The KGB did some of its finest work here."

He stood and extended his cuffed hands to shake. Bruno took his hand and bowed, surprised by the strength in the grip. He now remembered the man's face from articles in the *Economist*. He was much smaller than the photos suggested. Still, he bore the confident manner of someone who had run one of Russia's largest natural gas companies. His name was Anatoly Varushkin, and he'd once been the second wealthiest man in Russia.

"Mr. Tannenbaum, what a pleasure," Varushkin said, leaning back and expelling a cloud of smoke.

"I'm humbled you know my name."

"I may appear to you to be a simple convict, but in a past life I had a taste for finer things. After the Soviet collapse, it was possible for a clever man to make a very large amount of money in Russia. I was one of those clever men. I read your novel about the French vineyards. It was very good."

"I'm surprised. And honored."

"We are both wine people. In my day, I was quite a collector.

Maybe too zealous. It seems that I forgot to pay some alcohol tariffs, and then"—he gestured around him—"I found myself in here."

"I thought Butyrka no longer held tax criminals."

"They conveniently adjusted the charges. You may have read that I once had political ambitions. They accused me of being a Fascist and a member of the Nazbol. But not to worry. I'll have my chance to defend myself. I'm awaiting trial, which may happen anytime within the next twenty years or so. Fortunately for me, Russia is a civilized country and we no longer have the death penalty."

"Indeed."

"So, you have a question for me?"

"Yes. I've been told you may know something about the Constanoff Collection."

"Ah, so that's what it is. Of course I know of it. I purchased much of it at a state auction. Like the auction where I acquired my company, it wasn't exactly open to the public."

"So it exists?"

"Very much so. Most of it, anyway. Wine, as you know, was meant to be consumed. 'Drink the good stuff first,' an accountant friend of mine once told me before he took off for the States, coincidentally a short time before I was convicted." Varushkin narrowed his eyes. "Maybe you know of him? In any case, I should have listened to him. Little good all those bottles I saved are doing me now."

"Let me ask you," Bruno said, leaning forward and licking his lips, his heart pounding. It was all coming together for him. The locker in Chicago must have belonged to this man's accountant. He'd never felt closer to his treasure: "Were there any Burgundies in the collection?"

"Burgundies, Chiantis, Bordeaux, Rhônes, Champagne, Barolos. Constanoff was quite a connoisseur."

"War vintages?"

"Of course."

"Are there any left?"

"Those were the glory days, Mr. Tannenbaum," Varushkin said, ignoring Bruno's last question. His eyes were glassy. He stubbed out his cigarette on the table. "I can remember opening bottles that were worth many times more than my father's entire state pension. Every morning I would open five or six bottles . . . mostly just for a taste, and I'd give the rest away to my staff. Can you imagine my yardman bringing home a three-hundred-euro bottle of Cannubi to his family?"

Varushkin smiled without humor. He fished with his cuffed hands in his shirt pocket and pulled out his cigarettes. Bruno helped him retrieve one and lit it for him.

"Thank you."

He dragged deeply.

"So, Mr. Tannenbaum, is there a particular wine you are seeking?"

Bruno studied the closed door for a moment and then decided to trust Varushkin. What other choice did he have? "Yes. A Trevallier. From the war. Do you know of it?"

"Of course. That same accountant of mine first told me the story of that famous lost vintage. About how it had vanished into thin air. He became obsessed with finding it. He could never have afforded it, so he used my interest in wine to further his desire to locate it. In time, I also became obsessed with it. I always wanted what I couldn't have. I was the second wealthiest man in Russia. But it wasn't enough. I also thought I should be president. And that ambition led me to this . . ." He waved his hands at the wall. "The ruling party does not care for well-funded competition."

"So you found the Trevallier?"

Varushkin blinked. "I'm sorry. You see, in my 'stone sack'—that's what we call our little homes here—I don't speak to anyone. Sometimes for days, weeks, on end. If you'd just met me now you might think I'm a rambling, doddering fool. But when I practiced business, I was focused. I preferred one- and two-word answers, because they were the most efficient. Look at me now." He puffed on the cigarette and stared at the ceiling for a moment. "I just babble on and on."

"That's okay. Take your time. I'm not in a hurry," Bruno lied, leaning back and smiling.

"You know, when I was sent to prison, they took everything I had. My company is now in state control again. And who's in charge? Some bureaucrat, a friend of the president. Just as in the Soviet days. It's like nothing changed. My wife, Katya, was quite distressed by how quickly we lost all of our liquidity. You can't imagine how that makes her feel. She's a good deal younger than I am and she married me for my money. I think she respected me once . . . was impressed by the authority I commanded. But in here . . ." Varushkin held up his shackled hands. "Toward the end I took to hiding things from her, lest she spend what I'd put aside for my legal defense—should my case ever come to trial, that is. I should have let her have the wine. My loyal accountant took most of it when he fled west."

Bruno politely cleared his throat.

"Ah, yes, my wine. I still have some hidden away, even from him. And Katya, she never appreciated the finer bottles. Oh, she has taste, but she would never recognize the significance of a . . . say . . . '59 Bordeaux. So I've tucked a few bottles away, just in case I am ever to leave this place, which seems more unlikely by the day. You know, every sensation in the back of your throat, every rattle in your chest . . . it all feels like the onset of consumption. In the business world I based every decision on probabilities. I know the odds now are greater that I die in here than that I eventually get released. Anyway, back to my collection. The best of it is safely tucked away where only I can find it. And the Constanoff bottles are there as well."

"And there's Trevallier among it?"

"You want to know if it exists, don't you? That is your quest?"

Bruno nodded.

"I'm a caged rat. But I'm also still a businessman. I have something you want. So you must give me something in return. That's how it works. Even the guards here understand this. They are more entrepreneurial than our nation's leaders."

"I'm almost out of money."

"Aren't we all? Money is of limited use to me in here, anyway. But still, I should get something, don't you think?"

"That would only be fair."

Varushkin's eyes grew distant again. "Everything I own has been taken. There are the few hidden treasures. The wine, for instance. But now I can only close my eyes and open those bottles in my imagination. But you . . . you could derive actual pleasure from those wines, eh? You could profit handily should I decide to lead you to them."

"That's true. And I'll do whatever I can in exchange."

"You could help me escape?"

Bruno looked alarmed and Varushkin laughed.

"No, I don't think you could. But I've been giving this some thought ever since they told me you wanted to speak to me. You see, my wife is finally divorcing me. She realizes that I'm going to die in here and that I won't share with her the last vestiges of my fortune. It's not out of spite that I'm withholding what remains from her. But it's true that we have grown estranged. That's what happens when you marry for money and the money's gone.

"You wrote in your book that you believe in the transformative power of food. You said, and I quote, that, 'A single meal can change your world, heal your wounds, set you free, if only for a moment.' Do you truly believe this, Mr. Tannenbaum?"

"I do."

"Good. A man who stands by his word. I want you to prove it to me, then. I want to dine with my wife one last time. Here. You cook. You make all the arrangements with whatever resources you have available. I want one final memory . . . one last meal with my wife. Something that they can't take away from me. If you can do this for me . . . transform my circumstances for a moment, help me convince my wife that I love her still and wish her well, then I will give you the answers you seek." Varushkin's gaze had grown distant, but Bruno's heart was racing. The Russian had laid out a challenge for which Bruno had been preparing his entire life. If he failed now, he had only himself to blame. The hair on the back of his neck stood on end.

"Mr. Varushkin," Bruno said, thrusting out his hand, "we have a deal." Varushkin took it, offering an unreadable smile, his grip strong, almost painful. In his mind, Bruno was already planning the menu.

NINETEEN

Losos

The mighty salmon is known for the strength of its flavor and the epic nature of its journey. It is as forgiving as it is difficult to prepare well, which is why it is a staple at mediocre restaurants, corporate luncheons and catered weddings. But locked within the salmon's genes is the greatest story in all of nature. The odyssey of its exile to the open ocean waters and the return journey of a thousand miles upstream to its mountain brook to spawn and then die: this is as bittersweet and lovely a tale as ever spun by any bard, priest or poet. Cook a salmon well, and her sweet song will rise from the table.

—Bruno Tannenbaum, *Twenty Recipes for Love*

Every meal tells a story. When you cook for someone, you are communicating more directly than you can through any other means. You could make love, whisper in ears, taste skin, exchange pleasure, but that is only a moment of transient sensation. They say we are reconstructed at a cellular level every seven

years, and the fiber of our makeup through that cycle is knit
together and sustained by what we consume. What you make
when you cook is taken within the sacred vessel of the body. It is
the most intimate, delicate conversation that can be held. When
you feed someone, your creation becomes a part of her body and
the very fabric of her being. The cells of what you create merge
with her cells for that seven-year journey they make until they
are expunged and replaced.

It was Bruno's charge to create such a conversation between
Varushkin and his estranged Katya. Varushkin was a titan.
Swamped by the Mikhail Khodorkovsky saga, Varushkin's tale
was similar and only slightly less epic. A Western-style dissi-
dent and champion of free-market reforms, he founded a small
investment firm in the early days of economic liberalization and
rose to acquire the country's second-largest natural gas holding,
as well as a number of other privatized resources. When he
started backing the wrong party in regional and then national
elections, he found himself charged with corruption and tax
evasion. Butyrka Prison has been crushing reformers since the
times of the Czars, and in Russia, it seemed, few things had
changed.

Katya, a Ukrainian national with a résumé as a minor
celebrity, had spent time as a television reporter, hosted a short-
lived reality television show about Chechen War veterans who
kickbox for insubstantial cash prizes, and had endorsed a line
of cosmetics and lingerie. She was twenty years younger than
Varushkin and gorgeous. Bruno put the Internet skills he had
learned from lovely Lisette in Beaune to good use by browsing
through Katya's online photos, making his heart patter. There
was something in the cool, feline greenness of her eyes that
made him wonder if he was up to the task of creating a meal

that would leave any sort of impression, let alone convince her of Varushkin's love.

He sat on the edge of his bed composing a shopping list in his journal. He considered building the menu around pan-seared salmon with a brown sugar and balsamic glaze. This was a clear risk in that it was such a common, even pedestrian, choice. But the salmon's story in nature is such a heart-wrenching saga that he believed some of this epic narrative, if prepared correctly, would find its way into the ambient moment of the meal.

He scratched down what else he would need: fresh lemons, several varieties of wild mushrooms, truffles, caviar, good bread, probably asparagus, and then, of course, the perfect wines. It was then that his phone rang, startling him.

He stood and stared at the receiver for a moment before picking it up. But then he softened immediately as he heard the voice on the other end.

"Daddy?"

It was Claire, and before he could consider how she'd tracked him to this hotel, he blurted out, "Claire! Claire-ified butter ball! How are you?"

"I'm okay, Daddy," she said, her voice on the edge of a sob. Something was wrong.

"Oh, gosh. What's the matter? Are you okay?"

"I'm fine, really."

"Your mom, is she okay?" Panic swelled in his chest. He could hear the pain in her voice.

"Mom's fine. She's standing right here next to me, actually."

"Oh?"

"She wanted me to call you and tell you . . ." She sobbed now, unable to finish.

Bruno waited in patient terror.

"Daddy. I wasn't telling the truth. About the money."

Bruno swallowed.

"It wasn't Mom's money. And she had no idea that I'd given it to you."

"Then where did it come from?"

"My college fund."

Bruno gulped.

Her college fund. All those nights watching snot-nosed toddlers for the Mangussens next door. The Goldfarbs' spoiled brats. The Christmas checks and Hanukkah gelt that could have been spent on bicycles, iPods or clothes but that Claire diligently took to the bank instead. He remembered when she came home with Anna one afternoon when she was six or seven, proudly displaying her new balance book. All the dreams Anna ever had for her. All of Claire's dreams. Culinary school. College. Bruno felt his throat closing. He had to force himself to draw breath.

"Bruno?" It was Anna now. He could hear Claire sobbing in the background. "Bruno . . . ?"

"I didn't know, Anna. You have to believe me."

"Well, now you know. What are you going to do about it?" She was trying to sound tough, but underneath he could sense something else. Sadness? Disappointment? Despair?

"I was so close."

"Close to what?"

"I don't know. To finding . . . my story."

"Have you been listening? The money belongs to Claire."

"I know."

"So . . . what are you going to do about it?"

"What should I do?"

"Pack up and come home and bring her whatever's left. That money was her best chance at a future."

"It's still her future. She can have every dime I make off of the book. I'm so close, Anna."

"I've heard it all before, Bruno. I'd like to believe you."

"I can see the end of the story from here. The whole book . . . it's in my head. And the conclusion is right there in front of me, locked in a prison. And only I can let it out the right way. This will be different."

"How much is left?"

"One chapter, maybe two."

"No, I mean how much of Claire's money?"

"A little."

"You know what you need to do," Anna said, resolute.

Bruno stood in front of the window and looked at the lights reflecting on the shimmer and ripple of the water in the bend in the river. The absurdity of it. Claire had saved for her entire life simply to bring him here. For what? He had no book. He had notes and postcards: that was all. He could feel the weight of his delusion pressing down on him. "Did you read the postcards?" he asked after a long pause.

"Yes."

"What do you think?"

"You're a fine writer, Bruno," she said with a sigh, "but postcards aren't a book. You've had quite an adventure. But your adventure should not be subsidized by your daughter."

"Do you believe in me?" Bruno asked, hungry for any sign of hope. Any hint. To let him off the hook. To convince him that he hadn't misled his daughter, that her faith in him was justified.

"No."

The receiver trembled in Bruno's hand. There was silence and static on the phone. Then Claire's voice.

"Daddy? Daddy?"

"Yes, Claire. Claire-ified butter ball."

"I still believe in you, Daddy."

Bruno smiled. Sadly. And the line went dead.

*   *   *

Bruno wept quietly for a time into his pillow. He grew tired, and he wanted to sleep but couldn't. He thought that if he could find slumber he would be able to see a clear course of action in the morning. Maybe he had a book in him after all. Maybe returning home and handing back what remained of Claire's money was an ending he could write about. Maybe the Trevallier was meant to remain a mystery.

But if he did go home, Parker Thomas would eventually find the end of the real story and he'd write the book, and Bruno's role in the whole endeavor would be forgotten. Claire's money would have been wasted. Had he known it was his daughter's and not Anna's, he would not have taken it, but that's what had happened, and now the question before him was to either throw away everything he'd spent so far, or bet the little that remained on a long shot that just might put them all in the black.

He cursed himself. He should have known. How could he allow a sixteen-year-old to finance an expedition to Europe? Why hadn't he confirmed with Anna like any responsible adult would have done? But Bruno knew he had never once in his life acted like an adult. Or like a parent. And thinking of the last ten years made him shudder.

But that was all behind him and the choice that remained before him was either to continue with the delusion and finish the journey and write the book, or to head home and begin to make amends some other way.

He tossed and turned and by two in the morning he was nowhere near sleep, so he went down to the hotel bar. It was closed, so he wandered to the kitchen, which had already been cleaned for the evening. He inspected and admired the cookware and also poked his head in the pantry and walk-in cooler. In the back of the kitchen he heard some noise of conversation, and he found a table of Kazakh men in cooks' whites surrounding a loaf of black bread, some caviar and a bottle of vodka. They invited him to join them and he didn't hesitate.

The caviar reminded him of Anna. He recalled the first time he'd brought some to her when they'd been dating. "You're trying to seduce me, aren't you?" she'd said with a laugh. Of course that was true.

They were sitting at a table on the terrace of her tiny apartment. It was more of a sunken stairwell than an actual terrace, but it had afforded them a glimpse of the sky and the sounds of the city at night: the screech of the El, the wail of a siren in the distance. A bottle of inexpensive but very good Pinot Blanc from Alsace stood on the table between them.

"Am I that transparent?"

"Positively translucent."

She scooped out a tiny spoonful of luminescent globes and smeared it on a toast point. She bit and concentrated on the tiny pops, the little explosions of concentrated sea life spilling onto her tongue.

"So is it working?" he asked.

"Yes," she said, leaning over to kiss him. "But it's not the caviar."

Later, in bed, the two of them tangled in her sheets, her hand was pressed to his chest, and his heart thumped against her palm, almost with fear. "There's nothing to be afraid of," she'd whispered. He wanted that assurance now. He wanted her to tell him that his fear, the sinking feeling that he'd just thrown away everything of value in his life, was unfounded.

Fortunately, the Kazakhs provided distraction. He didn't understand them, but he was familiar with the sorts of conversations kitchen help had around bottles of liquor at two in the morning, and they were soon all laughing and swapping stories. The bread was obviously from the previous morning, and it was just beginning to dry, but it was still excellent slathered with mounds of good butter, and of course the vodka settled Bruno's nerves and returned some of his conviction.

The Kazakhs told more jokes and punctuated them with such infectious laughter that Bruno couldn't help but join in. By the time the bottle was empty they were all fast friends, arms around one another, singing songs in nonsensical words that Bruno could only attempt, though nobody seemed to care. His head was swimming by the time he returned to his room, and before he passed out he remembered vaguely that he had some sort of mental conundrum to sort out in the morning, though not the specifics of it, which was just the sort of numbing bliss he needed.

When he awoke the next day, he had a splitting headache and a stinging conscience. He sat up and took out his slim envelope of cash. Removing the bills, he laid them on the bed and stared at the pile for a long time. His stomach growled and he thought about ordering breakfast before counting, but then bit the bullet and started in on the math. After sifting through the bills in the pockets of his dirty laundry and jacket, he had a grand total of twelve hundred euros and around ninety-five hundred rubles, which was roughly another three hundred bucks. He also had some U.S. cash set aside for the return flight.

It wasn't much, but if he left right now he'd at least have something to return to Claire.

He considered what had been in the envelope Claire had originally given him and compared that to what was before him now and he thought he would retch.

Then inspiration struck. If he left and flew standby on the first available flight, he could be home in two days. It would be a Sunday. Monday he would start going through the newspaper and looking for something useful to do beyond just playing at writer. What other skills did he have? He could cook, that was something. Maybe Aleksei would hire him as a sous chef. He could test the depth of their friendship. Or he could work for his mom. She'd take him in if he begged a little. Even though the image of his father's lifeless body on the floor of the butcher shop still filled him with a lifelong dread of being a shopkeeper chained to some storefront, if it was the right thing to do, he would do it.

If he worked two jobs at slightly above the minimum wage in Illinois, and if he lived the spartan life of a monk, he could replenish most of Claire's savings by the time she started college. He could work all the way through both of the girls' college careers, and then, after twelve or so years, he would have accomplished something more substantial than his entire life's work at the keyboard and notebook. By then, Anna may have even warmed to him and they could reunite for the final, downhill slopes of their lives.

Before long he was packed and whistling the prelude to *Le maçon*, a lesser-known *opéra comique* from Aubert. It was wonderful to have a plan. He was thrilled that he would soon see his girls again.

Bruno tipped the doorman and then paid the cabdriver in

advance, acutely aware now that his dwindling funds belonged to Claire. He continued to whistle as they crossed the Krasno-luzhsky Road Bridge over the Moskva, but then as he took in the skyline he realized that this would be his last trip abroad for quite some time and he experienced a momentary sadness. He also felt bad for Varushkin, who would be sitting in prison hoping for one last decent meal.

As they approached Vnukovo Airport, Bruno grew steadily more morose. He became in turns angry and frustrated with Anna for crushing his dreams and the faith of his daughter. He was also bitter with himself for leading the poor girl to believe that putting her life savings into his project was somehow a good idea.

They stalled in traffic alongside the runway at Vnukovo and Bruno watched planes taxiing. He was in for a full day or more of endless lines and standby flights.

They funneled down to a queue leading to departures. Bruno spotted a family getting out of a cab. A little girl stood next to her father as the driver hoisted their suitcase out of the trunk. The girl looked up at the man and reached out, smiling. The dad lifted her to his shoulders and they disappeared into the crowd.

A thought suddenly struck him.

"My daughter . . . she looks up to me."

"Excuse?" the driver said, looking at him in the rearview.

"She's sixteen years old. A teenager. And she looks up to me. That's strange, isn't it?"

"I no understand."

"Me, either. Teenagers just don't do that. Look . . . I sleep on my mother's couch. I don't have a job. I tend to drink too much. I haven't written anything worthwhile in ten years. She's a smart girl. You might even say wise. But she decided to underwrite my whole career. She made a decision to put everything she had in the world on the line . . . for me. How do you explain that?"

The driver shrugged.

"She still believes. 'I believe in you, Daddy.' She said that, just last night. It's that simple. She believes in me." A hot tear slipped out and trailed down his cheek into his beard. He didn't wipe it.

The cab pulled to the curb.

Bruno tightened the grip on his suitcase.

"So where's the best market in town?"

The driver shrugged.

"You know. Market? Shopping. Where can I buy fresh ingredients?"

"You want airport, no? Is here."

"No. I changed my mind. I want to shop. Fish. Food. Vegetables."

"Okay. Danilovskii Rynok is best. I take you?"

"Drive on, driver!"

The cab peeled away from the curb back into the honking stream of airport traffic.

*   *   *

Bruno smelled the market at the same time he saw the huge building's rumpled dome. He crossed the street and walked into a wall of smells: dill, dried fruit and sweat. This trip was just for planning. He would scout the ingredients and allow them to dictate how he would prepare the salmon. It was far too late in the day to buy fish, but he would investigate the location of the best market for seafood the next morning.

Slipping under the white dome of the Danilovskii was akin to walking into a cathedral for Bruno, and his soul immediately began to levitate. The reverent murmur of voices, the red-coated butchers lifting pork shanks from hooks and slapping them on blocks, the clink of jars of candied fruits, carefully arranged pyramids of fruit, mounded cones of dried spices displaying every earthy hue and aroma: all of this was the language of Bruno's religion.

He inspected the stalls and aisles carefully. As he expected, the fish here was questionable, too pungent and the flesh soft to the touch.

He spotted a round, red-faced woman with the double-buttoned jacket that gave her away as kitchen staff or a culinary student, and he approached her. "Excuse me, but do you cook?" he asked in French and then German. She stared at him, not understanding. "I'm sorry, but I don't speak Russian," he said in English.

"That's fine by me, because I'm American," she replied, beaming at his surprise. "And yes, I do cook," she said, after he repeated his question in English.

"So, I've got an important meal to fix, and I'm in desperate need of a guide."

"Well, you're in luck, because I was just going to pick something up for dinner. Come along!" She offered her arm, which he seized and they squeezed into the crowd.

"Restaurant?" Bruno asked, gesturing to her jacket.

"Catering," she answered, dragging him through a thicket of bodies outside a produce stand and wending into the heart of the market until he was completely lost. "I'm Janice, by the way."

"Bruno," he said.

She led him to her favorite herb vendor, a wizened old woman with papery skin and bright blue eyes wearing a white smock and a babushka. Bruno bought fresh dill that had a sharp, clean tang, and then some ripe ginger that made his eyes water when he cupped it in his hands and pressed his nose to the root.

He scraped the ginger with his fingernail to release more of the aroma and breathed in the sweet bite of it, which was rich and layered as if it were a library of the concentrated, autumnal fragrances. That settled it! He would make a simple honey-ginger glaze for the salmon. Janice suggested visiting the Dorogomilovsky Market the following morning as early as possible, as that was where professional cooks went prior to dawn to haggle over the best fish arriving overnight.

They bought sweet pirozhki from a stand and sat on the market steps. Janice was a young woman with a quick laugh, a self-described "food nerd" and medical school dropout.

"One thing led to another and I somehow wound up stuck in Moscow," she said.

"That's precisely the situation I find myself in now." Bruno explained his predicament of having checked out of his hotel before a change of plans, wondering if she knew of an affordable place to stay.

"You're welcome to stay with me," she offered. "I've got a couch and an Internet connection at your disposal." He allowed himself to imagine a romantic dinner and was only a little disappointed to learn she was happily married to a Russian cook named Dima.

At the market, Janice also bought dill, green onions, cucumbers, turnips and cuts of beef for an *okroshka*, a cold soup based on kvass, a drink of fermented rye bread.

They ate the soup later on the couple's tiny balcony in an old stone building in a middle-class neighborhood and then Bruno used their telephone to make arrangements with Khramov.

Dima was a gregarious collector of Moldovan, Greek and Georgian wines, and they stayed up far too late drinking and talking about the meal Bruno was planning for Varushkin.

"You have luck," Dima said, clinking glasses. "I go to Doro-gomilovsky in morning. I take you." They finished the bottle and Janice was already asleep on the couch, but Dima merely threw her over his shoulder and hauled her off to the bedroom without even breaking her snore. Bruno was asleep in moments, feeling the lingering warmth of Janice's imprint on the couch and sensing Dima tucking a blanket over him.

It was pitch-black when he was shaken awake, and he was still foggy when they reached the market. There was already a fleet of restaurant vans, and a low rumble of haggling, and Bruno worried that they might be too late or that a vendor wouldn't be willing to part with only a small amount of his best fish.

He tasted and sniffed his way through the fishmongers' stalls, reveling in the beauty of the blue and silver creatures lying on their beds of ice, and then the bright colors of the salmon flesh. He finally was able to intercept a delightful steelhead that smelled precisely of pure seawater. He was only a tad reluctant to give up on the symbolism of the salmon, because steelhead don't die after spawning, instead returning to the sea, but maybe that meant that Varushkin might eventually be set free . . . Why not be hopeful? Most of the salmon he encountered were spent and soft despite good flavor. When Bruno pressed the steelhead's flesh with his thumb, it had a buoyancy and character that hint-ed at good texture and mouthfeel. It's always a mistake to rely too heavily on aroma and flavor at the expense of texture when cooking. The ginger glaze would work equally well on the steelhead.

With the fish in hand, he was free to concentrate on the rest of the meal. Free to improvise: he was inspired by the availabil-ity of good oysters at Dorogomilovsky, so he purchased them and eventually decided on a French bisque recipe that he hadn't made in years but would fit the meal perfectly. He gathered more ingredients and then asked around for the best wine shops.

Bruno bought a cooler with wheels and a pull-up handle for twenty-five hundred rubles from one of the vendors for transporting the fish. He filled the cooler with crushed ice and dragged it to an electronics store across from the market that was just opening for the morning, where he bought a disposable cell phone.

He called Khramov to finalize arrangements.

"Kitchen is five hundred. Interrogation room, five more. Table and chair rental, two hundred," Khramov said, as if the price list was in front of him. "One thousand two hundred total. Plus tips for guards. Is okay?"

"Is okay," Bruno said with a gulp, doing the math and realizing he was stretching his budget dangerously thin. "Can you guarantee that Varushkin's ex-wife will be there?"

"No problem. Is already arranged," Khramov said. He explained that she had been making regular visits trying unsuccessfully to extract information on the whereabouts of some of the hidden assets. The fact that Khramov knew all this confirmed Bruno's suspicion that he had listened in on the visit, and he made a mental note to be careful. He didn't want the corrupt prison official to get the jump on him in locating the Trevallier.

TWENTY

Roux

Making a roux is the culinary analog to raising a child. It demands your absolute love and attention. If you allow it to burn or crust over, even slightly, your soup will be flavored with a touch of unwanted bitterness that you may never be able to remove. If made properly, with the utmost care and delicacy, it will become the foundation for something brilliant.

—BRUNO TANNENBAUM, *TWENTY RECIPES FOR LOVE*

Bruno went through the list of ingredients in his head as he crossed the courtyard toward the prison. He was sure he was forgetting something. Once inside, he wouldn't be able to leave again until the meal was over . . . Khramov had made that very clear.

He hugged a sack of groceries and dragged his cooler behind him, which also had his suitcase strapped to the top. An old woman in a gray overcoat with a red headscarf dragged a battered grocery trolley with a squeaking wheel in the other direction, and she eyed his cooler with envy. He winked at her and she seemed startled and then offered a hesitant, toothless grin.

Focus, Tannenbaum, focus! He reviewed the list again: fish, *check,* oysters, *check,* ginger, *check,* caviar, *check.* He'd found a specialty vendor who sold Italian truffles and also truffle oil. He'd found excellent butter and cream, thick-shelled eggs (he had to crack a couple to be sure), parsley, shallots, black bread, brown sugar, clover honey. Four outdoor markets and seven specialty shops later, he now had a working map of the city's Métro system in his head.

Claire's money was basically gone when he discounted the envelope for Khramov, gratuity for the guards and what he needed to fly home. He was officially living without a net. But with a sack of good groceries and a cooler of fresh seafood, he still had at least one good meal ahead of him. It didn't matter if he was cooking or eating . . . he enjoyed both equally. What else did you need in life?

Well, wine, of course.

After a quick call with Nikolai, he learned of a shop just off the subway line where he selected a bottle of white Rhône, which cost him dearly but was necessary, and an Oregon Pinot Noir. It was a risk, to be sure, to go red with seafood. But he thought he could pull it off with just the right amount of glaze on the steelhead and not a touch more. Bruno always dismissed the silly rules and advice for wine and food pairing they had started publishing on back labels. The only rule was harmony, patience and a little love. If the whole world strove for this combination, there would be no trouble, at the table or beyond.

But trouble loomed ahead of him now, with the barbed outer walls and short round crenellated towers of Butyrka rising before him. It was dim and gloomy and smelled of must, rot, cold stone and a trace of raw sewage. How could he make such a place inviting?

A flea market had helped.

Tablecloth, *check*. Candles, *check*. Good china. *Check*.

He was led into the barred holding cell and locked in. He sat on the wooden slab of a bench feeling trapped, the walls pressing in. How could he relieve Varushkin from years of this? How could he make Katya feel comfortable in this prison? Had everything he'd ever written been hyperbole? After all, a writer can say anything with the tap of a few keys or the stroke of a pen. Now he had the chance to back up his words. And it seemed fairly impossible.

One meal. Just make one good meal, old fellow, he told himself.

A guard opened the door, startling him. Khramov stood in the corridor, motioning for Bruno to follow without meeting his eyes. After the guard unlocked the door to the next hallway and slammed it behind them they were alone for a brief stretch and Khramov unceremoniously held out his hand. Bruno handed him the envelope . . . the last of Claire's money, save for a supply for a return flight and some random bills for the guards.

"You can serve in the room where you met Varushkin before," Khramov said. "Katya arrives in three hours." He then pulled his key ring from his belt and unlocked a narrow, stained door, swinging it open to a narrower room. "Here is the kitchen."

Bruno's heart sank.

It was a tight galley with a few rusted pans, a pair of hot plates, a double sink and what appeared to be a toaster oven. There were a few indecipherable cans on a shelf above the sink, and some random, battered implements on the counter.

Bruno refused to enter.

"Something is wrong?"

"No, no . . ."

"Is okay?"

"No, this won't do at all."

"This is what we have."

"I said the prison kitchen."

"This is guard's kitchen. It is the best we can do."

"I need a real kitchen. With a broiler, professional cookware, open flames. Salt and pepper, even." Bruno felt the weight of the impossibility of what he was doing pressing down on him. He'd once done a column on prison kitchens, and those he visited could have been the envy of any restaurant. That's what he'd been expecting. Things were evidently different in Russia. He cursed himself now. Why hadn't he planned a simpler meal?

"There has to be something else."

"There is no place else."

"What about the main prison kitchen? There must be at least one, if not several, that are better equipped than this."

Khramov scratched his chin and thought. "That would be very difficult . . . and expensive," he said.

"How expensive?" Bruno asked, reaching for the inside pocket of his jacket where he'd stashed the money for his return flight.

*   *   *

The second kitchen was perfect. The stainless steel gleamed. Towers of battered but scrubbed pots stood awaiting orders. Implements of every configuration hung from racks. Industrial-sized cans lined the metal shelves like soldiers, labels all facing outward. The head cook was a former member of the Russian Ground Forces, and it was clear he brought military precision to the prison kitchen. Bruno ran his hand along one counter, his heart swelling. For the next few hours, this would be his domain. And he loved it.

Khramov haggled with the cook for quite some time before dividing the last of Bruno's funds down the middle. The cook pocketed the cash and ushered his staff toward the break room, where they removed their hairnets and turned on the television, glaring through a fogged glass window back into the kitchen.

"I will send for you in two and one-half hours," Khramov said, and then was gone.

Bruno couldn't help but whistle while he unpacked his things and arrayed them on the long central counter, composing a sort of still life and timeline of all of the meal's ingredients, arranged in the order he was to work. He mentally sifted through the prep process, deciding what should be shaved, shredded, chopped, pinched and rinsed, and when. From the bottom of his grocery sack he pulled out a white cotton chef's jacket he'd purchased at a restaurant supply stall at the Dorogomilovsky Market, hoping that Varushkin and Katya would appreciate the touch.

*   *   *

At the same moment that Bruno was admiring his *mise en place* and worrying just a little about doing irreparable damage to the meal through some clumsy misstep, Varushkin was in his "stone sack," a tight three-man cell, where he had a small sink, a mirror, a seatless toilet and two mute, shirtless, tubercular cell- mates covered in tattoos of Russian Orthodox religious themes. They lay on their bunks smoking while Varushkin unfolded a clean, ironed white shirt that he'd bartered for from one of the kinder guards.

He'd done his best to make himself presentable through a sink bath, and he wet and combed his hair with his fingers. He felt like a schoolboy on his first date. For a man used to control, this may have felt like a failure of his confidence, but since his confinement he had so rarely felt anything at all that this youthful confusion was a sort of tonic. Varushkin generally dismissed writers as opportunists and self-proclaimed experts. But he had actually read the man's novel, and for a moment after finishing it he had wanted to sell everything and move to Burgundy and take a seasonal job as a vineyard laborer. Tannenbaum could weave a spell. Maybe he could transform the prison enough to bring husband and wife together one last time for a civil meal. But then, Varushkin knew his Katya well, and he expected that she would stand for none of it. She would likely leave in a huff as soon as she learned that her husband had no intention of divulging information on the last of his fortune. And then the deal would be off and the writer would have to poke around in other dark corners if he was ever to find this wine he was seeking.

"Katya, my dear Katya, look at me fumbling like a love-struck youth." Varushkin buttoned his clean white shirt and studied his pale face in the mirror.

And at that same moment Katya Varushkin Ivanovich was in the backseat of a limousine with the appropriately named Igor, her hulk of a driver and all-around errands man, behind the wheel. She stared out the window at the traffic, wishing that she could just scrape together enough money to live comfortably abroad and leave this wretched, crowded, expensive, dirty city. One hundred million rubles would do. Well, perhaps two hundred. She had her designs set on Milan or maybe Florence, though the latter was somewhat touristy and provincial despite the better weather.

Katya resented Varushkin for a number of reasons, but chiefly the fact that he'd always treated her like a trophy. When they first met, she'd so hoped that he was attracted to her not for her youth and beauty, but out of respect for her accomplishments. From humble roots as the daughter of a low-level party functionary, she'd staked out a career as a journalist. She'd liked to think that they were a power couple . . . equals. But it was soon clear that she was considered mere decoration. The fact that he'd always assumed she married him for the money was an insult. She'd loved him at one time, but she doubted he'd ever loved her, despite pretending to for so long. And for that crime, and for robbing her of her most productive career years, and forever associating her name and reputation with his ego and overreach, forever taking from her what remained of her independence, she was determined to extract a fee, a pound of flesh from her former husband, a sting that he would feel, even in prison, to know that she'd escaped and carried on and was living happily without him. "I want to spend no more than twenty minutes in that stinking cesspool," she said to Igor. He cast his steel-gray eyes into the mirror in acknowledgment and nodded.

In the prison kitchen Bruno was making one more round of the ingredients, sniffing the dill, petting the truffles. Ah, the truffles! "Children of the Earth," Cicero had called them.

The steelhead still lay on its bed of crushed ice, its flesh taut and firm under his thumb. The oysters smelled like the sea so many thousands of miles away. It was a risk to bring that sea, in the form of a meal, this many miles inland. But like the journey that the steelhead takes, it would be a transformative experience for the unhappy and beleaguered couple, or so Bruno hoped.

He scanned his ingredients once more and his stomach suddenly dropped.

He gulped.

He'd forgotten something.

Bruno believed that there were certain select recipes that required the delicate presence of a good fresh olive oil. He simply couldn't work without it. How could he be so forgetful? It was usually the first thing he purchased. Even when he knew he'd be cooking in a well-stocked kitchen, he would purchase a small bottle of quality oil just to ensure its freshness.

He did another check of his bag, cooler and the ingredients he'd laid on the counter to be sure, and then he began systematically tearing through the kitchen. He inspected the tall stainless-steel cupboards and the walk-in cooler. There were various cans of industrial vegetable oil, but nothing even remotely close to what he sought.

He ran to the break room where the kitchen staff lounged.

"Olive oil!" he said. "Do you have some?"

They shrugged and looked at each other. Bruno went to the head cook.

"Speak English? Do you know olive oil?"

The man said something in Russian and waved him off, as he was blocking his view of the small picture-tube television.

"Yes," a skinny, toothy young man said, smiling awkwardly. He was standing in the corner away from the others, leaning against the wall. Bruno rushed up to him.

"You speak English?"

"Yes," the kid said.

"Can you show me to the olive oil? Please?"

The kid led him back into the kitchen toward a series of cabinets in the corner. He dragged a stepladder over to it and climbed to retrieve a small bottle from the back of a top shelf.

"Is good?" the kid asked as he came down.

Bruno hugged him and nearly wept.

"What is your name?" Bruno asked.

"Vasili," the kid said, tapping his chest and smiling.

Bruno grasped the youth's shoulders and held him at arm's length. *Vasili.* It was a good name. A fortuitous name. A Czar's name. Bruno knew its Greek origins. It meant "basil." "Vasili, eh? Well, we've got olive oil. If we had pine nuts we could make a decent pesto, no?"

Vasili looked at him and blinked, not getting the joke.

"Well, Vasili, can you cook?"

Vasili nodded vigorously.

"You want to help?"

He nodded again.

"Let's get to work, then, shall we?"

* * *

Varushkin sat on the edge of his bed, waiting. He closed his eyes and leaned his head back, breathing in a rhythm. He tried to remember Katya's smell. Spending so much time locked in a cell had sharpened this sense. He knew by scent which of the guards had passed outside his cell. He could smell the mud on their boots and know if it was raining outside. Sometimes he smelled blood.

When Katya came for a visit, he smelled her. Beneath the must of her fur coat and the perfume and antiperspirant. Under the soap and the jasmine bath oil, he could smell the real Katya. It was the rich, intoxicating, animal odor of her.

In his mind he tried to trace that scent. It conjured the shape of her. She was taller than him. Her body, the curves and slopes of it . . . the only word he could think of to describe it was lush.

He wondered if things could have been different. What if they were some aging middle-class couple, their children grown, spending their summers in a dacha on the river? Could she have

been happy? With what he had hidden away, in bonds, international bank accounts, cash deposits . . . and wine . . . they could
live comfortably, albeit humbly, for the rest of their lives. Maybe
somewhere in northern Italy. The south of France. Mexico.
Would she agree to this? If he could somehow escape or arrange
a release and flee the country? It had been done before.

Could that charlatan writer weave some kind of magic and
convince Katya that Varushkin loved her? That he'd always
loved her? Or was he deluding himself? The businessman in
him, the one used to calculating risks and odds, would have
judged this deal he had made with the writer as a romantic folly.
There was no practical value in one meal. If he were ever to
escape, or, by the whim of those in power, be released, then he
would want his wine. It was worth a considerable sum. He sat
motionless on the edge of his bunk with his eyes closed in a deep
state of contemplation.

At the other end of the cell block, Bruno began to work. Vasili was scrubbed and busily grating the ginger (work slow, make
a fine paste, remove all liquid and fibers), while Bruno melted a
touch of brown sugar with honey.

He'd already started a fish stock after he'd removed the best
cuts from the steelhead, and in another pot he was stirring a roux
he'd begun with shallots and butter once he had confidence in
the intensity of the flame. He was careful. To brown the shallots now would destroy the dish. He sifted in flour a touch at
a time, eyeing the color. It could swing from tan to the color of
dark mud in an instant, and the visual effect of the lovely golden
oyster bisque would be lost. As the aroma of the bubbling stock
began to rise in the steam, his belly rumbled and he suddenly
wished that he was preparing this meal for, or rather with, Anna
and the girls instead of for two strangers who no longer loved

one another. Bruno wondered at his chances of creating some warmth between this Katya and her estranged husband. Hadn't he at least managed this much with Anna, restoring civility around the table?

Bruno's mind drifted from Anna to Sylvie. He realized that he might be missing the mark entirely. Maybe the key to his happiness didn't lie behind him in Chicago, but rather ahead in Beaune.

He wished he could stare at Sylvie as she blew smoke rings after they made love. He wanted to rinse barrels at her side until his back ached and his fingers were pruned. He wondered how long she might be willing to tolerate him. He thought of the angled bones of her hips, the faint blue vein he could see deep within the flesh of her left breast as she lay back and it flattened against her rib cage, the muscled knots of her forearm, the surprisingly soft touch of her cool, callused hands. She may be brusque and aloof, but this was all on the surface. Bruno found her gorgeous, no less so for making some of the greatest wines on the planet.

Bruno felt a jab at his side as Vasili elbowed him and pointed at the roux. "Make sure not burn," he said.

"Good call!" Bruno replied, stirring the whisk.

It was time to slowly add the stock to the roux, and as he did so he instructed Vasili to shuck the oysters and separate them from their liquor with a strainer.

He would serve the bisque first, then the salmon with white asparagus and paper-thin slices of truffle added at the very last moment so that the warmth of the fish would release their aromatics, and then also a crust of *lepeshka* brushed with the olive oil, garlic and a touch of the ginger and toasted for only a moment over an open flame before being topped with the red caviar.

Bruno was soaring now, in that magic kitchen dance, when everything he needed was a single step and arm's reach away, as a mound of pans accumulated while dishes slowly and steadily coalesced and the shape of a meal began to form like a shimmering, effervescent sculpture made out of something delicate and temporary.

He instructed Vasili to carefully snip the parsley with kitchen shears, leaving a V shape at the bottom of each leaf with no remaining stems. He whisked egg yolks for the bisque into froth the consistency of golden sea foam. He added the ginger to the glaze and turned up the heat until the bubbles just started to rise in the melted sugar, then set it aside to cool and thicken. He laid the lovely steelhead steaks on waxed paper and brushed them with the olive oil. They lay glistening like thick slices of apricot, radiant in their warm color despite the unflattering lights overhead. He checked the broiler flame and readied the truffle oil to drizzle as a final touch onto the steelhead as soon as it finished cooking. It was all in balance, ready for its strange and magical transformation caused by the precise application of heat.

Cooking, Bruno thought, *is the greatest artistic achievement.* The original biped back in the murky depths of the Pleistocene who first laid her (for Bruno was sure it had been a woman) skinned slab of gazelle on a dark rock next to the open flame and reveled in how it bubbled and oozed and life returned, the smells drifting across the savanna in a siren call to the council fire—she was the first true pioneer, mage, priestess and artist of our species. It was cooking that increased our proteins, in turn increasing the size of our brain and granting us the luxury to dream, imagine and create rather than dig roots in the cold hard ground until our fingernails bled, or spend moonlit night after moonlit night tracking the herd. Around that fire, where the members of the clan lingered in the aroma of the first meal, was where our first true sacred act as a species had occurred: the telling of a story. And that moment, that first primordial dinner conversation, was perfected only a brief moment later in geological time, when someone in the clan had buried bunches of grapes wrapped in animal skins in the ground in an attempt at preservation, and dug them up weeks or maybe months later to find that the juice had changed. The addition of patience, the luxury of time, had transformed yet again, and those grapes had become something to revere, something to complete that campfire circle . . . to loosen the tongue and lift worries and give strength, comfort. Community.

Vasili touched Bruno's elbow, rousing him from yet another reverie. Bruno scanned the final preparation and then turned to his *chef de partie*: "Time to cook!" he said. He brushed the asparagus with butter and dill, the steelhead with glaze and cracked pepper, sliding them all under the open flame of the broiler, an aria from Puccini suddenly bursting from his heart. *Who am I? I am a poet,* he sang in Italian, *and how do I live? I live in carefree poverty. I live songs and squander rhymes like a lord.* Vasili was likewise inspired and he sang something in Russian. They traded phrases as the flames worked their transformative spell.

TWENTY-ONE

Caviar

Red caviar may be the poorer cousin, the humble substitute for the pearly black onyx of the real thing. But her color is more brilliant, her flavor more overt and the epic odyssey of her species more inspiring. A circle of red caviar, gleaming little bulbs on a slab of bread torn freshly from the loaf and toasted only momentarily. This, like the three simple words "I love you," has a power and humility that is difficult to describe. So forgive me for trying.

—Bruno Tannenbaum, *Twenty Recipes for Love*

Varushkin shuffled down the corridor, guards on either side. He tried to stand erect, proud. But the chains binding his hands to his feet sapped his dignity. The cold stone floor pulled his spine to a curve and his chin toward the earth. What had he become?

He didn't want Katya to pity him. He wanted her to know that he had once loved her, and that perhaps a part of him still did. And that he would never break. He would die in here clinging stubbornly to what he was, not what they were trying to bend him into. This arrangement with the writer . . . it was Varushkin's last business deal. It was the final application of the power he once held. He had helped to transform an entire country out of the dark ages of an idealistic but ultimately corrupt and untenable idea. He had transformed a company employing seventy thousand workers from a clumsy, bankrupt state enterprise to a gleaming example of efficiency. And he had then stepped too far in an attempt to transform his country's politics. But now he had painfully learned that the black souls of politicians were beyond reform and it had been futile for him to try.

Now, here, he could only attempt to transform a little cell in the darkest hole in Moscow. And in the process, endeavor to warm Katya's frozen heart only a little. If anything the writer had claimed in either of his books held a shred of truth, then the ice would begin to melt. And if not . . . well, then he had exposed another great lie.

They reached the door to the interrogation room. A guard unlocked it and let them in, clicking on the buzzing fluorescent lights. There was a wobbly metal table with a stained wooden top and two folding chairs. The stains on the wall seemed darker and more ominous than the last time. He wondered if this was all some cruel trick of his political enemies and he was in for interrogation instead of a reunion with his wife and a fine meal.

He sat down at the table and extended his cuffed hands to the guard.

"Would you mind?"

The guard looked at Khramov, who nodded, so he reluctantly twisted a key into the cuffs, which then dropped to the floor in a pile on top of the chain that affixed them to his leg shackles. Even this small touch of freedom was something to savor. He closed his eyes and leaned his head back, inhaling deeply.

* * *

At the same moment, Katya was working her way into the guts of the grim institution, twisting down long, antiseptic hallways, hearing only the sound of the red-lacquered soles of her shiny black knee-high Christian Louboutin boots and the soft tapping of her guard's shabby loafers. They mustn't pay these men anything, she thought, noticing that she could see his socks through the holes in his shoes.

There was a distant iron clang and some echoing, angry voices. She'd wanted to bring Igor, but it was clear the guards wanted nothing to do with that grim-faced hulk. Katya had quipped that as a former soldier, he was fully house-trained and wouldn't bite without her permission. She laughed at her own joke, but nobody else did. Igor never so much as smiled, and she wondered what went on behind those opaque, steel-gray eyes. He took a seat at the reception and inspected a week-old newspaper.

Katya caught a sound echoing in the distance that was like music. She thought she recognized the tune. "Is that opera?" she asked the guard. He shrugged and then paused before a plain door, one of many, set in the narrow hallway, fumbling with his keys. She smiled warmly and folded a ten-thousand-ruble note into his shirt pocket, saying, "For you . . . and your family." He nodded at her blankly.

She drew a deep breath and clenched her fingers into fists, bracing herself. She tried to determine what she wanted out of this meeting. She'd been summoned abruptly. She had been in the midst of packing for a trip to Saint Petersburg when some low-level prison administrator had phoned to tell her that her husband required her presence immediately. *Required?* She'd hated how her body responded, pulse quickening, face flushing.

It had once thrilled her . . . that ambiguous mix of feelings she had around Anatoly Varushkin. Now it made her feel like a confused girl. What was once mysterious about him had morphed into manipulation, what was authoritative and wise now seemed mostly old and stubborn. Inspirational had become egomaniacal.

What she wanted now was a final ultimatum. Either he would make some grand gesture, release some of the hidden wealth she knew he had squirreled away, enough to allow her to live comfortably for the rest of her life, or she would hunt down what she could herself and liquidate it immediately, using whatever she found to finance the best attorney she could acquire, and Anatoly would never see her again. And she would do this with a clean conscience. It wasn't wealth that she was after . . . it was autonomy.

Against her will, her pulse began to pound and her scalp warmed. Her breath drew short and she felt momentarily unsteady on her feet. Why was this so hard? She placed her hand on the guard's arm to steady herself as he opened the door. Then she smiled broadly even as her heart sank to see her husband in a clean but cheap shirt sitting at the little table in a bland, empty room like some bad schoolboy sent into isolation for punishment.

*　　*　　*

Varushkin stood. His chest warmed as it always did at the shock of seeing Katya. He wasn't sure if it was emotion or just surprise because she was so out of place against the drab landscape of the prison. She wore tall, shiny black boots that reached to just below her knees, and a black trench coat short enough to expose centimeters of exquisitely tanned knee and thigh. Her hair was pulled back in a tight, protective ponytail. He was disappointed because he preferred it falling loose, brown and glossy around her shoulders. Only her bright red lips and the red-lacquered soles of her boots provided any relief to the serious tones of the ensemble. This must be her prison adventure outfit.

She smiled upon seeing him and he rose to meet her. She kissed the air on either side of his face, their cheeks touching slightly, a strange electric tingle in the sensation worrying him that he was becoming sentimental.

He gestured to the seat across the table.

"I'm glad you came."

"Thank you. I was surprised. Is something wrong?"

"No, things are . . . as fine as can be expected."

"Really?" She glanced around the room, frowning. She sat down reluctantly, not removing her coat. He could tell that she was angry already. In the past, this would have aroused him ever so slightly. Disarming her was an unpredictable game, one he enjoyed.

"Kind of you to join me."

"I'm not here out of kindness. I actually don't know why I'm here."

"I wanted to see you. To join me for dinner."

"I'm in no mood for joking. Anatoly, I am going to be frank. And I am not going to beg. I know you have the power, and the remaining means, to either leave me destitute or provide for my comfort. I can't spend my life waiting."

"I suppose not. But there is only so much I can do from in here. Outside, everyone has abandoned me. My friends have renounced me. Even my accountant fled to America and disappeared . . . with a handsome commission and not a few bottles of my wine, no doubt. Only you, my dear wife, have remained loyal."

"And what reward is there for my loyalty? I'm flirting with poverty."

"I can see that," he said, tipping his head to look at her boots under the table.

"I know you have a little something hidden away. An account in Basel. An apartment building in Paris. Something."

Outside, the sound of opera drew closer. Varushkin was enjoying the game. But he was also famished.

"Let's save this talk for after dinner."

"Don't be absurd. I'm not eating with you. Not here."

"I assure you it won't be prison food."

"I've no patience for your games."

"Once you leave through that door, I expect that I will never see you again. Isn't that true?"

Katya didn't respond. She glanced to her lap guiltily. She looked up at him with a momentary flicker of defiant fire in her eyes, and Varushkin knew that it was true. She would leave him . . . whether or not he gave her what she wanted. He pressed his hand gently against his chest as if to dampen the pain.

"So humor me this last time. Please."

Katya stiffened. There was a commotion outside the door. A clank. A laugh. "Room service!" someone called in English.

"Ah, and here's the chef," Varushkin said.

*   *   *

Bruno pushed the squeaking, rickety cart into the room past the guard. The place was more dismal than before. The stained white walls were oppressive, the sickly fluorescent lights making Varushkin look even more shriveled and tubercular.

But the woman, Katya, Bruno presumed, seemed unaffected by her mean surroundings. He caught his breath as she glanced at him, her perfectly almond-shaped eyes lined in dark pencil, her brow in a furrow, her lacquered lips pursed with skepticism.

He caught a glimpse of thigh where her short trench coat ended and before her tall boots began. She shone, and it was like stumbling across a jewel in the gutter.

"My wife, Katya," Varushkin said.

Bruno extended his hand and bowed with ceremony. Katya gently placed her fingers on his and he brushed them with his beard. "Delighted. Bruno Tannenbaum, at your service," he breathed against her hand.

"Of course, I know who you are," she said, and he could see that she was surprised as she glanced from Bruno to Varushkin. She cracked an unreadable smile. Bruno was baffled, and also pleased, that his dubious celebrity seemed to even penetrate to this darkness.

Then he burst into action. He snapped his fingers and Vasili unfolded a white tablecloth, shaking it out and letting it drift down on the table and then smoothing it. When the table rocked, he pulled a stick of chewing gum out of his pocket and knelt to prop it under one leg. He set out two candles and lit them.

"The lights," Bruno said to the guard, who ignored him. "The lights, *pozhaluysta*," Bruno said, and the guard then shook his head. Vasili put his hands on his hips and said something in Russian, and finally the guard complied and the lights were switched off, leaving the couple isolated by the candle flicker. Katya's shoulders seemed to ease immediately. The room was now filling with aromas, and Varushkin inhaled and smiled.

Bruno pushed the cart to the corner. From the bottom shelf, he lifted a sickly rubber plant, which he stood against one wall to break the monotony. He then switched on a small transistor radio he'd found in the kitchen, and the room filled with crackling Prokofiev, Kutusov bellowing the aria from *War and Peace*, his voice grandiose and haunting.

Bruno set two glasses before his guests. They were, of course, his guests now that he had taken over the room. This little cell was his. He had joined them. What he had made would soon sustain them. And, if he was successful, transform them.

"May I pour the wine?"

Varushkin nodded.

Bruno popped the cork with the silver eagle corkscrew that he had had since the beginning of the quest. He felt kind of attached to it now, even though he still had no idea what the inscription said. He made a note to ask Vasili about it later. He showed Varushkin the label of the bottle.

"Chateau de Beaucastel Chateauneuf-du-Pape Blanc Vieilles Vignes," Bruno said with a slight bow and a smile. Varushkin sniffed and contemplated. He furrowed his brow. He sniffed again and tried to suppress a smile. He sniffed a third time, and then sipped. He slowly lowered the glass from his lips. His eyes glistened. "It's quite good," he said, with emotion in his voice.

"Madame?" Bruno asked.

"Please."

He poured and she drank and smiled, looking now at her husband as if surprised by the effect the wine had had on him.

"Delightful," Varushkin said, recovering. "I'm excited to see what you will serve with it."

"Ah," Bruno said, snapping his fingers. Vasili uncovered the bowls of oyster bisque with snipped parsley arranged in a nautilus pattern, setting the bowls down gently. Bruno presented the torn bread, toasted golden, a careful dab of salmon roe caviar glistening like a sunset captured in tiny shining orbs that reflected the candlelight and seemed to illuminate the whole room. Bruno stepped back into the shadows, smiling and waiting patiently.

Katya removed her coat, deciding she was going to stay and humor her husband. The sparkle in his eyes, the precursors to tears that he had exhibited when tasting the Chateauneuf . . . that emotion was so unlike him that she had to wonder if he had learned he was dying. Or maybe they had finally broken him. He was too stubborn to have changed any other way. The stone room was still cool on her bare shoulders, so she took a sizable gulp from her wineglass to warm herself, taking a whiff of the bisque and inhaling the rich, milky cream of it, beneath which was the clean smell of the ocean. Her stomach growled audibly and Varushkin laughed.

"Will you be joining me after all?" he asked.

"I could never resist you, could I?" she said with a sigh.

As she ate she was aware of two things: the circumstances and surroundings disappearing, and also her estranged husband's careful attention. He seemed to search for some sort of reaction. She ate quickly and with little self-control, mainly due to nerves from being in the prison and also because the meal was excellent and she couldn't wait to find out what was next.

The chef served broiled asparagus with cracked pepper and a small slice of prosciutto. He poured more wine. Katya kept glancing at the American, who emerged from the shadows to attend to her every need, removing plates, brushing crumbs, arranging silverware, filling her glass, and she began to regard him as something of a sorcerer, more so after every bite. She could tell as she spoke to her husband that the American understood no Russian.

"Where did you find him?" she asked.

"He found me."

"That's quite interesting."

"We share . . . a common interest."

Katya smiled. She grew light-headed from the wine but didn't care. She stared at Anatoly now and squinted, trying to see the man that she had once found dashing. She knew when they'd first met that his age meant he would decline in desirability far more rapidly than she, even despite the societal double standard that accelerated that process for women. And she always told herself that she would look for other things to love about him. She was still searching, and she doubted that she could find them in here.

After the asparagus, the American laid plates of lovely pale pink fish before them, a cross pattern of glaze seared to the top, and paper-thin slices of fresh truffle arranged along one edge.

There was the pop of a cork in the shadows, and then glasses were set before them and Bruno presented the label of the new wine to Varushkin.

"Ah, a Pinot Noir," he said in English. "With salmon, eh? Something of a risk." There was a touch of condescension and skepticism in his voice that she recognized, a trait of his that had always annoyed her. He liked to flaunt his expertise, as if anything that didn't conform to his worldview should be called into question.

"It's actually steelhead, and I'd be happy to pour more of the Chateauneuf instead, which should also pair nicely."

"I'd love some Pinot," Katya said, thrusting her glass to Bruno and smiling at him, feeling her husband's eyes on her. "You haven't led us astray yet."

Bruno filled her glass and then Varushkin also nodded for some. In the silence that followed, Varushkin concentrated on his meal, taking a bite and a sip and a bite and a sip. The fish was stunning, and Katya reveled in the way, after breaking through the glazed, seared crust, it melted on her tongue almost like a salty seawater crème brûlée.

"Bruno," Varushkin said finally. "In my opinion, matching

this lovely fish with such a rich Pinot Noir is quite a risk, eh? A risk, and in this case, a triumph." He leaned back in his chair and raised his glass. "Katya here will tell you that I need to stop being such a pompous ass."

This admission surprised her. Was prison turning Anatoly into a different man?

"Pour yourself a glass, chef," Anatoly ordered. "To our chef," he said, clinking glasses with Bruno and Katya, and they drank. She thought the wine was quite good, though she still preferred Burgundies. She'd become quite a connoisseur in her own right, and it frustrated her that Anatoly never acknowledged this.

As they finished the fish, Bruno disappeared to the kitchen. They were both full and still eating for flavor rather than sustenance. Both of them quiet and contemplative.

Katya caught herself staring at her husband, or rather through him.

"What do you see?" he asked.

"I see the man I used to love."

"Used to love?"

"I believe love requires trust. But there were the other women, for example. You just assumed that I would take you back."

"I regret that. And I was wrong. You can at least trust me now, in here. The Russian state guarantees my fidelity."

Katya smiled. She took a cigarette out of her purse. She handed a lighter to Varushkin and he clicked the flame, leaning toward her.

"You haven't changed," he said as smoke curled out of her nose.

"That's not true. Besides, I'd like to return to the subject of trust. If you loved me, wouldn't you trust me with some of what remains of your fortune?"

"Let me ask you this. If I gave you what I have left, would you stay with me? Would you wait here in Moscow for me? Truthfully?"

Katya didn't answer. She leaned back, her elbow propped in one hand, holding her smoldering cigarette by her ear.

Bruno reentered with two cups of espresso. He seemed pleased that both of their plates were empty.

"Well, Mr. Tannenbaum," Varushkin said, taking a cigarette out of Katya's pack and lighting one for himself, "you've made us a splendid meal." He kissed his fingers. "How did you find dinner, my dear?"

"Astonishing."

"I wanted this evening to be memorable."

"How could I ever forget my first meal in prison?"

Bruno, who watched the exchange without understanding a word of it, saw Katya beam at her husband with a radiant smile and a sparkle in her eyes. He was a touch envious.

*　　*　　*

Bruno left them in privacy for their coffee and waited in the hall, smoking with the guard and Vasili. The guard, whose name was Evgeny, was having difficulties with his wife. Because of the ever-climbing rents, they'd recently been forced to move into a flat with his parents. Living in one room with his wife and daughter and sharing a kitchen and bath with the retirees had frayed her nerves. And he feared that she now looked at him as a failure.

Through Vasili's translation, Bruno recommended that he send the old couple and the child out to the park, or perhaps the Obraztsov Puppet Theater and ice cream, and then prepare a late afternoon meal just for the two of them. While Vasili was excited about the glazed salmon, Evgeny said his wife's favorite dish was stroganoff, so Bruno suggested a small cheese course, *boef bourguignon,* a salad with pears and black walnuts, and the cheapest bottle of Volnay he could find.

"I've never cooked a thing for her before," Evgeny said.

"All the better," Bruno replied.

The door opened and Katya emerged, her eyes smoldering, tying the belt of her short trench coat. She was about to storm past when she paused by Bruno, leaned close and straightened his collar. She smelled like cigarette smoke and expensive perfume.

"The meal was extraordinary," she said, in almost a purr that made Bruno's knees wobbly.

"It was a pleasure serving you."

"Hmm. A pleasure." She smiled, a twinkle in her eye, and then she left, with Evgeny at her elbow. He watched her walk the entire length of the hall and disappear around the corner.

The guards went in to fetch Varushkin, and he emerged in shackles with one guard on either side. He looked small and weak again. He shuffled up to Bruno, his eyes vacant.

Bruno's stomach had risen to just below the bottom of his throat. He was dizzy. Here was the moment. The instant that could define the rest of his life. He had put his trust in this wasted and shrunken soul. Was Varushkin still even sane after years of confinement and isolation? Had everything that Bruno hoped for—for his career, for his daughter's future—really come down to this instant? Varushkin was pale, with a greenish cast, in the fluorescent light.

"That was brilliant, Mr. Tannenbaum," Varushkin said, the words forced.

"Thank you."

"I've caused my wife an enormous amount of grief over the years. That's why I wanted your help to convince her that I still love her."

"So, were we successful?"

"No," Varushkin said, and Bruno clenched his fist to keep it from trembling. "But through no fault of yours. The meal was a triumph. In truth, I don't love Katya anymore. I'm not sure I ever did."

"So where does that leave me?"

"Oh, don't worry, Mr. Tannenbaum. You've convinced me of the transformative power of food. To restore love, a meal, a glass of wine, must be given with all the heart. And love must still exist in the hearts of the participants. But between strangers, the most we can hope for through the breaking of bread is to create a space for civility and discourse. Perhaps Katya and I finally know one another for the first time."

One of the guards coughed. Bruno fidgeted.

"I must thank you," Varushkin continued. "I had, you know, a spectacular collection once."

"Had?"

"Some may have considered it obscene . . . the amount I spent on wine. It was worth a substantial fortune."

"Was?"

"My accountant made off with a good deal of what was left after the other vultures had their share. The state repossessed whatever Katya didn't drink."

"It's all gone?"

"Why, no. There's some left."

"The Trevallier?"

"We all have our oases, don't we? Those places we run to for comfort when the world spins too quickly and the heavens begin to collapse. For me, it was a little café below street level. Good meals. Intelligent friends. An impressive cellar of just the right temperature. It was there that I stored my favorite wartime vintages. Those Burgundies were a small obsession buried within a larger compulsion of mine."

"The café?"

"I know. There are thousands in Moscow, no? But the description I've given so far . . . this should be enough. With a little effort, and a few weeks' time, you'll be able to find it, I'm sure. A resourceful writer like yourself?"

"I don't have a few weeks."

"It's funny. All I have is time. But for the rest of the world, it's such a precious commodity. It's interesting that you've had the answer in your hand the whole time. That puzzled me. I almost thought you were toying with me."

"What do you mean?"

"It's all so strange."

"An address?" Bruno said in a harsh whisper as Varushkin was about to shuffle away, a guard tugging at his arm.

"Oh, of course," he said, reaching for Bruno's hand with both of his, clasping it, chains rattling. He palmed a square of paper into Bruno's hand and pressed his cheek close to one side of Bruno's face and then the other in the traditional Russian kiss, whispering as he did so, "I've written down the address and some instructions for the sommelier. He'll allow you into my vault when he sees my handwriting. You'll find your answer there."

The guards tugged him away and he laughed. Bruno thought that the man's mental state had visibly deteriorated in the two days he'd known him.

"You're suddenly in possession of a small fortune, Mr. Tannenbaum. How does it feel?"

"I don't know," Bruno said, slipping the paper carefully into his hip pocket.

"Neither do I," he called as he disappeared around the corner.

Bruno was tempted now to rush from the prison. As Khramov returned to lead him out, he embraced Vasili and promised to write him letters of recommendation for a kitchen job with any of the chefs he knew in Europe. As he left the prison he wanted to skip, which somehow didn't seem appropriate. So instead he surprised himself by whistling the pop song that had been on Anna's kitchen radio the last time he cooked with his daughters.

TWENTY-TWO

A Single Glass

Wine is meant to be a humble companion to food. Yet there are times and wines that call for a single, solitary glass, due to the greatness of the vintage or extremity of the circumstances.

—Bruno Tannenbaum, *Twenty Recipes for Love*

The sun had slipped low behind the neighboring tenements when Bruno exited the outer gate to an empty street and the smell of sewage. As soon as he turned a corner and was out of the sight of the guard towers, he ducked into a doorway and reached into his pocket to look at the slip of paper. Of course it was written in Cyrillic cursive and he had no hope of making any sense of it. He wondered whom he could trust. Certainly not Nikolai from the hotel. He'd look for some studious young person at a coffee shop, and failing that he'd return to his friends Janice and Dima, if he could find his way back to their flat.

He was in something of a predicament. He had only his suit-case and a few hundred rubles. His airfare home had been spent.

He spoke no Russian. But for some reason he was certain that fortune had smiled upon him. Varushkin had left him something of value. Whether or not he found the Trevallier, there would at least be an answer, an end to his tale—and a small fortune in wine. He had a set of tasks ahead of him now, a few steps toward his future, which now looked brighter than it had in many years. He should translate the note, find the sommelier, secure the wine, sell two bottles for cash and then contact Morty to arrange transport and auction. Morty would want a big bite, but he could be trusted.

Bruno started walking with a primary goal of finding a Métro station. For the first time in many years he felt fortunate and filled with purpose. He tucked the note in his breast pocket next to his heart. A middle-aged woman passed him in the opposite direction and they smiled at one another. The sun behind him caught the glass side of an apartment building ahead, illuminating the street in golden light.

He didn't notice the long black car until it had pulled up alongside him. He stopped and looked at his disheveled reflection in the mirrored rear window. It rolled down and his visage was replaced with the much lovelier Katya.

"Mr. Tannenbaum!"

"Mrs. Varushkin."

"If I had money, I'd hire you for my cook."

"I'm flattered."

"But, alas, the most I can do in exchange for that lovely meal is offer you a ride."

The rear door opened and Bruno couldn't believe his continued good luck.

Katya lounged on the spacious backseat as if on a sofa. She had removed her coat and sat with her legs crossed and the tops of her boots unzipped, revealing a smooth length of tanned calf. Bruno tried not to stare but was caught in the act. He blushed and she smiled and seemed pleased.

"These boots are so uncomfortable. I'm going to get rid of them as soon as I get home. I should burn them. That place was filthy."

"Quite," Bruno said, blushing more and using the excuse to inspect her footwear as license to ogle. She smelled wonderful. As the driver pulled away, she leaned close.

"So," she said conspiratorially, "what do you think of my husband? Do you think he's gone mad?"

"Seems pretty stable, all things considered."

She shrugged and looked out the window as they drove on. Bruno cleared his throat.

"Oh," she said. "So where are you going?"

"You can drop me near Lomonosov Moscow State University, if you would." He didn't want to trust her with the translation of the note, and he figured that near the university he could find someone who spoke English to help him. He knew nothing about the area other than one guidebook's recommendation of the nearby cafés.

"Are you staying there?"

"I wanted to try the restaurants."

"There are some good ones. It's a wonderful area. Igor . . ." she said, getting the driver's attention. Then she spoke in Russian and he merely grunted in return.

They drove on in silence for a while. Bruno watched the apartments give way to an industrial landscape.

"Tell me," Katya finally asked, "why did you go to see my husband?"

"To research a book I'm writing."

"What is it about?"

"Wine."

"Why him?"

"You must know that he was once known as quite a collector. To have had some of the greatest wines in the world, and then to have lost them . . ."

"Of course. How poetic and sad. So what did he tell you?"

"I've got a responsibility to my sources."

"I'm sure you do. So what did you really think of him?"

"He seems intelligent. His eyes . . . that knowing smile. It's like he always knows more than he's telling you."

"Exactly!"

"But he also seemed worn and tired."

"He did, didn't he? He's the most manipulative man I've ever known. You'd be surprised how much he controls, still, even from in there. I think I loved him once. Very much."

"I'm sure he would like to know that."

Katya laughed. "You've fallen under his spell, haven't you? So tell me. Did you learn what you wanted?"

"I'm not sure yet. But I'm hopeful."

"That's good. Very good."

She slid closer to him and touched his leg. It was like a light shock, and he flinched. She smiled and he felt her breath in his ear.

"You know, you could come stay with me. For a little while. I'm fairly impoverished, but I still try to live comfortably. You could have a few quiet rooms to work on your writing. And in exchange you could cook for me. And I'm sure I could find other uses for you."

She turned to him. One hand inched up his thigh and the other was now pressed against his chest. Every cell in Bruno's body wanted to press his lips to hers, but for some reason he exerted an unusual amount of self-control. Some small voice in the back of his brain was shouting and waving its hands in warning.

"And I haven't properly thanked you for that wonderful meal."

Before he kissed her, Bruno thought that something in his recipe must have been misdirected: she was supposed to have these feelings for Varushkin. Perhaps Varushkin should have prepared it and Bruno merely coached him.

She sat astride his lap now, and she was touching him all over in a way that was odd but that he also quite enjoyed. Her mouth and tongue were salty, her hard breathing through her nose tickling his beard. One moment a hand was twisted in the hair at the back of his head, another by his hip and then against his chest again.

Bruno began thinking that this was the most odd, fortuitous and wonderful day he'd yet experienced.

But then suddenly she sprang off of him and scooted back to her side of the car.

"Aha!"

She held the slip of paper. Bruno didn't have time for anger; he was too bewildered. He realized that the car had stopped on a road shaded by trees. And then his door was ripped open and he fell halfway out.

Standing above him was the driver, the man's face fully visible for the first time. He recognized the square jaw, the short blond hair, the scar along the side of his face. It was the man from Germany. From Chicago. The pieces of the puzzle were coming together in Bruno's mind: the accountant, the locker, Scar . . . It must have been Katya hunting Varushkin's treasure all along. And Bruno had led her right to it . . .

He now saw a small leather club, looking silly in the driver's
thick fingers, descending rapidly toward his temple.

A flash.

And the world went dark.

*　　*　　*

There are moments in your life when you awake with a splitting head, not knowing where you are, or anything at all, really,
beyond the suspicion that something momentous had transpired.
And Bruno had had many such moments over the years. Some of
these had fueled the decline of his marriage.

After one evening that began with a panel tasting of Burgundies (Bruno did not believe in spit buckets) at a hotel in San
Francisco, he'd awoken stuffed into a double sleeping bag under
a row of Gewürztraminer vines in Sonoma County with a member of the waitstaff, a hearty ranch girl originally from western
Nebraska named Lorrie who had a thick waist and a lovely
snore and who smelled nice and kept him warm as he watched
the ocean fog slowly seep out of the river valley with little idea of
what had happened between hotel and vineyard. On the other
end of the spectrum, after a book signing at some minor Mid-
western state university, he'd awakened alone in a dorm room
wearing clown makeup and a pirate suit stolen from the theater
department. After his ensuing discovery by the floor RA and
arrest, he swore off binge drinking with college students.

But this time was different. This time there had been no alcohol employed. And this time he couldn't call Anna to come bail
him out.

The first sensation he experienced was sound. Children's
laughter. Wistful music. Then there was the splitting pain as he
cracked open his eyes to see cement, and, in shallow focus, a wad

of spent chewing gum hardened and smeared across a crack, the imprint of the sole of a tennis shoe on its surface like the pattern of a fossil.

Then came the sinking realization that something was wrong. An overwhelming sense of loss. A pair of blinking toddler's shoes ambled past. The wheels of a stroller. The elderly shuffle of loafers.

He opened his eyes all the way and lifted his head, and the world spun around him, a stabbing pain between his temples. Between bright flashes of light he could see that he was in a well-lit park just after dusk. The music came from a carousel that spun lazily in the periphery. People circled a fountain.

He stood carefully. He was in a copse just at the edge of the park, and as he stood and brushed leaf litter from his jacket, a nervous mother picked up her toddler and edged away. An old man paused and jabbed his cane in his direction, muttering.

Once he'd gained his balance, everything came back to him. He was in Moscow. He'd been to the prison. He'd fixed a meal for Varushkin. Katya had picked him up. She had been sitting on his lap . . . and then suddenly it struck him: he'd been mugged. He rifled through his jacket pockets just to be sure, but it was true . . . the slip of paper that held the code, the key to his treasure, was gone.

Nowhere to be found.

All was lost.

He stalked into the plaza surrounding the fountain, unsteady on his feet like the drunk that he sometimes was, though wasn't at the moment. More people moved out of his way.

He had to think. He'd lost the paper. But Varushkin could simply share the location again, right? He paused. With only a handful of rubles remaining, he couldn't bribe his way back into Butyrka. And even if he could, Katya was already minutes, hours maybe, ahead of him.

What could he do? Who did he know? Perhaps Aleksei could help? No. There was no time. What else? What had Varushkin said? Any hints or clues?

Of course. There'd been one.

You've had the answer in your hand the whole time, Varushkin had said.

What answer? What had been in his hand?

He sifted through his pockets. A few coins. Some wadded ruble notes. The business card Parker Thomas had shared with him.

And then, of course, the corkscrew.

He pulled it from his pocket. He extended the gleaming screw and turned it over, examining it in the lamplight. Inscribed on the handle were words. Cyrillic letters. They said something.

"Excuse me," Bruno shouted, staggering toward passers- by with the corkscrew thrust before him. People parted. One woman shrieked. "Excuse me . . . does anyone here speak English? English? Translate? I need a translator."

He wasn't having much success when he heard a voice behind him.

"I speak English. Some," said a thin, youngish fellow with a backpack and headphones draped around his neck. He looked to be a high school student.

Bruno showed him the handle and he inspected it carefully.

"It says here," the student said, tracing the words, "Two Eagles . . . Two Eagles Café. Yes. Is from a café. From a restau- rant."

"Do you know it?"

"Yes. Is not so far. Four streets this way." He gestured with his hand in one direction. "And three, maybe four streets this way." He gestured in a perpendicular direction.

"Thank you!" Bruno said, kissing him on both cheeks.

He was off at a sprint, light on his feet now. He threaded the sidewalk traffic, dashed across busy streets. Drivers honked and people turned. The world streaked past, but he didn't care about anything other than his target. It was a refuge, as Varushkin had said. A small café where he hid from the world. And it was close.

Bruno counted off streets in his head. He turned. He raced on and then slowed to a jog, finally stopping because he recognized the place now. It was just as Varushkin had described it. He needed only that one word: refuge. A warm light radiated from a pair of windows flanking a set of stairs descending to a terrace-level café. Outlines of diners filled the windows, and even from outside and across the street he caught the scent of a good, working kitchen, a combination of aromas that always reminded Bruno of roasting game hens and baking bread.

He descended the stairs as if in a trance. He could feel heads from the diners turn to watch him. The café was perfect. It was Hemingway's clean and well-lighted place, or even Joel Berteau's cozy restaurant under the El station in Chicago. It was the stool in the corner behind his mother's deli where, after his father's death, he would sit as a young boy and read Jack London and Robert Louis Stevenson stories, and later scratch poems onto the backs of sheets torn from the receipt pads.

The place was narrow, with only a few tables along either side. A small bar stood at the back with a pair of stools and a selection of wines in a rack. He looked for stairs or doors in the back but there was nothing, so he pushed his way into the kitchen.

An assistant cook stood dicing at a stainless-steel counter, and a large man with tattoos rolled a pan of mushrooms in oil at the stove, flames licking the underside of the pan. Bruno nodded to him and pointed to the pan, kissing his fingers, and the man nodded back, not asking questions.

Bruno scanned the room quickly and saw a narrow hall at the back of the kitchen, and so slipped through past an office and down a set of stairs that breathed of cool, earthy air and had the clean and slightly sour must of a good cellar.

At the bottom of the stairs was a long corridor lined with cans of kitchen stock and a door to a walk-in cooler, and then around another bend it opened into a vaulted room that felt more ancient, as if it had a different provenance than the rest of the building.

Here there were wooden wine crates, all stamped with names that Bruno recognized, stacked in neat rows, and then alcoves along the far wall, each with a formidable, thick-timbered door set into it. One of these doors stood open and two burly men were carrying out unmarked and antique wooden cases and stacking them onto a hand truck while others watched. Two of the faces Bruno recognized immediately, with Nikolai from the hotel holding a clipboard and pen, making notes. And Parker Thomas stood to the side, observing, hands on his hips and a wide grin on his lips.

A dignified old man with slicked-back white hair and a trim mustache approached Bruno.

"May I help you?" the man asked in English with a heavy French accent.

"This is Anatoly Varushkin's wine?"

Nikolai approached now.

"No . . . it belongs to a young woman, and this gentleman

will be arranging the auction," the sommelier said, gesturing to a short, bearded Russian.

Nikolai grabbed Bruno's shoulders and gave him the double air kiss of his countrymen. "Bruno! I knew a writer of your stature would sniff out this story! Incredible, isn't it?"

Bruno turned from him and took the sommelier to the side and whispered low to him. "I think there is some mistake. I just spoke with Mr. Varushkin and he said he was leaving his collection to my care . . ."

"Do you have any documentation?"

"No, I, uh . . ."

"Very well. You see, his wife contacted me only a short time ago. She possessed a handwritten note which I verified myself against an entry by Mr. Varushkin in my ledger. It clearly stated that everything in his locker is the property of the note's holder. I'm afraid you are mistaken."

Nikolai had followed them and was slapping Bruno on the back now. "Mr. Tannenbaum, you can help me. What an amazing turn of events . . . We spoke about this, I know, only a short time ago, and now it has come to fruition. Katya Varushkin contacted me about the auction of her husband's collection, and of course I said yes immediately. Now we will have a splendid new event on the calendar. Perhaps the best one of all. And of course we will need publicity . . ."

Bruno walked away from him and squeezed into the locker. It had been mostly emptied, but some aged bottles still stood on the racks. The two large men were packing them efficiently. Bruno plucked one bottle. A '43 Bouchard.

"An entire collection of war vintages," came a voice at Bruno's shoulder. Parker Thomas. "Can you believe it?"

"I'm not sure," Bruno said sadly.

"This is the story you've been following, isn't it?"

"Partly."

"Nikolai called me right away, and I tell you, I'm itching to do it. But since you've obviously been on the case, the article is yours. Fair's fair. But if you snooze, I'm going to jump on it. Can you believe it? Some kind of defrocked gas baron is sitting on the greatest stash in the history of wine and then he finally decides to hand it over to his estranged wife after years of rotting in prison? Wow. And you got an interview with Varushkin, didn't you? In Butyrka? I can't touch that. What an incredible story, man. Let me know and I'll connect you with my editor at the *New York Times*."

He squeezed Bruno's shoulder and walked out.

Bruno hunted down Nikolai and took the clipboard from him.

"Yes, yes, look at these. Can you believe them? Romanée-Contis, Pommards, Gevrey-Chambertins . . . you name it. A great story, no?"

"What about Trevalliers?"

"Ha, ha, now, that would be amazing. But I'm afraid—"

"No Trevalliers?" Bruno asked, incredulous, flipping through the sheets.

"I logged every bottle myself. I'm afraid that particular vintage will remain just a legend. But still . . . quite a story, eh?"

As the workers carted the cases to a bay door at the rear of the cellar, Bruno made his way back up the stairs toward the kitchen. Each lift of a foot to the next tread required enormous effort. His reversals of fortune had been so frequent and absolute that he was numb and bewildered. It was all absurd . . . especially the profession and calling of the writer. To what purpose? What expertise or experiences did he have that mattered to the world, this broken, frumpy fellow with a cheap coat and no suit-case and a splitting head lifting himself out of a cellar where he didn't belong, in a city he didn't know? What right did he have to think that other humans should spend a portion of their pre-ciously limited time on this lovely earth with their noses buried in pages that he had written, sentences and words leading them on a fool's quest? He was a hack. A charlatan. A huckster. And the greatest travesty wasn't the countless readers he'd deceived and led on aimless rambles, but the fact that he'd somehow inspired Claire to invest her entire future in an unwritten book.

That lonely, somber walk up the back stairs of the café was the lowest of the extraordinary array of low points that punctuat-ed the dubious chronology of Bruno's life.

So he did what he always did in such moments. He headed for the little bar at the back of the restaurant.

He found the sommelier there gazing out over the dwindling clientele. Bruno took a stool and the man regarded him with a mixture of professional indifference and boredom.

"Pouring anything?" Bruno asked.

"I have very nice bottle of Montrachet open."

"You wouldn't happen to have a '43 Trevallier, would you?"

"That's not possible."

"No?"

"In my not-so-insubstantial lifetime in wine, I've seen no evi-dence of that vintage. It's a rumor. A legend. If it ever did exist, it was consumed a long time ago by those who stole it. There is a good chance it was never even produced or even just blended in with the regional swill in an act of contempt or defiance. Many vignerons did this. I've talked to most of the older ones in my travels."

"Humph," Bruno said. Here was the man who should write

the book about the Trevallier, he thought. He fished around in his pockets, turning up a last, wadded hundred-ruble note. He unfolded it and laid it on the counter.

"Will this get me some of that Montrachet?"

"I'm afraid not."

"Well, what, then?"

"*Vin de la maison.*" The old man retrieved a magnum bottle from the counter behind him and poured a glass for Bruno, taking the note. "A glass of *vin ordinaire* for the gentleman," he said in French.

The phrase struck Bruno. He'd heard it so often before, but perhaps because of its humility he'd never really dwelled on it.

"What was that?" Bruno asked.

"Oh, pardon, I said a glass of our *everyday wine* for the gentleman."

"*Vin ordinaire?*"

"Correct."

Bruno laughed and the last two remaining customers turned and looked at him. He seized a glass from behind the counter and took the bottle from the sommelier, pouring a second glass and placing it in the man's hand.

They clinked a toast, and Bruno tossed his back, slapping the sommelier's shoulder and heading for the door, the wine tracing its way to his belly, warming him, helping him to lift the dark veil of defeat from his shoulders just enough to let in some light.

Despite all of the wrong turns this story was taking, he felt it still tugging at him. And he had to follow it to its conclusion, wherever that would lead.

TWENTY-THREE

Dessert

Dessert isn't a course. It's the end of a process. It's been unfairly caged as an excess, as gluttony topped with whipped cream and chocolate sprinkles. But it needn't be. Its role is to merely complete the cycle, and to bring harmony and closure to the orbit of the life of a meal.
—BRUNO TANNENBAUM, *TWENTY RECIPES FOR LOVE*

Bruno rang Morty again and waited for him to pick up. The phone booth was on the center aisle of a boulevard, with three lanes of traffic on either side. He finally made a connection, though it was difficult to hear between the cars and static on the line.

"Yeah?"

"It's Bruno."

"Where the hell are you?"

"I'm in Moscow. Long story."

"I'm not even going to ask. Well, what do you want this time?" Even through the bad connection, Bruno could pick up the impatience in Morty's voice.

"I need some info. On the Trevalliers."

There was a pause. Bruno heard Morty already flipping through catalog pages. "Don't tell me you found the '43 . . ."

"I think I'm getting close."

"Well, why didn't you say so?" There was a long pause, the sound of Morty rifling through his bookcase. Then came a thump and the crackle of a spine. "Okay, I got the book out."

"Tell me, did Trevallier ever put their name on *vin ordinaire*?"

"In the old days . . . sure. But that's their rotgut . . . why would anyone care about that?"

"But they stopped?"

"Yeah. Lot of the fine brands did that. They don't want their name on the cheap shelf. They just sell the worst of it off to a negotiant. Or sell it under a different label."

"Or pour it down the drain like Sylvie Trevallier?"

"Right . . . in fact, the last year they made the table wine was . . ."

"The year Sylvie took over."

"Bingo."

"That's what I needed to confirm. Thanks, Morty."

"So you're going to find it? For real?"

"I think so. I have one more stop."

"What else can I do to help?"

"Well, since you asked . . ."

"Uh-oh."

"I could use a loan. I'm flat broke and stuck in Russia."

There was a pause as Morty thought. "My usual percentage? On the whole thing?"

"Sure."

He heard Morty punching buttons on his calculator.

"Okay. How much you think you need?"

* * *

At the airport, Bruno picked up a Sunday edition of the paper. He pulled out the *New York Times Magazine* and dropped the rest in the trash bin. While he waited for the train he read Parker Thomas's article in its entirety. It was well done, dipping into the history of the Constanoff Collection, some background on war vintages, the free market free-for-all that created Varushkin and his ilk, and then the final rediscovery of a treasure trove in the basement of a "shabby bistro in Moscow's student quarter." Overall, it was a nicely written travelogue. Thomas dropped in a gratuitous tip of the hat to Nikolai's auction and tourism racket, and then he focused the remainder of the article on the modern and more affordable counterparts to these classic wartime vintages, complete with scores and a helpful sidebar mentioning where to find them in some of the larger liquor store chains like BevMo! and Binny's.

Bruno wasn't angry. Thomas had offered the story to him first. And he had even mentioned Bruno in the piece and hinted that he was working on the larger story: "The path to the Constanoff Collection is still shrouded in mystery and legend. With characters like the oligarch Anatoly Varushkin and noted novelist and food essayist Bruno Tannenbaum lurking in the shadows, this wine critic can only guess what the next chapter will be for the world's lost vintages."

Bruno left the magazine next to his empty espresso cup on the café table when he heard the track called for his train. He sought an empty car so that he could be alone.

It was early afternoon when he arrived in Beaune and he was unimpressed as always with the sleepy train station for what was the epicenter of the wine universe. He was one of three passengers who disembarked, and he walked the ring road along the old medieval city walls and then veered southwest on the D974 toward Pommard.

It was hot, and a dog lay panting on the cobbled street in the shadow of the fountain in the village square. Bruno wiped sweat from his brow as he headed upslope west of the village. When he reached Sylvie's she was in the courtyard working on the Bobard tractor, and the sad blue machine looked as if it hadn't moved in the weeks since Bruno had left. She pulled her hands out of the tractor's entrails, her arms and face covered in grease and sweat, and she allowed a half smile of disbelief when she saw him.

"Where's your mechanic off to?" he asked.

"Claude left me," she said, wiping her hands on a rag and walking toward him. "He's now working for the Bouchards for twice the salary. I'm fairly sure he doesn't get to fuck the owner, though." She offered both cheeks to be kissed, which Bruno did, breathing in the delicious tang of oil mixed with sweat rising from her body. "And I'm terrible when it comes to machinery. This godforsaken thing. How are you with tractors?"

"I understand that this is how you steer it," Bruno said, tapping the wheel. "Otherwise, I'm relatively useless."

"That's unfortunate."

He followed her to the shade where she had a jar of well water. She drank from it and offered it to Bruno as they stood watching the heat shimmer rise off the vineyards beyond the stone wall.

"So what can you do?"

"Well, I can cook . . ." Bruno said, furrowing his brow and thinking hard. "Light household chores. Shopping for groceries. Laundry, though it tends to get away from me. I'm also open to performing any sort of unskilled labor providing there's not too much heavy lifting. Oh, and I'm pretty good at whistling opera."

Sylvie thought for a minute, frowning. "I suppose that'll have to do." She smiled briefly and walked back toward the tractor, calling over her shoulder, "You can stay in the room above the garage. If Claude left anything, just throw it out. See if you can find something to fix in the kitchen. I expect I'll be famished in two hours."

Claude's room was perfect. There was a simple writing desk, a single bed and an old picture-tube television, which Bruno turned to face the wall. A pinup magazine lay on the nightstand, which he tossed in the trash only after leafing through it briefly. The airbrushed models, while glorious in their nakedness, were also as sexually appealing as plastic dolls. Bruno thought of the three moles on Sylvie's rib cage below her left breast, her collar- and hip bones, the rolls on her stomach that hid her navel when she sat up in bed, and lust began its stirrings somewhere in his bottom half.

He whistled as he crossed the courtyard to the kitchen, where he found a package of ground lamb and some lovely tomatoes in the refrigerator. He then checked the cozy kitchen garden that Sylvie kept behind the main house. It was weedy and neglected, but there was a drip irrigation system and several unkempt rosemary bushes. He dug out a few new potatoes and brought it all back to the kitchen, where he blanched, seeded and peeled the tomatoes, then blended them into a puree. He added crushed rosemary, some diced garlic from a basket hanging over the sink and then made another trip to the garden for basil and thyme. The lamb was lean, so he warmed it in olive oil until the color just started to darken, and then he drained it and added it to the puree. There was an unlabeled bottle of Pinot Noir on the counter that he assumed was for cooking (though he drank a full glass and it was delicious), so he added two cups to the puree, simmered to reduce some of the alcohol, then added the rest on a low flame before walking back down to the village for bread, claiming their very last baguette and a pink meringue to munch on for strength on the way back up the hill.

When Sylvie finally came into the kitchen it had been closer to four hours than two. She had showered and now wore jeans and a clean white T-shirt, and she'd put on simple gold hoop earrings, which was all the elegance she needed. Bruno's spine tingled at the sight of her and he folded the newspaper he'd been reading and stood and bowed.

"It smells fantastic. I'm starving," she said, looking at the soup and bread, quite pleased.

They carried the meal out to the shaded patio behind the house. They could see the evening light on the vines, the leaves curling in the heat.

"I hope it cools tonight. I'm worried about the acids. If they drop too far and the fruit is cooked, our wines will lose all their structure. Every year it's a touch warmer. It frightens me. We could use a cold spell, as long as there's no hail. If it hails again this year, we're finished."

"There must be times when a grower feels helpless."

"You have to be humble and fatalistic to make wine. *This is the year we were given,* you say. But you also have to be stubborn and have an ego to think you can make something good every year. I think that's why most vignerons are half crazy."

They ate in silence and sat comfortably together until the sun had set completely. She lit an oil lamp in the center of the table while he made coffee, and moths began to dance around the light. As they sipped the coffee she said, "I know why you've come back."

"Do you?"

"You think you've figured it out?"

"I think so. But I respect your privacy and I'll question you only if it's okay."

"Are you going to write about it?"

"I haven't decided."

"It doesn't matter. You can do as you wish. We haven't had any wine yet. Come with me."

She led him into the courtyard and around the building. The moon had climbed and now cast their shadows across the grass. She veered to the wall and leaned over, pressing a vine leaf between her palms.

"They're breathing again now that it has cooled off a little. Feel." He followed her lead and pressed a grape leaf between his hands. It felt cool and smooth, alive against his skin, and the leaves were no longer curled as they had been in the heat of the day.

She led him around to the cellar, pausing along the way to wind up a hose. She clicked on the lights inside before securing the door behind them. The air was thick with oak and must, muted and weary in anticipation of harvest, which would bring the sulfurous, yeasty bubbling of fermentation. Bruno wondered what it must be like, being able to breathe this ancient cellar air every day, to wake every morning and gaze out over vineyards. His mother's couch was comfortable, but how was that life? His cubicle at the *Sun-Times* had guaranteed him a regular paycheck, but was it worth the time he spent in that cell? How was all that any different from the life Varushkin lived now? Some live their entire lives inside a great big Butyrka. The magic of food and wine, the well-laden table, the puff of steam as the lid is lifted off a dish of cassoulet, the reflected candlelight in the sparkle of a freshly poured Pinot Noir: these are the things that offer us a

daily glimpse of the wonder that now surrounded Bruno. This
was how humans were supposed to live: in fear and humility
beneath the threat of hail. In reverence over the cool touch of a
breathing leaf in your palm. In the surety that you can pull something wonderful from the soil.

He now understood why Sylvie was so protective of her life.
And why she didn't do interviews. She wanted to merely exist,
vintage to vintage, and earn enough simply to make it through
another year. From the outside, someone would look at her
vineyards and the incongruity of the broken Bobard tractor
and wonder how her wines could be in such demand. It was no
vision of success. Or luxury.

Bruno understood her, and he was no longer angry. For
a while he had been. On the plane from Moscow to Paris, he
stared out the window and gritted his teeth as he thought about
how she had deceived him, sent him on a fool's quest, when the
answer had been here all along. But then, the journey is the destination, as all the new age pseudo-Buddhists liked to say. And in
truth he had learned a lot on his quest.

"Why didn't you tell me?" he asked as they wended their way
around stacks of barrels to the far recesses of the cave.

"Tell you what?"

"About the *vin ordinaire*?"

Sylvie smiled and clicked on a light, illuminating a narrow-
ing corridor sided by barrels that had been aging for a decade or
more.

"Ask me anything now."

"*Vin ordinaire*. Table wine. Your grandfather never bottled
Premier Cru '43, right?"

"That's true."

"Von Speck . . . he stole only the best. The Premier Crus and up. He left the plonk for the locals. He never took your grandfather's wine, did he?"

"No."

"Then what did I follow to Naumburg? To Moscow?"

She shrugged. "Who knows . . . maybe it was some other Pommard. Bouchard's, perhaps. Or a Volnay. Gevrey-Chambertin. The Nazis loved their wine, and they took a lot of it."

"So what happened to yours?"

"My grandfather was outspoken and stubborn. He got into trouble with the occupiers and decided to go into hiding with relatives in the south. Many of the men were hiding, fighting or with *la Résistance* then. The women and children were left behind."

"So he didn't make any wine that year?"

Sylvie brushed her hand absently against the barrels as they moved farther back in the cellar. "No, he didn't."

"So what happened, then? Was the fruit just left on the vine? Did someone else take it?"

"My grandmother made the wine that year. With help from her sister." Sylvie paused by a misshapen wooden door that plugged a natural hole in the side of the cave. "When my grandfather returned, he wouldn't allow the premium designation. He wouldn't allow the family name on the label: his father's name. His grandfather's name. But this wine was made by the women. So it was labeled *vin ordinaire* and sold cheaply."

"Does that make you angry?"

She shrugged. "That is just how it was back then. Later, when neighbors found out what he'd done with the labeling, they said, 'How clever of Clement Trevallier, to outsmart the Germans by calling his Premier Cru *vin ordinaire*.' I assume this is the same conclusion you came to."

"So it wasn't about fooling the Nazis. It was about pride?"

"Mostly. Afterwards he was ashamed—about going into hiding, about leaving the women and children behind, about not giving his wife credit for the vintage. That was when his philosophy changed: all wine was *vin ordinaire*. Everyday wine. His ego and family name became less important. And his wife and family more so. Great men learn from their mistakes."

"But when you took over, you stopped making *vin ordinaire*?"

"Yes. When I took over, both of my grandparents were gone. It was time to follow my own vision. I suppose I am more like my grandfather when he was young. I wanted all of the wines made by Trevallier to only be the best. If it is not good, I pour it out, even though it is expensive to do so. Every wine we make will be extraordinary. And from now on, until the name Trevallier passes into memory, all of our wine will be made by a woman." She smiled.

"What about the wine your grandmother made?"

"It was all consumed years ago. Nobody saves ordinary table wine."

"Not even the producer?"

Sylvie smiled. "We may have a few bottles lying around somewhere."

She unlatched the door and led him into a low-ceilinged room with a barrel standing on end, along with two stools. The walls were lined with racks and dusty bottles. A low shelf held clean glasses.

"When I was a girl I used to dare myself to come back here. I thought that this was where the ghosts lived."

She lit a candle that was stuck in wax to the barrel and took two glasses and gestured for Bruno to have a seat. She pulled a bottle from low on the rack and wiped the dust and mold with the hem of her shirt. The bottle had no labels or markings of any kind. She took a corkscrew from her pocket and effortlessly pulled the crumbling cork that was a twin to the one that Bruno had carried for so long. The room filled with the aroma of earth and just a hint of ripe fruit. The air felt ancient, and Bruno thought that this was what it must have been like for those adventurers who first opened the tombs of the pharaohs.

She poured, swirled and sniffed.

"This one is still good. Here."

She poured some for Bruno. He was afraid to touch the glass. He felt weak. His stomach fluttered. He thought he might fall off the stool.

"So it was here the whole time?"

"Yes."

"What of this?" Bruno held out the cork he'd been carrying for so long.

"My grandfather or father may have given some bottles away over the years. Maybe it is from one of those gifts. Or perhaps it's a fake."

"Who knows about this?" He gestured to the rack of wines.

"My father did. My grandfather. Of course, my grandmother as well. People tried to guess what happened to that vintage, and we let them. Was it stolen by Hitler himself? Or had my grandfather called it *vin ordinaire* to hide it from the Nazis? We allowed people to wonder."

"Who else knows the truth?"

"No one. Not Claude or my ex-husband. I'm the only one left. And now there is also you." She winked at him. "Well, I suppose you want to try some?"

Bruno's hand trembled.

"It's okay. Go ahead. Don't wait too long. Wines this old lose their magic quickly. Sometimes in minutes. Like life, it's fleeting. Then it truly becomes just everyday wine," she said.

He smiled and swirled. He sniffed the air above the glass. Tears brimmed in his eyes. He held it to the light a long moment and then sipped.

"How would you describe it?"

"I don't think I can."

"Sometimes it's fine just to drink it."

They both sipped in silence. Bruno knew as well as anyone that the pseudo-scientific formulae for evaluating wines were something of a sham. Life isn't as empirical as we all pretend it to be. French wines are extraordinary because they make us think of France, whether we've been there in reality or only in our imaginations. Great wines are about the people we shared them with, the meals we drank them beside and the location where we pulled the cork. Wine tasted from brown paper bags standing next to scorecards in some publisher's office is a practice in absurdity. Bruno sipped again and fought to contain the emotion.

It was extraordinary not only because it was so utterly unlike anything he'd ever tasted in his life, so perfect in its composition, so rich and deep with layered meaning, but also because Bruno knew its story. This wine was a story, a voice that had been calling him from even before he'd stumbled across the cork in Aleksei's locker. It wasn't the story of this mysterious cellar, of an occupying army or of the women who'd brought in that harvest under Nazi occupation. Not the story of the year's worth of weather, or the soils, which had once been the bottom of an ancient sea, then slowly raised to hillsides of millennia to clutch the roots of the breathing vines. The story of the monks who had spent centuries painstakingly crossing and selecting this single cultivar to be grown in this exact spot on the globe.

Or even the story of this strange, beautiful, complex and ordinary woman who sat across from him now.

This wine was none of these, and all of these, because it was Bruno's story. It had led him here, to this place, to be with Sylvie. And because of this, it was perfection captured in a glass.

"What would they write about this?" Sylvie asked. "Would they say it tastes of raspberries, pencil shavings, a hint of chocolate? Maybe they'd make up new words for it, if they were particularly clever. But do you know what I think of, when I drink this? I think of my grandmother. My grandfather was called by some the greatest winemaker of his generation. But my grandmother's wine was even better. Don't you agree, now that you've tried it? And in the end, both of them were humble farmers. Nothing brought them more pleasure than to sit down at a meal with their family. Tell me, what do you think of as you taste this, Mr. Tannenbaum?"

He thought for a long moment, the silence settling down around him.

"I'm thinking of my daughters," he said, finally.

She smiled. "That's good. Maybe you really do understand more than the others."

"I'm trying."

"So, do you have an ending to your story now?"

"Yes, but it's not the ending I expected."

"It never is."

Bruno watched the candle flame flicker on the rim of his glass, his palms cupped around the bowl as if in prayer.

*   *   *

Bruno didn't return to his loft apartment above the garage that night, but instead shared Sylvie's bed. They made love and then he fell into a restless and fitful sleep, but when he awoke it was just before dawn and his head was in her lap as she sat up in bed, smoking with one hand while combing his hair with the fingers of her other.

A plan began to form, and he discussed it only in part with her, but it seemed perfectly reasonable, simple and attainable. Here, in this tiny village in Burgundy, he'd written his first novel all those years ago. He had been able to do so only because of the simplicity of life. To work in the vineyards all day and then stumble bone-tired to his empty room where it was all he could do to hover over his notebook—these were the conditions under which he'd crafted his best words. Back in the city there would be distractions. There was too much shame. Guilt over his poorly lived life. He could never write there. So he would stay here. He'd cook for Sylvie and help her around the vineyard and winery as he could and provide as much companionship as she'd allow.

He'd finish his book and sell it for what he could and then give all of it to Anna, Claire and Carmen, and then he would hire on with a restaurant in Beaune and work at the bar or wait tables until they trusted him enough to help out in the kitchen. And then next year during the bacchanal, he'd stand off to the side with the other vignerons instead of mixing in the churning mass of revelry.

He looked up from Sylvie's lap, between her breasts to her absent smile and the mess of morning hair. They made love again after she finished smoking, and then they walked down to the village for a coffee, stopping at the *boulangerie* to pick up *pain au chocolate* and bread for later in the day. She spotted a flatbed truck pulled to the side of the road in the first terrace of vine-yards, and she cut through the vines until she found an old man stooped and slowly pulling leaves to allow more light to reach the grape clusters. He looked up and smiled and they talked for a long time about the weather, reviewing what the season had given them while the sun climbed and drew the damp warmth from the earth and began to cook on the back of Bruno's neck. He watched a moth flutter between the rows and a dragonfly buzz past on the hunt. Back in the direction of the village, a cat slunk along a stone wall, then sat abruptly to clean its paws. He knelt and picked up a golden, chalky stone, putting it in his pocket. On the way back to the house, Sylvie took his hand and listed everything she wanted to accomplish that day. "Then after that we'll go out," she said. "My friend Agnès serves *lapin à la moutarde* in her restaurant on Tuesdays."

In the evening Sylvie drove her compact Opel aggressively, grinding the clutch, slamming the gearshift and squealing around corners so that Bruno gripped the dashboard and she laughed out loud. The bistro was a comfortable room off the Rue des Tonneliers, and Agnès came from the kitchen and hugged Sylvie while they chatted like sisters and Bruno was introduced, much to the chef's pleasant surprise and also a few winks and raised eyebrows.

The waiter pulled out a table, and Sylvie sat along the wall and she and Bruno talked about their favorite books and writers from when they were younger, both lamenting that they hardly seemed to have time to read. Sylvie also confessed that she hadn't been to see a film in more than ten years, so after the amazing rabbit and a spectacular bottle of Montrachet they walked to the Cap Cinéma and selected a comedy with Pascal Légitimus. The forty percent of the film that Bruno could actually understand seemed somewhat inane, but what he enjoyed was Sylvie's easy laughter and the way she absently put her hand on Bruno's leg without looking at him as if she could transfer some of her mirth.

On the way back they stopped at a café and drank Kronenbourgs, not talking because they didn't need to. Bruno felt comfortable and satisfied being near her. That night it began to cool as a front was moving through, pushing dark clouds past the moon.

In bed he lay close to her under the covers, warm where their skin touched as the night air slipped in through the open window. He couldn't sleep again because he was excited by the notion that he was happier now than he had been at any time in his life.

Searching for the lost vintage had not been so much a universal story as it was a personal question. He knew that now, which made it all the more wrong to expect Anna to finance it, and doubly so now that he knew it had been Claire's money all along. But he'd found happiness, and this happiness was lying right next to him. He could feel her heartbeat through the back of her rib cage.

He suddenly wanted to write and he needed a walk to compose his thoughts. He kissed Sylvie's bare shoulder and she sighed and turned and he got up and took her pink robe and walked out into the brisk night. Clouds slipped over a crescent moon and a haze blanketed the valley between the village and the pale glow of Beaune.

He walked across the grass and then into the soft and stony earth of the vineyard. He tried to think when he'd been so happy before. As a young man he'd graduated college with no idea what he would do with his life, but a need to see the world he'd read about in his literature classes or on the backs of jars in Ma's deli, far beyond the blue-collar streets of Chicago.

He scraped together some money he'd been saving and took it to Woolworth and bought an external-frame backpack, then a plane ticket to Amsterdam and a rail pass.

He'd somehow wound up in Burgundy out of money during harvest, and winemaker Michel Leroux hired him on for the vineyard crew and kept him around that winter for odd jobs. Living in France without a television was all the education he needed. The winter was slow, so when Leroux gave him a hard-bound notebook for Christmas, Bruno started rewriting the journal he'd been keeping on cheap spiral pads. That rewriting had somehow turned from a diary into a semi-autobiographical novel, and the next thing he knew he was almost famous, with a fledgling literary career.

He'd been happy then, he now understood, as a young man in France sitting in his bunk room emptied of the harvest crew, huddling near an electric space heater, gripping a pencil in a hand sore from pruning. Finally, after so many years, he was back, and now had Sylvie to keep him warm.

And he'd never been happier.

Bruno stopped short as the clouds disappeared and the moon-light now shone unobstructed over the silver vines.

He was fooling himself.

There'd been other moments.

Like when he'd looked up from his table at the steakhouse and first spotted Anna in her apron and she smiled at him.

And then a few weeks later when she invited him into her semi-private apartment in the basement of her parents' town house in Skokie, and she took his hand, leading him down the steps, the stirring feel of her skin for the first time, the innocence of it all.

And then the terror of Claire's birth, the glorious mess of it all, this slick little wailing pink bulb of a child, Anna's elation and exhaustion as the nurse handed the newborn into the trembling hands of the new mother.

And then Carmen's somewhat more dubious initiation into the world of the breathing. The umbilical cord had wrapped around her neck, so it was a cesarean, and this little blue beetle of a creature was extracted rather violently through the incision, and as she sucked breath and the warm color of the living began to seep into her flesh: in that instant, he'd been happiest.

And then that last dinner with his family, before he'd come to Europe this time, where they all sat around the table and the awkwardness of the estrangement had melted, the tension between Bruno and Anna abated ever so slightly so that it felt, for an instant, like any meal they'd had together as a family. Then, also, Bruno had been happiest.

Bruno felt that he was falling in love with Sylvie. And though she was hard to read, he could see her falling for him, too. And this life, here on the vineyard, was what he wanted more than anything. But he did the math, and there were four women whom he loved back in Chicago when he counted his mother, and here there was only one.

He thought of old Clement Trevallier, who allowed pride and ego, and perhaps fear, to remove his family name from the wine his wife had made and sell it as cheap swill rather than give her the credit she deserved. And how he had regretted what he'd done and had changed afterward. What was it that Sylvie had said? *Great men learn from their mistakes.* Bruno would never be a great man. But perhaps he could become a better one.

The notion of what he had to do brought him to his knees, the dry stones clacking. He clutched at the trellis and sank into

the moonshadow of it and then he began to weep; hot tears, pro-
fuse and swollen, dropped to the thirsty soil.

He pulled himself together after a few moments. His cheeks
were tear- and dirt-streaked. He went back to the house and had
a shower and then as the sun began to rise he went through the
kitchen planning a breakfast. They could at least share another
meal together before he told Sylvie that it was time for him to go
home.

Bruno sat on a stool in the corner behind the counter of the deli just as he had as a boy. He wrote on the back of a receipt pad, his face scrunched in thought, tongue pressed between his lips as he concentrated, searching for just the right word, when the bell above the door rang and an elderly man wearing a raincoat and a tweed fedora shuffled in.

"You still open?"

"Just barely, Klaus," Bruno said, hopping off the stool and wiping the counter next to the cash register.

"Good, because I need your help," Klaus said, blinking at Bruno with pleading eyes magnified to an absurd degree by glasses with lenses as thick as his German accent.

"What did you do this time?"

"Went out with the boys and had a little too much to drink. Gertrude found me passed out on the couch."

"That doesn't sound so bad."

"It was our anniversary."

"Oh." Bruno paced behind the counter. He was thinking that a roasted squab would fit the bill, but that would likely be too difficult to prepare for poor old Klaus.

"And you know I'm not much of a cook. Unless I can throw it on my Weber."

"Ah! I have something for you!" Bruno said, suddenly stabbing the air with his finger. He raced through the deli. He cut slices off a pistachio-and-duck terrine. "Serve this cold first, with a slice of orange." He then wrapped a pair of wedges of a *tourte aux pommes de terre* that he'd made the day before. "Just warm this in the oven, two-fifty for ten minutes."

He disappeared into the cooler and emerged with two half duck breasts. As he wrapped them, he scribbled notes onto the paper. "Here's where it gets tricky. Score them, salt them, pepper them and then render the fat side on a very low flame for twenty minutes. Then when the skin is gold, clear and crispy, grill it on both sides just long enough to cook through. You want it rare. Can you handle that?"

Klaus blinked and nodded. Bruno could see that he was a little bewildered, so he gave Klaus a friendly sock on the shoulder. "Don't worry, you'll do fine. I'll fetch some Black Forest cake for dessert, right?"

"And the wine?"

"Absolutely!" Bruno slid his ladder along the wine shelf and reached for a bottle high up in the corner. "Here's where I keep the special stuff." He pulled down a Riesling from the River Nahe. It was valley floor, low alcohol, and the sugars were balanced by an acid backbone. That particular wine turned out well maybe one out of every three years, when the region received more than a hundred days of sun in a season. It was ten years old and deep rich gold in color, and when the cork was pulled a faint whiff of diesel engine would emerge ahead of the more floral bouquet. He explained as much to Klaus.

"It's expensive. But you haven't steered me wrong yet," Klaus said, pulling off his glasses and pressing the label to his nose, squinting at the Gothic lettering. "One in three, eh? Seems like this wine is all about looking past the bad years."

"Precisely."

"You know, Bruno, I think a great wine is all about forgiveness."

Bruno, who was punching numbers into the register, stopped short and looked at Klaus. "What did you say?"

"Great wine . . . is about forgiveness."

"You're brilliant!" Bruno reached over the counter and pulled Klaus's hat off, and then planted a kiss on his bald forehead. He scribbled the phrase on the receipt pad, then rang up the order, ushering the old man toward the door.

"Tell your mother I hope her retirement is treating her well," Klaus said as Bruno held the door open.

"Good luck with Gertrude!"

As soon as Klaus was gone, Bruno switched off the light in the window and locked the door. He pulled out the register drawer and took two twenties off the top, stuffing them into his hip pocket. He scooped up the rest of the cash and carried it back to the cramped office.

The simple desk had a ledger pad, a calculator and his father's typewriter in front of a stack of manuscript pages. He raced through his tasks: the balancing, rounding the daily deposit, rolling the coins haphazardly and then zipping it all in a bank bag and tossing it to the side.

He turned his attention to the typewriter. There was a half-written sheet in the carriage and a facedown stack of pages behind the machine. He took the slip of receipt paper out of his pocket and read Klaus's words a few times over, thought a moment, then began typing. He typed a line. The bell rang.

He pushed the carriage over, shifted down two more lines and typed, *THE END.*

He smiled and laughed to himself. He wanted to uncork one of the nicer wines in the shop to celebrate, but he restrained himself. He was already running late.

He pulled the page from the typewriter and laid it on the stack, which he lifted and shuffled, flipping it over and laying it gently in a manuscript box. The title page read *Vin Ordinaire.* He addressed the box to Sue Brown, his new editor in New York by way of introduction from Parker Thomas, who had been talking up Bruno's story. Parker had even done some copyediting on an early draft, and the critic's amiability puzzled Bruno until he realized that the problem had always been his own, not Thomas's.

Bruno had reunited with Harley after six months of the agent's pleading and an epic lunch at Cicchetti. He said he'd make it up to Bruno, and he did by securing a larger advance that hadn't been in the offing originally. The advance check, minus Harley's commission, now sat on the table next to the typewriter. Bruno had called his mother and Anna and suggested a meal to celebrate, though he didn't say why.

He grabbed a sack of groceries he'd prepared earlier and then locked the store and tucked the manuscript box under his arm, hoping he wouldn't be too late. The pages weighed heavy under his arm. What bothered him was twofold: Now that he'd taken over daily operation of the deli since Ma's retirement, he didn't think he'd have time to tour or promote the book. Also, there'd be expectations of a follow-up book. With his plans for expansion of the shop, he just couldn't see finding the time to write or travel, at least for a number of years. But was that really a bad thing?

The manuscript grew heavier still when he thought of Sylvie.

The normally reticent winemaker had been very open about her family's history while he'd been researching this final draft. They'd spoken for hours on the phone and she shared old stories, journals and photographs. Most of their conversations strayed from the business of the book, though, into the personal details of their daily lives. She talked of the weather and how the year's vintage had progressed after harvest. It'd been hot, and the acids lower than hoped. The wines would be bigger, more robust, but with less of the depth, layers and arability that she always sought. "The Americans will like it, though, so we'll sell it to them," she'd said with a laugh.

Bruno talked about his daughters, his mother's retirement and how he took over the business to keep out of trouble and was finding it quite enjoyable.

But they'd always avoided the subject of what would happen after he published it. It would expose a number of details the reclusive Sylvie had shared in private. Old family wounds would be laid bare for the world to see. Publishing the book could change their relationship.

He stood wavering now by a mailbox. A taxi slid past on the road and the El train squealed around a bend a block away. He smelled the kitchen of a Thai restaurant across the street and his stomach growled its empty song. It had been a long day at the store and he dreaded the next morning, but it always felt good to lock the door and count the positive balance in the till. Anna had started doing the books and she said the balance sheet was looking good and the three-year financials looked even better. She said she'd help him work out the details with the bank when and if the time came for the expansion.

He pulled open the door of the mailbox and the package hovered above the abyss. There was always one more option.

He could shelve the manuscript and return to live with Sylvie in France. He missed her dearly, and she had left the door open for his return. But then, he could no more leave Anna and the girls than Sylvie would be able to leave her family's vines. He hoped she'd understand.

He dropped the manuscript in the box and it clanged shut. He trotted toward the El stop, an extra skip in his step.

At the house, all the women were in the kitchen, cooking. Bruno set the grocery sack on the counter. Carmen jumped in his arms and kissed him on the cheek. Claire ignored him.

He took the two twenties out of his pocket and stuffed them in a jar Carmen had decorated that read *My College Fund*. It was a relief to have all the transgressions and the penance so obviously displayed. Bruno's scarlet letter was a liberation rather than a burden.

Greta spotted him and came over wearing a grease-splattered apron. "Bruno, I need you to look at the duck for me," she said, a worried tremor in her voice. She was still the better cook, but her confidence had been waning. He pulled the oven door open and poked the bird quickly with his finger. It glistened gold-brown, drips of fat rolling down its side, the pan sizzling.

"Look's perfect, Ma. Let's just give it a few more minutes."

He hovered over Claire, who was making a yogurt dill sauce for the potatoes. He was going to suggest more black pepper, but then he bit his tongue. She could decide for herself.

He had a few minutes, so he snuck up to Claire's room to leave some postcards he'd collected on his last adventure in Europe as a surprise. The postcards were still a sore spot with Anna. He set them on her desk, and when he turned, Claire was standing in the doorway with her arms folded. She smiled and they hugged. She smelled like the kitchen.

They sat on the bed and Bruno took out the check.

"Can I open it?" She grinned.

He nodded and she ripped open the envelope. Harley had worked some of his magic on the back end, but it was modest. The publisher was being cautious. Still, Claire was impressed.

"My gosh, this is amazing!" she said, hugging him again and kissing his cheek. Then she snapped a picture of it with her cell phone.

"Hey, don't you put that on Twittergram or whatever."

"I won't. Just want a picture of my first investment profit."

"That should cover what you threw into the kitty and a little bit more. And if the book does well, who knows . . . ?" he said. With this check and what he'd been saving over the past few months, he was not only returning all of what he'd borrowed from Claire, but padding the college accounts for both girls as well. A weight was lifting from his soul. He took a pen from her desk. "Here, I'm going to sign it over to you, and you decide what to do with it. And maybe you should invest it a little more wisely this time around."

"Goodness." She held it in her hands, and he could see the wheels turning. "Maybe we could take that trip to Europe together, the one that we always talked about."

"Your decision," Bruno said, thinking that that was probably how he would spend it.

"Mom would kill us, wouldn't she?"

"Or at least stop talking to us for a while."

Claire sighed and then brightened. "Oh, well, savings it is. Let's go show her."

"Wait until I leave."

"You sure?"

"Yeah, I'm sure."

They went downstairs and Anna asked Claire to help set the table. Carmen brushed bread with olive oil and slid it under the broiler while Greta sliced the duck.

Bruno thought through the final few pages of his book as they all bustled around him, feeling that he had finally arrived at a sort of wisdom. He wasn't a brilliant writer, or perhaps he was. Either way, it didn't matter much because of this meal that was coming together: five people from three generations with complex interrelations, rancor, love, desire, disappointment, hope, were all about to commune and enjoy a few moments of harmony amid the maelstrom of life. This is what food can do. This is what wine can provide. It gives you a moment, a fleeting instant that you can live within, if you choose.

Dear Claire and Carmen, he had written.

I am learning that we not only eat for pleasure, but, like our Pleistocene ancestors, we still eat to survive. The only way we can ride out this mad, strange existence is by reaching out to one another, across the table.

Bruno helped Claire arrange the toasted bread on a platter while she chopped parsley for the presentation. She poured the yogurt sauce in a bowl and made a swirl on the top for effect. They carried it in and sat.

Greta brought in the duck, sliced and glazed, with spiral-cut orange peel on the side and a dusting of the parsley. Everyone applauded.

There is no more significant or intimate act than cooking for those you love.

As they sat, Anna rose to pour wine. A tiny splash for Claire, a bit more for Greta and a healthy pour for herself. It was an Alsatian Gewurztraminer, and Bruno could smell the citrus bouquet, the lemon meringue above a layer of spice and clove. It sparkled in the flame of the candles that Claire was lighting. Anna had only poured a little in Bruno's glass when he raised his hand. She seemed surprised, though she should have been growing used to his moderation by now.

I've come to learn that the best wine doesn't leap out of the glass at you. It doesn't knock you to the floor. It doesn't conjure a decadent collection of saccharine adjectives.

They raised glasses for a toast.

"So, Bruno," Anna said. "What's this all about? You said you wanted to celebrate something."

Everyone looked at him. Claire met his eyes and then looked away.

He smiled and thought. He hadn't mentioned anything about the book or the advance to Anna, or anyone in his family outside of Claire. He could make a triumphant announcement, but that didn't feel right. This wasn't about him. He thought of old Clement Trevallier. He raised his glass. "I just wanted to celebrate you, my lovely family. *Santé.*"

"*Santé!*" They clinked glasses. Carmen swirled and sniffed her skim milk. They sipped, then attacked the meal.

And maybe the greatest wines are hardly even noticed at all. They are mere accompaniment. Vin ordinaire. *They have the dignity to allow what's most important to take center stage during our brief spin on this great blue-and-green rock.*

Carmen began telling a funny story about her class's rehearsal for the spring play, and everyone was smiling. Anna laughed. Bruno took a bite of the duck, his mother watching out of the corner of her eye, smiling and nodding, patting his forearm absently.

Great wine is the ordinary. It is the everyday. It is family. It's another meal. Another shot at grace. It's love. It is life. It is . . . forgiveness.

Acknowledgments

We writers often complain that ours is a lonely pursuit. But don't believe us! Any book is brought into the world with the aid of a small army of selfless people. In the case of *Vintage*, here are just a few: I'm grateful to my beautiful wife, Nancy, for being my first reader and overall foundation, and this book wouldn't be here without a solid quarter-century of her patience and encouragement; I thank my daughter, Bailey, for loving books and reading with me, the best part of every day; my parents, Don and Karin, and sister, Jill, all bookish people, ensured that I was always surrounded by stories; filmmaker Justin Smith helped me work out the plot, lending his cinematic take on the story; Angela Yeager, Kegan Sims and the talented actor Seth Allen all played a role in helping me find Bruno; Chef Jack Czernecki, Joseph Krause, Derek Whiteside and Scott Wright offered advice on truffles, French language, food, cooking and wine; so many teachers and fellow writers taught me to love language and want to make words and sentences happen, and a few of them include Suzanne Ryan, Carole Maso, Shelby Hearon, Patricia Ann McNair, Eric May, Randall Albers, Joe Moore, Lein Shory, Daren Dean and Nina Furstenau; winemakers and wine people Alan Baker, Serena Lourie, Mike and Kendall Officer, Michael Amigoni, Jim Day, Mary Olson, Todd and Kelly Bostock, Jay Selman, Katherine Cole, Jimi Brooks, Janie Brooks Heuck and so many others have offered the inspiration of their passion, craft and celebration of the world's greatest beverage; far too many authors to name, dead and living, have been my heroes, beacons and silent friends, but I do have to thank Jim Harrison for writing so long and well with ferocious appetite, heart and spirit; my agent, Scott Miller of Trident Media, believed in this story from the start and found the perfect home for it; and last, but not least, everyone at Simon & Schuster and Touchstone who lent their professionalism and energy to this project, especially my editor, Etinosa Agbonlahor, who poured her enthusiasm, insight and passion for food and stories into this novel. Editors are the unsung heroes of literature, and our books would be sorry things without them.

About the Author

David Baker attributes his fascination with wine to a chance train stop in Beaune, which led to time spent working in commercial vineyards, a film, a novel and a dozen years making passable Pinot Noir in his garage. He holds an MFA from Columbia College Chicago, and is the director of *American Wine Story*. He lives in Oregon's Willamette Valley with his wife and daughter.